# DREAM OF DESIRE

Lily had known this moment would come. She had seen it in her dreams for a long time now. She had seen this man, Harte Delaney, taking her in his arms, to make her his.

Now it was actually happening. He was exploring her body, his mouth and fingers touching everywhere with slow and thorough reverence, her breasts, her stomach, sampling every inch of her trembling flesh. Then his lips found hers.

Lily slid her arms around his neck as he caressed her with his fingertips until she felt she would surely not be able to bear the pleasure. His mouth found hers again, hot and hungry, forcing her to respond, making her forget everything but him and the exquisite feelings exploding inside her.

"Now you know how love feels," Harte whispered, and she could only nod as he took her once more to a place beyond her wildest dreams. . . .

# WHITE LILY

by

Linda Ladd

A TOPAZ BOOK

TOPAZ
Published by the Penguin Group
Penguin Books USA Inc., 375 Hudson Street,
New York, New York 10014, U.S.A.
Penguin Books Ltd, 27 Wrights Lane,
London W8 5TZ, England
Penguin Books Australia Ltd, Ringwood,
Victoria, Australia
Penguin Books Canada Ltd, 10 Alcorn Avenue,
Toronto, Ontario, Canada M4V 3B2
Penguin Books (N.Z.) Ltd, 182–190 Wairau Road,
Auckland 10, New Zealand

Penguin Books Ltd, Registered Offices:
Harmondsworth, Middlesex, England

First published by Topaz,
an imprint of New American Library,
a division of Penguin Books USA Inc.

First Printing, August, 1993
10 9 8 7 6 5 4 3 2 1



PRINTED IN THE UNITED STATES OF AMERICA

To my good friend,
Laura "Bullet-serve" Dowd—
who graciously puts up with me
on the tennis court

With a special thank-you to
Debbie Pickel Smith
and
Vernon Clemans of Austin Books
for their friendship and support

And to Bill, and Laurie & Bill—
Again, and with love

# 1

*Confederate North Carolina*
*October 1864*

Harte Delaney was taking one hell of a chance. The men who rode down the deserted country lane with him were Australian blockade runners, any one of whom would enjoy plunging a bowie knife into his back. His masquerade as a Confederate buyer of goods smuggled through the Union blockade had served him well for three years of undercover missions into enemy territory, but Jacob Ringer, the captain of the Australian frigate *Sea Rover* was no fool. His shifty black eyes missed nothing, and Harte wasn't stupid enough to let down his guard.

As Ringer turned his bay mare off the rutted dirt road onto an overgrown path, Harte gauged the terrain and took note of landmarks that could guide him back that night to dynamite Ringer's ship and its illegal cargo. Once his objective was accomplished, he would have to make his way up the Cape Fear River toward the Federal blockader awaiting him off New Inlet.

Ringer rode directly ahead of Harte, and the two other men pressed close behind him. Nearly twenty minutes passed before Harte picked out a farmhouse and ramshackle red barn about a quarter of a mile ahead. Just past the rickety structures lay a rectangular field of cut tobacco, and beyond that the Cape Fear River shone in the sun like a silver ribbon. The *Sea Rover* was anchored at midstream.

By tomorrow morning the sleek blockade-running vessel would be rotting on the bottom, he thought, his blood pumping with exhilaration. He liked balancing on a tightrope of danger. The constant possibility of detection made his heart race and his brain sharp and clear. He enjoyed taking risks—the more perilous, the better. But Ringer and his men would never have an inkling of his inner excitement. He prided himself on his icy composure and the ability to hide his feelings, even in the most precarious predicament.

"The booty's in the barn, mate," Ringer told him, jerking on the reins and pulling his mare to a brutal stop. His Australian brogue was so thick that the word "mate" sounded more like "might."

Intentionally relaxing his tight muscles, Harte controlled his black stallion with his left hand so his right palm could rest on his upper leg, comfortably close to the well-oiled, pearl-handled Colt revolver he had worn strapped to his thigh since he was seventeen. A derringer lay in a hidden shoulder holster. He had learned early in his career as a detective that it paid to be ready for a trap or a double cross. More than once he'd had to shoot his way out of trouble, and he wasn't adverse to using a gun when the need arose.

When Ringer and his men dismounted, Harte swung out of the saddle himself and glanced around in a casual survey of the farm. Five more men lounged on the back porch of the house. All were armed, their postures indolent and relaxed; they seemed confident that they were safe from attack here, so deep within Southern territory.

Harte took notice of where each man sat, where his horse was hitched, and whether he carried one pistol or two. He had discovered a long time ago, the hard way, that when outnumbered, it paid to be aware of every detail, no matter how insignificant it might seem. He had once been forced to spend long months in irons in a filthy Mexican prison because he had been careless. Since that experience he had never left anything to chance.

The autumn day was peaceful, Indian summer, with only the droning buzz of a wasp and the chirp of a pair of blue jays in the pecan tree by the back door of the cabin breaking the early afternoon silence. Harte said nothing—the fewer words uttered, the less opportunity to betray his real mission. Instead, he watched Jacob Ringer's every move.

Ringer looked unconcerned. Standing two or three inches over six feet, he was almost as tall as Harte, which was unusual; Harte towered over most men. Ugly in the face, Ringer had a beefy complexion and build, a big belly and bowed legs. His stocky frame was as strong as a prizewinning bull, and he had a habit of pulling the end of his waxed handlebar mustache. His eyes were as hard and black as lead musket balls.

Although Ringer was more intelligent than his men, he was greedy as hell. That shortcoming made him sloppy. Harte had approached him as a complete stranger in the taproom of a Wilmington tavern, and without verifying Harte's credentials as a Confederate buyer from the Richmond government, Ringer had foolishly agreed to conduct him to the location of his ship—a stupid thing to do in wartime.

The two men who had ridden escort with Ringer were young and green. Sailors off the ship, if Harte's guess was right. One's name was Clyde. He was clean-shaven and had long, stringy brown hair tied back with a leather thong. He clutched his rifle like it was a naked woman, but he was too dumb to cause Harte much trouble.

The third man was probably the most dangerous. They called him Brute, and it wasn't hard for Harte to guess why. Small, lean, and mean as a snake, he resembled a reptile with his wide-set dark-blue eyes and swarthy, triangular-shaped face. He wore matching revolvers and a long knife strapped in a fringed scabbard to the back of his wide black leather belt.

Watchful and alert, Harte flipped his reins over the hitching rail and followed Ringer into the barn. The interior was dim; all the doors and windows were bolted tight against the late-afternoon sunlight. The cloying odor of manure and straw saturated the air, heavy and tangible. Several stalls were built along both side walls, but only one of them housed a horse—a silky-coated white Arabian. A ladder rose to a hayloft at the rear of the center aisle, and there were boxes and crates of supplies stacked in every corner and nook, upstairs and down.

"Show me what you've got for sale," Harte said to Ringer. He placed one hand on the butt of his gun. "If it's not good quality, I'm not interested."

"No need fer you to get yer dander up, mate. We brung in a special haul of Bahama Rum that goes down smooth as molasses and coats your stomach like you got a fire burnin' in yer innards. Share a pint or two with us, then we can get down to brass tacks."

"I didn't ride all the way out here to drink with you," Harte responded coldly. "Let me see what you have or find yourself another buyer."

"Ain't a sociable sort, are you, mate?"

"No."

Ringer looked over at Brute, who leaned against a post between two of the stalls, cleaning the space between his two front teeth with a piece of straw. Clyde was standing to Ringer's right. Harte kept his back to the wall.

"All right, it's business first, if that's the way you gotta have it." Ringer flung a hand toward an empty stall to Harte's left. "Over there be the flour, seventy danged barrels of't. There's half again that much sugar, and we got some tea 'cause we heard it was goin' for near a hundred Confederate dollars a pound in the streets of Richmond. We picked up some velvet cloth, too, fer the ladies, and some fancier dresses for the whores."

"You said you have guns you could sell me," Harte said, thrusting his hand into an uncovered flour barrel to check for weevils. He found plenty.

"That's right, I got some pistols, but they'll cost you more'n the flour and sugar put together. They be prime stock, Federal issue straight out of Massachusetts. Got'm off'n a Federal gunboat we found run aground offshore to the Florida Keys. Killed us a whole hassle of blue-bellies that day, we did. Like shootin' fish in a barrel, weren't it, Clyde?"

*And you'll hang for it, you bastard,* Harte thought as Clyde affirmed his captain's remark with a hearty guffaw.

"How much?" Harte asked without a change of expression.

"Twenty dollars each, and I'll throw in a couple of crates of ammo 'cause I support the cause you people are fightin' for. Never could see treatin' black-skinned devils like normal human bein's. They ain't even got no souls in 'em."

Brute made a noise that probably signified his agreement with Ringer's bigoted remark. Harte glanced at him, anxious now to settle on a price, then get out fast so his men could round up the lot of them, haul them to jail, and throw away the key. He was about to utter his first offer when something rustled in the straw behind him. He swiveled quickly.

"A mite jumpy, ain't ya?" Ringer grinned down at the Colt revolver already clutched in Harte's hand. "But tain't nothin' to worry 'bout, mate. Just a purty little gal we got tied up back there for safekeepin'."

"A girl?"

"Yeah. We got her down on the docks of Melbourne. The minute I seen her I knowed she'd bring a purty price on the slave block in Damascus."

*Slavers,* Harte thought in disgust, but he wasn't surprised.

"Wanna see'r?" Clyde seemed overly anxious for Harte to take a look at the woman. "We got her all dressed up for showin' off."

Harte looked at Clyde, pitying any poor girl being held by such crude, loutish criminals. No telling what she had already suffered from them on the long voyage from Australia.

Harte gave a noncommittal shrug. "I guess I can have a look at her, but I've got plenty of slaves back home to do my washing and cooking."

"You ain't gonna want her for that kind of

work, mate," Ringer proclaimed with a suggestive chuckle. "But it don't matter no way, 'cause she ain't for sale. I'm savin' her for some pasha's harem. She's gonna make me a rich man."

Always aware of Clyde's and Brute's positions, Harte followed Ringer to the stall at the base of the ladder leading up to the hayloft. "There she be. See for yerse'f if she ain't worth her weight in gold."

Harte peered into the dim cubicle, then started in shock at the small figure kneeling in the dirty hay. There, dressed in a scarlet gown so low cut that it could only have been designed for a whore, was the most beautiful woman that Harte had ever seen in his life.

She said nothing, just stared back at him without a trace of emotion. Her eyes were large, an odd golden color as pure as topaz, and ringed with incredibly long lashes. Harte found himself unable to tear his gaze away from her skin, as white and flawless as priceless marble. Her features were small and perfectly formed, and her hair was long and golden-blond, unbound and cascading over her shoulders in soft, silky curls that hung to her waist—the kind of hair a man would want to bury his hands in. When she moved slightly and put her hand to her throat, he saw the iron slave collar fastened around her neck.

Inside him, rage leapt and burned through his soul at seeing a woman chained to the wall like some damned dog. But he kept his voice unemotional. "Selling white women is against the law, Ringer."

"Not with them crazy Arabs, it ain't. They buy and sell white women all the time, especially them rich merchants over in Damascus and Baghdad." Ringer's eyes narrowed appreciatively as he looked down at the girl. "And I can tell you for a fact that there ain't none anywheres near as good-looking as this little gal. I been there and watched them sheiks lay out fortunes for harem girls nowhere near as beautiful as her."

"Don't get too close or she'll put a hex on ya," Clyde advised, sidling up close enough to make Harte uncomfortable. "I heard them abos she was with when she showed up on the docks say she got magic in her."

Harte looked at him, unable to hide his distaste. "Abos? What do you mean?"

"Aborigines. Them's the black savages we got down in Australia," Ringer answered for Clyde. "But the government's got the right idee usin' the law to control the abos."

"What law?" Harte asked, but his eyes were drawn back to the girl. There was a look in those big eyes of hers now, something unsettling that he couldn't quite figure—almost as if she recognized him. But that was impossible. He hadn't met her. He would have remembered someone who looked like her.

"Down our way, when the abos give the herders trouble, they can just ride out and shoot dead as many of'm as they want to.

Works real good. Almost like one of your American turkey shoots."

Harte merely stared at him until Clyde stepped closer to the captive girl. "C'mon, little gal, talk to the mate." When she didn't look at him, he grabbed her chain and jerked hard. She cried out and fell forward on her hands and knees. Before Clyde could blink, Harte had him by the throat and was slamming his back up against the rails of the stall. He put the barrel of his gun on Clyde's bobbing Adam's apple.

"We don't treat ladies like animals here in America," Harte said in a low, conversational tone that was so full of menace that Clyde's eyes bulged with fear.

Ringer laughed. "Now let me boy down, mate, he din't mean no insult to you. You ain't got nothin' to worry about. I been takin' real good care of the laidy. I sure ain't gonna let nobody hurt her before I get her to Damascus. Them Arabs don't want nothin' but innocent little virgins. Not that I ain't been tempted to have her meself. She's got a soft little body just waitin' for the right man to pleasure himself on her."

Harte reholstered his gun. "I want her. How much?"

Ringer smiled, showing a set of very bad teeth. His tiny eyes got tinier. Before he could formulate an answer, the sound of a galloping horse arrested their discourse, and Harte was immediately wary. Tensing, he prepared himself for trouble when he recognized the man who came running through the door as the one Ringer had left behind at the tavern in Wilmington.

"He's a goddamned Yankee agent!" the newcomer cried without preamble, pointing an accusing finger in Harte's direction. "We just got the word from one of our army contacts outta Richmond."

Lunging to one side, Harte went for his gun, but before he could squeeze the trigger Brute's rifle butt came down hard against the side of his head. Light exploded inside his brain—white, hot, blinding—then all went black, as deep and impenetrable as an ocean chasm.

"Let's kill the bloke now, Captain," Clyde growled, giving the unconscious man a kick in the ribs.

"We can't," said Gilley, the one who'd brought the news from the tavern. "The man from Richmond said we couldn't kill him. He said to keep him here 'til they bring someone down to fetch him back to the capital for questioning. He must be somebody important 'cause they're gonna pay us more if he's alive than if he's dead."

"Then we'll keep him alive," Ringer said with a greedy glint in his eye. "I don't want nobody touchin' him 'til they come get him. Clyde, you stay here and keep an eye on him."

Lily Courtland sat very still as her captors tied up the big American. He was so tall and muscular that they had trouble dragging him into the stall across from her. They left him where he lay and moved toward the front of the barn, where they conversed for a few moments. Not long after, Ringer and the other men left the barn, but Clyde came back and sat down at the bottom of the loft ladder, where he could see both her and the unconscious man. A moment later, he took a bottle of rum out of the crate beside him, uncorked it with his teeth, and tipped it to his mouth.

Lily inched back into the shadows so Clyde couldn't see her face. She stared disbelievingly at the Yankee agent, who lay on his side facing her. There could be no mistake. She had known he was the one from the first moment she had heard his voice. Swallowing hard, she let her gaze rest on his coal-black hair, which lay thick and wavy against his nape. He was bigger than she had thought he'd be, and his eyes were filled with a hard, cynical look that she hadn't noticed in her dreamings. When he had looked at her the first time and she had seen the pure sea-green color of his eyes, her certainty that he was the one was confirmed.

Her heart began to thud as the realization took hold, and she felt her throat tighten with emotion. Finally, finally, after so many years of waiting and hoping, she had found him. He would help her escape from Ringer and his men. He would help her find Derek. Tears of joy burned like fire behind her eyelids, but she didn't make a sound to alert Clyde. The Kapirigis would come soon. All she had to do was wait.

# 2

Harte roused slightly. When he moved, it felt as though a meat cleaver had split the back of his head into two parts. He blinked hard and tried to lift eyelids made of stone. Agony thudded and reverberated through his mind like angry Comanche drums.

He lay still, desperately fighting to harness the bleary, disjointed thoughts bouncing around inside his head. He was lying on his side, he realized groggily, and his arms were bound behind his back. There was the rusty, unpleasant tang of blood in his mouth, and the acrid, dusty odor of straw filled his nostrils.

Helplessness assailed him. He forced himself to open his eyes, and then he saw the beautiful girl with the golden eyes watching him from the opposite stall. Oh, God, now he remembered. The man, Gilley, had identified him. The Australians knew he was a Federal agent. Awareness of his own peril cleared his blurry vision. Clyde sat nearby with his back against the loft ladder. He was drinking rum.

Harte looked back at the girl. She hadn't

moved. He tried to ignore the pounding behind his ear where the gun butt had slammed into his skull. He was in trouble, big trouble. If he didn't find a way to escape, he was a dead man. Behind his back he twisted his wrists, endeavoring to loosen the cords without alerting Clyde.

For ten minutes he struggled to free himself, but whoever had tied him up knew what he was doing. When a board creaked directly over his head, he froze and listened as someone crept stealthily through the dry straw littering the floor of the hayloft.

Muscles tight, he strained upward from his cramped position, relieved to find Clyde still blithely guzzling rum and completely unaware that someone was on the upper level of the barn. When Harte glanced back to the girl, she lifted one forefinger to her lips and warned him to silence. She pointed to the hayloft, and Harte's gaze followed the furtive gesture.

Just above the place where Clyde sat drinking, a small Negro boy stood at the top of the ladder. The child looked to be around seven or eight years old. He wore nothing but a brown loincloth, and his face was painted white. He carried a short spear made out of a sharpened stick, and he had something else tied at his waist, a curved object that looked like a boomerang. Harte blinked in disbelief. Then, to his further astonishment, a second child stepped into view, one who was absolutely identical to the first boy. Harte squeezed his eyes shut.

Oh, God, he was seeing double. The blow to his head must have given him a concussion. He opened his eyes and watched warily as one of the half-naked children retrieved a pint of rum from the crate stored beside the ladder. The boy squatted on his haunches, carefully aligned the bottle with Clyde's head, then let the missile fall. The vessel hit the top of Clyde's skull and shattered into a thousand shards of brown glass. Clyde keeled over sideways and lay still.

The boy who had dropped the bottle scrambled down the rungs and snatched Clyde's knife from its fringed scabbard. The other twin stayed in the loft and watched the barn door. Harte struggled to his knees as the first boy hurried toward the girl, still clutching the dagger in his hand.

"Don't be afraid of us," the girl whispered in a cultured accent that sounded more British but had some Australian brogue. "The Kapirigis have come to free us. As soon as they cut you loose, you must find a way to break my chain so we can escape."

"The Kapirigis? Who the hell are they?" Harte muttered as the little boy ran to his side and began a furious sawing motion against the thick hemp rope binding his wrists.

"They're my aboriginal friends. We tried to escape when they took us off the ship several days ago. The boys got away, but Brute caught me. That's when they chained me up in here."

Aborigines were the natives Ringer had said

were hunted for sport down in Australia, Harte remembered. When he felt the ropes on his arms begin to loosen, he jerked his hands free and shook off the bindings. He took the knife from the little black boy, who grinned at him, revealing a gap where his two front teeth had been.

"He be the green-eyed one, Lily?" the boy asked the girl softly in broken, heavily accented English.

*So her name is Lily,* Harte thought, as the girl nodded, but he didn't waste time puzzling over their cryptic conversation. Gritting his teeth against the pain from his head wound, he quickly made his way to Clyde and jerked the six-shooter out of the Australian's holster.

"Is there a key to this thing?" he asked softly when he returned to the girl and went down on one knee to examine her shackles. The iron ring around her neck was narrow but heavy, and he frowned when he saw the raw skin where the metal had rubbed away the soft flesh of her slender throat.

"Ringer keeps it with him," Lily answered as Harte lifted the chain to gauge its weight.

Bracing one boot against the boards of the stall, he pulled hard. His injured head exploded with arrows of agony as he exerted all his strength. A second later, the wood began to splinter and he was able to pull the chain out of the anchor ring. As soon as the suspended chain fell to the floor, Lily picked it up in her hand and jumped to her feet. She grabbed hold of Harte's arm.

"Some of Ringer's crew arrived from the ship while you were unconscious," she whispered urgently. "Come, the Kapirigis can lead us out through the woods."

Even armed with Clyde's pistol, Harte knew he wouldn't have a chance in hell against so many men. Lily was right. Their only choice was to make a run for it.

"If we can get to the river, there's help waiting for me downstream," he muttered, but Lily didn't stay to hear more. She and the boy were already halfway up the ladder by the time Harte stuck the gun in his belt and swung up the rungs after them.

Lily stopped in the loft to stuff the hem of her full scarlet skirt into her waistband. A shaft of smoky light flooded downward from a hole in the ceiling, and when he had almost reached her, she pulled herself lithely up through the opening and out onto the shingled roof, then hunkered down to await him. Harte forced his way through the broken slats, relieved to find that the sun had gone down and twilight was deepening into night.

"Ringer's got the dingoes penned up behind the barn," she whispered. "They'll set them on us as soon as they know we've escaped."

"Dingoes?"

"Dogs. They run wild in packs in Australia, but Ringer's trained them to hunt the abos.

The Kapirigis are terrified of them. That's why they aren't waiting for us to catch up."

Without another word, she turned and crept down the steep-pitched roof to a gnarled white oak tree that grew close to the barn. Harte could hear a group of men talking somewhere, probably in front of the barn where he had left his horse at the hitching rail. Luckily, they couldn't see him from their position.

As soon as her feet touched the ground, Lily took off in a crouched run toward the trees behind the barn. Harte could barely make out the two aborigines waiting in the cover of the trees; only their painted faces were visible in the growing dusk. When he and the girl reached them, they took off like pursued rabbits through the woods toward the river.

Within minutes they reached a shallow creek, but neither the girl nor the boys slowed their flight, splashing along the rock-strewn bed of the rippling stream, their feet churning the clear water and causing a huge crow to caw raucously and flutter off a cedar limb. Harte hastily followed their lead, then froze in midstride at the sharp crack of a rifle report.

Lily looked back at him, her face twisted in horror as a frenzied barking and baying echoed from the distance. "They're setting the dingoes loose!" she cried in terror. "Hurry! Run! They'll tear us apart if they catch us!"

The two boys were still sloshing down the stream at a full run, and Harte grabbed the girl's hand and bolted through the shallows.

He had ridden in enough fox hunts in his youth to recognize the excited yelping of hounds on the scent. The pack had picked up their trail, all right, and it wouldn't take the dogs long to catch up with them.

Harte changed his course, dragging the girl up the bank into a copse of evergreens. About fifty yards away through a thick undergrowth of brambles and bushes, he could see the river where it flowed below the anchorage of the *Sea Rover.* As he turned to look back, the first howling hound lunged into sight. The agitated animal ran up and down the bank, his nose sniffing the ground near the point at which they had entered the pines.

Harte pulled out his pistol, but before he could use it, he heard a *whooshing* sound and saw a boomerang pass by on his right side, rotating end over end down the creekbed until it struck the dingo's head hard enough to knock the animal off its feet into the water, where it lay still. By the time Harte could look back downstream, the young aborigine who had hurled the weapon had turned and was fleeing again toward the river.

Lily was running through the trees ahead of him, her scarlet dress a bright patch in the dusky gray light. Harte dashed after her, but halfway to the river a second dingo caught up to them. As Harte turned to fire, the dog veered away from him and toward Lily, leaping onto her and knocking her to the ground. Harte pulled the trigger, to stop the vicious, blood-crazed animal's attack, then yanked Lily to her feet as three more snarling dingoes with bared fangs sprang toward them in long-legged pursuit.

Harte thrust Lily behind him, aimed, and fired in rapid succession, wounding two of the animals before he ran out of bullets and a huge black mongrel hit him full force from the side and knocked him to his knees. Grappling desperately with the infuriated dog on his chest and trying to protect himself from its snapping jaws, he somehow managed to get a grip on the knife in his belt. He plunged the sharp blade deep into the dingo's side, then sucked in air and fought to regain his breath as the animal fled, yelping and dragging its back legs.

Harte got hold of the terrified girl again and ran for the river. When they reached the high bank, he jumped without hesitation, taking Lily into the water with him. They broke the surface within seconds, choking and gasping for air as he pulled her into the swiftest part of the stream, praying that the current would carry them far enough downstream to get them out of rifle range.

To his dismay, they were washed up on a shallow sandbar only ten yards from the point where they had entered the water. Well aware that Ringer and his men would show up at any minute, he looked around frantically and spotted a downed tree bobbing in the current near a logjam of branches and driftwood. He sloshed through the swift water and put his shoulder to the log. He shoved hard, trying to dislodge it, and Lily came quickly to help. Then they heard a man's shout echo over the water.

"That's Brute," Lily whispered fearfully as Harte pushed her toward the exposed rootwad of a weeping willow tree that overhung the water near them. Holding her back tightly against his chest, he clamped his hand over her mouth.

"Don't make a sound," he whispered against her ear. "They're coming down the bank looking for us."

"They must've got away, Captain," Brute called out not long after that.

An indistinguishable answer sounded from farther upstream. Harte pressed deeper into the recessed bank. He pulled out the long bowie knife again and held it in readiness.

"Spread out and beat through them bushes from here up to where we found them dead dingoes," Jacob Ringer ordered, his voice very close now. "They couldn't've gone far. He's probably hiding somewhere along here."

Every nerve on edge, Harte tensed when he heard low splashing sounds coming toward them. Within seconds, a rifle butt slashed through the willow fronds not a foot from Lily's shoulder. The next jab would hit her.

When the gun reappeared, Harte grabbed the barrel and jerked as hard as he could. His unexpected attack loosed the weapon from his stalker's hands, and Harte swiveled the rifle around, found the trigger, and fired up through the thick foliage toward the man who had been holding it. A hoarse scream ended abruptly as the bullet struck, and Harte wasted no more time.

"Grab hold," he muttered to Lily, grunting as he thrust the log out into the stream as hard as he could. The jammed driftwood broke loose, enabling him to maneuver the log into the swift current. Frantically kicking his feet, he propelled them out into the river.

Harte darted a look behind him and saw Ringer and a couple of his men running down the bank about twenty yards behind them. He pressed closer to the log as a slug hit the wood between Lily and him, throwing up splinters of bark. The second bullet was more accurate, and he groaned from the burning impact of hot iron ripping open the top of his arm.

"I'm hit, dammit. You've got to help me! Kick!" he yelled to Lily, gritting his teeth against the pain as he clung to the log with his good arm. With Lily's help, they finally reached the rushing current, which swept them into a wide bend in the river. Harte breathed easier and probed the bloody wound with his fingers. He wasn't hit badly. If he could hold on, they had a chance of making it.

After they had been swept about fifty yards downriver, he caught sight of the two young aborigines struggling through the dense growth on the riverbank. Unfortunately Lily saw them too.

"I can't leave the Kapirigis," she cried, letting go of the log and striking out for shore.

"Wait, it's too swift here!" Harte yelled after her, but she paid no heed to his warning and continued to struggle toward the bank, barely able to keep her head above water. *The heavy iron collar and chain are dragging her down,* he thought furiously. *She'll never make it.* He ought to leave her to her fate, dammit, but he couldn't just lie back and watch her drown before his eyes.

Cursing foully, he let go of the driftwood and managed to get to her before she went under. He set his jaw against the pain, got his injured arm across her chest, and began to tow her to shore. The moment he dragged her into the shallows, the little aborigine twins splashed into the water to help them.

Harte pushed his long hair out of his eyes and looked apprehensively back upriver. "We've got to get farther downstream. If they go back for their horses, they'll find us here."

Lily was staring straight at him, but she had a strange expression on her face, as if she didn't really see him. Then suddenly her eyes sharpened and seemed to regain their focus. She gasped.

"We can't! A boat's coming upriver," she cried in fright. "We have to hide! It's your enemies! The ones with a red flag with a big blue X on it."

"Confederates? Where?" Harte jerked around but saw no sign of any craft on the mile or so of river exposed before the next turn in the stream. When he turned back, Lily and the boys had disappeared into the bushes.

"Goddammit, they're going to get me killed," he muttered furiously, grasping his bleeding shoulder and pushing into the undergrowth after them. He found the three hidden in a thicket of vines.

"There. You can see it now," she murmured softly as he went down on his haunches beside her.

Harte followed her gaze and found that a small paddle wheeler had rounded the far bend and was slowly steaming upstream toward them. Just like she had said, it flew the Confederate stars and bars on its bowsprit.

Harte turned incredulous eyes on her. "How the devil did you know it was coming?"

"I knew because I knew."

Harte scowled and shook his head at her stupid answer, but then the aborigines began talking urgently together in their peculiar guttural language.

"The Kapirigis have been hiding near here. They say we'll be safe in their *wiltja,*" she whispered, then sprinted off after the little boys before Harte could object.

"Damnation!" Harte cursed under his breath, looking again at the gunboat chugging toward them, but he knew he had little choice. Not with enemies on both sides.

The aborigines and the girl were moving swiftly and silently through the fallen leaves and branches ahead of him. He increased his pace to keep them in sight. He followed them up a low hill and through a copse of thick pine trees beside another meandering creek. All three waded through the shallows and rounded a series of boulders that took them out of his sight. When Harte got to the same point, they had disappeared.

"Up here," hissed a low voice, and Harte craned his neck to find the girl leaning out of a small opening high above him. When he started his climb to reach her, she vanished into the side of the cliff. A cave, he realized, but once he scaled the rocks, he found that the opening was so small he had to squeeze sideways to get his wide shoulders through the narrow crevice.

Inside, the two little boys were hunkered down around a ring of stones in which banked embers smoldered, and Lily was shivering and shrugging a tattered blanket around her shoulders. The cavern was too low for him to stand, so he squatted down and looked curiously around the cramped chamber. Crude drawings of birds and animals decorated the ceiling and walls, strange elongated shapes etched in white paint.

"The Kapirigis say the dingoes can't find us here, because we crossed through water before we climbed the rocks." Lily's low voice echoed slightly off the sides of the cave.

Harte jerked off his black neckerchief and wrapped it around his wounded arm, a surreal sensation overtaking him as he pulled the makeshift bandage tight with his teeth. He stared at the trembling girl and the two little white-faced black boys, wondering how he had ever gotten himself into such a bizarre predicament. A coarse cry from outside brought him quickly alert. He pulled his knife and flattened himself next to the opening to the cave.

# 3

"Do you hear something?" Lily asked, huddling deeper into the woolen blanket wrapped around her. She winced as the iron collar rubbed painfully against her raw neck.

"Yeah, a shout, but it could've drifted in off the water," Harte Delaney answered softly from his crouched position near the entrance. "We're close enough to hear the men on the boat."

Lily thought he looked absolutely enormous in the small confines of the cave. His hair was still damp, and when he combed his fingers restlessly through it, the slicked-back wet hair accentuated the chiseled features of his deeply tanned face. One sleeve of his soaked, mud-spattered white shirt was torn and blood-stained, and the garment clung to his body, outlining the bulging bands of muscle across his broad back.

"Are you hurt badly?" she asked, watching the tiny rivulets of blood that trickled down his arm and through his fingers.

"No," he answered. He glanced briefly at his

wound, then absently wiped the blood on his pants leg.

Harte Delaney was even stronger than she had expected, Lily thought. She knew his face well and had longed endlessly to meet the man she had seen in her dreamings since she was a little girl, but her vivid visions hadn't prepared her for just how imposing he would be in the flesh. Although he stood four or five inches over six feet and had a lean, muscular physique, she was still astonished that he had possessed the strength to wrench the iron bolt from the wall of the barn.

Furthermore, she had begun to sense unsettling things about him. Often inside her mind pictures, he had smiled affectionately and easily, even laughed. At those times she had felt warm and secure in the knowledge that he was a good, kind man who could be trusted. But now that she had met him, she realized that he wasn't like that at all. He seemed hard and jaded, the sort of man who she feared could be quite ruthless and uncaring when he wanted to be. Now, so close to him, she found that he both frightened and fascinated her.

"I've got a skiff hidden downstream not too far from here," he told her a moment later, his eyes riveted on the woods below the cliff. "There's a Union gunboat waiting to pick me up just after dark, so we'll have to head out of here soon. Maybe we'll get lucky and Ringer won't come after us."

"He'll stop looking after the sun sets," she

told him at once. Silent and composed, the two aborigine children waited on either side of her, clutching their spears and watching Harte Delaney with wide, solemn eyes. "After the Kapirigis escaped, Ringer hunted them with dogs all through the daylight hours, but he always stopped looking at night."

Harte turned to face her. "How did they escape?"

"I distracted Clyde so they could get away. That's when Ringer put this on me." She pointed to the collar and chain.

A muscle jumped spasmodically in the lean contours of Harte Delaney's dark cheek. When he spoke, his voice was thick with suppressed anger. "I'll get that damn thing off you as soon as we reach the ship. How did they get their hands on you in the first place?"

"I bought passage on the *Sea Rover* to come to America. I didn't know they were slavers."

He looked at her in surprise. "You were going to make the voyage here all by yourself?"

"No, the Kapirigis were with me," Lily answered, encircling each little boy around with a protective arm.

"Why do you call them that?"

"They're identical twins. They believe they're the same person since they shared the same womb."

"They have the same name? Then how the hell do you tell them apart?"

"They're always together, so there's never

any need to tell them apart. But sometimes I call them Kapi and Rigi."

A faint frown brought Harte's eyebrows together before he turned to scan the outside terrain. "I guess it's dark enough now." He gestured at the boys. "Can you keep them quiet while we're on the move?"

Lily bristled at his patronizing tone, realizing again how different he was from the man in her dreamings, whom she had admired and longed to meet. She didn't like the real Harte Delaney much, especially now that he had spoken of the Kapirigis as if they were stupid animals.

"If you'll remember," she said coldly, "the Kapirigis kept quiet enough to free you from the barn after you carelessly got yourself caught by Ringer and his crew."

Her obvious sarcasm brought the big American's attention to bear on her. A faint expression of surprise registered in his pale-green eyes; then, to her surprise, he grinned, but only fleetingly. "You're right. I owe them. Now let's see if we can get the hell out of here in one piece before Ringer shows up and catches me again."

The moon had not yet risen to lighten the inky night, and Lily found the descent over the steep rock cliff a difficult maneuver in the darkness. When her foot hit a patch of loose shale and sent a small rockslide scraping down the cliff onto Harte's head, he took a firm hold of her arm and assisted her the rest of the way. When they reached the ground, he pulled her down beside him and waited until the Kapirigis descended with their agile grace and settled on their haunches beside them.

"Once we reach the riverbank, I don't want you to make a sound. Voices travel over water, especially at night, and the river's crawling with Confederate patrols," he whispered, his mouth so close to Lily's ear that his warm lips touched her earlobe. A flood of goose bumps swept down both her arms, and she was appalled at her reaction to his touch.

Apparently Harte Delaney was not similarly affected, because he struck off through the night without another word. Lily blamed her cold chills on the cool night air, then rubbed them away vigorously as she hurried after him. He moved swiftly and silently through the woods, at a pace relentless enough to eventually strain Lily's endurance. Although she had once been physically fit from riding horses and working with her father on Malmora, the inactivity of being locked in a cabin aboard the *Sea Rover* had taken its toll on her stamina.

A familiar wave of helpless grief gripped her when she thought of her father's death and the loss of the cattle station he had worked so hard to acquire. Six long months had passed since his death, and his murderers still went unpunished. She had to find her brother. Derek was the only one who could get Malmora back and see justice done.

Tears burned her eyes, and she willfully

forced the image of her father's beloved face from her mind. She couldn't let herself think about him right now. She was in enough trouble already. For the time being, her only concern should be keeping up with Harte Delaney's long-legged, tireless strides.

Glancing back at the boys, who walked behind her, she saw that they were having no trouble with the American's pace. A night trek over rough terrain meant nothing to them. While she had been lovingly brought up by doting parents in their comfortable station house, they had been born in the wilds of the outback.

From birth, their young lives had been filled with hardship and danger, not only from the snakes and crocodiles that inhabited the land but also from the cruel white men who hunted down aborigines and shot them like animals of prey. She shivered violently as the wind off the water cut through the damp fabric of her skimpy silk dress and penetrated her wet skin. Now she, too, knew how it felt to be hunted, then collared and chained like a wild animal.

To her relief, Harte eventually stopped and waited for them in a thicket of willows. "We're almost there. Can you make it?"

Lily nodded, but her chest was heaving with exertion, and the iron collar grew heavier with every footstep.

"Stay behind me and keep quiet," he ordered, moving out again.

After what seemed a long time, Harte finally

went into a crouch, and Lily collapsed gratefully on her knees. The Kapirigis squatted beside her, patiently watching Harte climb down the riverbank and pull branches and debris off the small boat he had apparently hidden earlier.

A moment later he returned, picked up Lily, and lowered her into the boat. He helped the Kapirigis scramble aboard, then stepped into the stern himself, his massive weight causing the light craft to dip precariously to one side. After using the oar to push away from the bank, he sat in the stern and bent his back to the job of rowing.

Huddled close to the two boys, Lily let Harte Delaney take them wherever he would, glad for the opportunity to sit and rest. After the long, terrible voyage with Ringer, she was in America and with the man of her dreamings. Once they reached safety, somehow, some way she had to persuade him to help her find her brother.

Several hours after they had climbed safely aboard the Federal gunboat *Integrity*, Harte made his way belowdecks and headed for Lily's cabin. He had spent the last hour debriefing Captain Richtner and his officers about the *Sea Rover* and her cargo, but his mind had been on the girl who wore the slave collar.

In his hands he carried the hammer and chisel he had obtained from the ship's carpenter, and he increased his pace, eager to get that damned collar off her neck. He knew the humiliation and degradation of being shackled and how it felt to wear heavy irons that robbed a man of strength and rubbed away his skin until it festered and oozed.

When he reached the door of the cabin to which Lily and the boys had been taken, he knocked and then entered without thinking to await permission. From her place at the washbowl, the girl whirled around, nude from the waist up. Harte stopped in his tracks as she quickly crossed her arms to hide her nakedness.

"Forgive me," he mumbled thickly, embarrassed by his own ill manners. As she hastily snatched up a blanket and wrapped it around her, he averted his gaze, but his body had been instantly affected by the brief glimpse of her full, bare, ivory breasts. He was aroused in a way he didn't like.

Frowning, he turned and shut the door. He saw that the two little boys were snuggled together sound asleep in one of the bunks attached to the wall of the cabin. When he looked back at the girl, she had covered herself with the blanket, but he still had trouble dragging his eyes away from her beautiful face. There was something about her that made him uneasy. She gazed at him with a strange, insightful expression in her topaz eyes, almost as if she knew something that he didn't. At that point he realized that he didn't even know her last name.

"I guess it's time we introduced ourselves," he said, his eyes drawn to her mouth when she wet her lips with the tip of her tongue. The innocent gesture was unbelievably erotic, a fact that was not lost upon Harte. "I'm Harte Delaney. What's your last name, Lily?"

"Courtland. How do you do, Mr. Delaney?"

Harte had to grin at her coy remark, more appropriate if they had been sharing tea and wafers than after the hair-raising escape they had endured only hours before. He was surprised when she relaxed visibly and gave him a tentative smile.

*Good God,* he thought in awe, *she has the face of an angel.* Her small, delicate features seemed almost too perfect to belong to a mortal woman, and her topaz eyes rocked a man's senses. Harte had learned long ago that beautiful women were created to enslave a man's mind and make him stupid and careless, and Lily Courtland had the face and body to do the job better than just about any woman he'd ever encountered. Although he was wary of her, she intrigued him.

"I've come to get that collar off," he said brusquely, annoyed with his overblown reaction to her beauty. "I know how degrading it is to wear irons."

"You've been a prisoner too?" she asked as he moved closer to her.

Harte's jaw clenched, unwanted memories stirring in the muddy depths of his mind where he kept his ancient pain and dark disillusionment. He didn't answer her question. "I think I can pry it off, but you'll have to hold completely still. Sit down and lean across the desk."

Holding the blanket around her torso, Lily obeyed. When she looked up at him, Harte avoided her eyes; he didn't like the way she affected him. He was drawn to her more than to any woman in a long time. "Put your head down and hold on to the edge of the table."

When she did as he asked, her long golden hair lay spread in soft waves across the top of the desk. He put his hand upon it to push it aside, and the thick blond tresses felt like silk against his fingers. He fought a nearly uncontrollable urge to gather the satiny strands in both hands just to savor the fine texture.

"Hold back your hair so I can see what I'm doing," he ordered in a sharper voice than necessary.

Obediently Lily pulled the long tresses over her shoulder and out of his way. She laid her cheek flat against the tabletop and squeezed her eyes shut. She was afraid; her lips were trembling. He stared down at her for a moment, wondering how old she was. Her skin was so smooth and white, so clear and unblemished that it seemed translucent. Ringer had been right. She would have brought a fortune on the slave block. Most men would sell their soul to have her, and unfortunately Harte was probably one of those men.

Muttering a curse beneath his breath, he went to work on the shackle. The task took a long time, but the lock finally came free, and he lifted the collar off her slender throat, wincing at the sight of her inflamed neck.

"I've brought some salve," Harte said, taking the jar from his vest pocket. "Hold up your hair, and I'll put it on for you."

Lily did as he bade her, and Harte unstoppered the bottle, very aware that she was nearly naked beneath the blanket. Trying to shake off his lascivious thoughts, he poured the oily ointment in his palm and gently smoothed it over the ugly welt that the iron collar had raised. She sighed with pleasure, her head falling back slightly as he reached the side of her throat. He could feel her pulse beneath his fingertips, rapid and erratic.

Harte's hand stilled as Lily suddenly opened her eyes. He wanted her, dammit, he thought furiously. He wanted to possess her. He wanted to be the first man who ever touched her, the only man who ever touched her. Disgusted with himself, he stepped back as if she were poison, deciding he had to put distance between them until he could purge the provocative thoughts dominating his mind.

"I guess we need to decide what to do with you and the boys," he said at length, taking a flask of whiskey out of his pocket. "Do you have anywhere to go? Or do you want to return home to Australia?"

"I came here to find my brother. I was hoping you could help me."

Harte took a swig of the liquor and welcomed the burning of the potent brew's course down his throat. "Is he here in America?"

"I think so. He's a ship's captain, and his last letter came from a place called Charleston in the Carolinas. Do you know of it?"

Instantly Harte was suspicious. If she had a brother fighting for the South, she could very well be a Confederate agent. She could have been working with Ringer all along. Although it seemed unlikely, Harte had learned a long time ago that things weren't always as they seemed. More important, he had found out that trusting women, even young ones who looked as innocent as Lily Courtland, was stupid. Careful to disguise his budding distrust, he sat down across from her.

"What's your brother's name?"

"Derek Courtland. Do you know him?"

"No."

Lily leaned forward eagerly. "Perhaps you've heard of his ship then. It's called the *Mamu*. It's very fast and sleek."

Harte's mind froze. It was difficult not to show any reaction to her revelation. The *Mamu* was the most notorious blockade runner the South had in her employ. Every man in the secret service, bar none, had orders to capture the *Mamu* and its crew, at any cost.

"Sorry, never heard of it," he replied coolly, but he watched her closely for any sign of deceit.

Disappointment that looked too genuine to be manufactured furrowed the smooth skin of her fair brow. "I have to find him. My father was murdered for his land. No one would listen to me when I said I knew who did it, but they'll listen to Derek. Is the city of Charleston in your half of the United States?"

"No. It's a seaport in South Carolina that's part of the Confederacy."

"Could you get me there somehow? If you'll help me, I can repay you."

Harte looked at the girl who sat across from him wearing little more than a woolen blanket, no other possession to her name. "How do you intend to repay me?"

"I can help you with your work."

Harte's suspicion intensified. "What do you know about my work?"

"You're an agent for the Northern states, aren't you? The ones fighting against slavery? I don't know much about your war, but I think all people should be free. The aborigines are treated abominably in my country."

"What makes you think I'm an agent?"

"Gilley told Ringer you were when he came into the barn, right before they knocked you unconscious. Don't you remember?"

Harte did remember, but he was more interested in how she thought she could help him. "If I should arrange for you get to Charleston, what are you going to do for me?"

For the first time, Lily's forthright manner became evasive. "I want to tell you the truth, but I'm afraid you won't believe me."

*And she's right*, Harte thought, but he only

lifted a shoulder in a careless shrug. "There's only one way to find out."

After a moment of indecision, she met his steadfast gaze. "I can identify your enemies for you."

"Is that right? How?" He tried to keep the mockery from his tone.

"It's hard to explain."

"Try."

Lily nervously moistened her lips, but this time Harte was not tempted to kiss her, nor was he fooled by her furrowed brow and troubled face. He knew how to handle enemy agents, especially female ones who were trying to insinuate themselves into his confidence.

"My brother and I were born with something that other people don't have," she said finally, very reluctantly, and she looked so guilty and uncomfortable that Harte was ready to disbelieve anything that came out of her mouth. "You see, my grandmother had it too." She looked at him, then cast down her gaze. "The aborigines think I'm a witch, but I'm not really one."

Harte could only stare incredulously at her. "What the hell are you talking about?"

"I see pictures in my head that come true," she admitted, as if quite embarrassed to be speaking of it. Her words began to spill out faster when she saw his annoyed frown. "I know things about people that I have no way of knowing. I don't know why. I just do. It's really sort of like . . . magic."

Harte had heard enough. He got to his feet. "Look, Miss Courtland, I'm tired, and my arm hurts. I can tell you right away that I'm not in the mood for stupid games, and I don't believe in magic. You can find someone else to help you find your brother."

"Please don't go! I can tell you things about yourself, right now, if you like. Would you believe me then?"

*Yeah, probably memorized intelligence straight out of the files of the Confederate secret service,* Harte thought, but he was curious to hear what she had to say. He sat down opposite her. "All right. Show me what you mean."

Lily hesitated momentarily, and Harte thought she looked nervous. He lowered his eyes to her hands. She clasped them tightly together on top of the table.

"When you touched my throat a moment ago to put on the ointment, I suddenly knew that you're wearing a medallion around your neck. One that you never take off. It's round and made of gold and set with a silver crucifix, and it's hanging from a chain with a repaired clasp. There are some words engraved on it, but they're in a foreign language, Spanish, perhaps. If you'll let me hold it in my hand, I can tell you more."

Harte stared at her in astonishment. She had described every detail of his gold Saint Christopher's medal. How could she possibly have known? Unless perhaps she had somehow managed to see it in the barn when he was unconscious. He hesitated, not sure what to think. Intrigued, he slowly pulled the religious ornament out from beneath his shirt, looped the chain over his head, and placed the necklace on the table between them.

Lily gazed down at the unusual-looking antique amulet, suddenly loathe to touch the burnished metal. Dark, sinister sensations emanated from the beautifully crafted object. What would happen when she picked it up? Suddenly she wasn't sure she wanted to know, not even to obtain Harte Delaney's help. She didn't want to sink into the darkness and lose control of her mind—what if she saw something awful, something terrifying and full of pain? What if the headaches came again and the shadowy places?

Harte was watching her closely. She was certain that he didn't believe her. She looked down at the gold medallion lying on the table just inches from her fingertips. Her throat felt as if it were stuffed with scratchy dry cotton. Fingers of fear closed around her heart, tight, constricting, stifling. *I have to do it, I have to,* she thought wildly, *or Harte Delaney will never help me.* She reached out and covered the medallion with her hand. She shut her eyes and spoke quickly, before she lost her courage.

"I see a pretty woman with dark hair and eyes. She has on a bright-colored dress—yellow with black lace around the neckline and black bows down the front. She's standing somewhere high up in the air, and the wind's blowing her hair and billowing her skirt, and I can hear a loud roaring. It's the ocean, the sound of waves against rocks. She's unhappy. She's weeping. She has a funny name. Calla—no, it's Camillia, I think." Lily opened her eyes and saw that Harte Delaney's face had blanched.

"Go on," he muttered, but his voice sounded strangled, as if he had to force out the words.

Slowly, so full of dread that she could barely breathe, Lily curled her fingers around the medallion and clutched it tightly in her palm. She closed her eyes and waited fearfully.

*Please, please, let the feelings be warm and good and kind,* she thought frantically as the cold darkness came rushing in at her, swiftly, faster and faster, hard, black, and so loud it seemed that the sound and fury of all the world's tempests whirled through her mind, until she felt caught up by a typhoon, alone and blind to all around her until the first image came surging at her. An animal, an enormous white stallion with flowing mane and flaring nostrils, swift and sleek . . . no, it wasn't white, it was lathered with sweat . . . the steed was black, as black as the night through which it galloped. Then she saw the other riders and horses and the darkness that had closed around her lightened to mottled gray and she could see the gore and blood, could hear the screams of dying, the firing of guns, and the clanking of heavy swords. *She felt the blood gushing through her veins, smelled the acrid smoke and swirling dust kicked up by the battle, heard the screams of agony and death, felt the sword as it sliced into her back, knocking her to the ground amidst the writhing wounded horses and dying men. . . .*

"Lily? What's wrong?" Harte's voice came from some far away place. "Can you hear me?"

*The smoke was clearing now—a different day—it was dawn—she could feel the cold air on her bare skin—could feel the wind raise the loose white shirt she wore, a camisa, it was called. Oh, God in heaven, they had failed, they had failed, the battle was over, the white-clad* campesinos *lying dead and bleeding on the desolate, wind-swept mountains near Veracruz—it was Mexico—it was 1858 and Santa Anna's soldiers were her captors, standing on the ground beside her horse—what was it?—why was she shaking?—why was her heart caught in her throat?—*

"A hanging, I'm going to hang," she whispered in horror through lips swollen from the gash made when one of her captors had struck her. She tasted blood, felt her eyes rolling up into her head, and heard the awful grinding voice that came from her mouth but was not hers: "Let me die like a man. Take off the irons, damn you—"

*The man was coming toward her, big, brawny, mustachioed, dressed in a tan uniform and a wide-brimmed white hat, the noose came down tightly over her head, a rope, thick, coarse, biting into her throat,* "Juarista *bastard . . . choke on your own tongue"—a growl, an oath, and she struggled to speak the words as the rope tightened around her gullet—*

"Camillia," she choked out, holding her throat with both hands. "Camillia—"

*The horse lurched from beneath her and she was plunged down into empty space, her body jerked to a stop and the cord cut into her neck, cutting off her air—she couldn't breathe! She couldn't breathe! She was going to die!*

*And then she was plunged into the blackness of the other side and she knew it was over, the battle for Mexico, her life, and she didn't want to die—*

The vision ended abruptly. Lily opened her eyes and found Harte's face twisted with revulsion. Obviously shaken, he pushed his chair back and staggered a few steps. Then, without uttering a word, he turned and left the cabin.

Lily's muscles, still stiff and tense from the brutal dreaming, finally relaxed. She lost her grip on the medallion, and the heavy gold medal clattered against the desktop. Lily waited with sick dread for the onset of the intense headache that always followed the most violent of her visions. When the jagged-edged pain slashed across her forehead with the force of a rapier, she groaned out loud, laying her head down on the table and clutching her pounding temples.

# 4

From his position at the stern railing, Harte saw Lily Courtland the moment she appeared abovedecks. As he watched her stroll with the Kapirigis toward the starboard bow, he absently massaged his bandaged arm and tried yet again to come to terms with what he had witnessed the night before. Even now, he felt shaken and twisted up inside because of Lily's trance—or whatever the hell it was.

Suppressed emotion wrapped his chest in a bond like a tight leather strap. God in heaven, she had seen the day Santa Anna's men had tried to hang him. She had spoken aloud his own last words. How in God's name could she have known that? And she'd mentioned Camillia, of all people. Harte hadn't spoken Camillia's name in nearly ten years, not to anyone. She was dead, the past over and done with. He hadn't thought about her in a long time, not until Lily had picked up his medallion and made him relive intimate details of his own past.

His attention sharpened as the first officer

of the *Integrity*, a middle-aged man by the name of Janzen, doffed his cap to Lily. When the two of them began a conversation, Harte wondered if she might be probing for details about the ship and its mission. If she really was Derek Courtland's sister, as she had said she was, Harte couldn't discount the possibility that she might be working for the Confederacy.

Since the beginning of the war he had dealt with countless Southern agents, both those spying on and sabotaging Northern cities and those trying to uncover his own allegiance while he was working as a Federal agent behind enemy lines. Since Sumter had been fired upon, plenty of women had used their charm and beauty to extract information from unsuspecting men fighting for the other side. Lily Courtland certainly had enough of those qualities to tempt any man into telling her whatever she wanted to know.

Somehow, though, his instincts told him a different story. Deep inside his heart, as incredible as her story seemed, he believed she was telling the truth—about being abducted, about coming to America to find her brother, and most surprisingly, about the fantastic ability she seemed to possess.

Harte had read about people who were supposedly gifted with a sixth sense that defied scientific reason. Seers of visions. Fortune-tellers. Although he had always scorned such stories as hoaxes concocted by charlatans, Lily's demonstration had been too powerful and too detailed to deny.

But apart from the possibility that she might be a true clairvoyant, there was an even more important issue concerning her brother. Allan Pinkerton, Harte's good friend and superior officer in the secret service, would no doubt be extremely pleased to have Derek Courtland's sister in Union hands. The *Mamu* had so far been able to elude Federal blockaders, and Lily could be invaluable in luring the blockade runner into a trap. The idea intrigued him, except for one thing: If he did use Lily to capture her brother, he would have to spend a good deal of time in her company. Given her gift to divine facts, could he keep such a conspiracy from her? Besides, the woman already affected him more than he liked, and he wasn't inclined to let her get too close to him. Personal relationships were dangerous. He worked alone, he lived alone—and that was the way he wanted it to stay.

Frowning, he watched a second crewman stop to chat with Lily and the boys. Even dressed in rolled-up trousers and a man's shirt, a woman as beautiful as she attracted attention. If he took her into Washington, she would not go unnoticed. He would have to keep her presence a secret, he decided, and the only good way to do that was take her to his house and keep her there until he and Pinkerton decided what should be done with her.

Clear on his course of action, he strode in her direction. What he was contemplating was not particularly honorable, but a lot of things he had done while with the secret service were shady at best. War was war, and a very dirty business, especially a bloody civil war waged in a country divided within itself.

As he approached, he watched the way her unbound hair billowed in the sea breeze and remembered vividly how soft and silky-fine it had felt in his hands. There was something different about Lily Courtland, some inexplicable quality that beckoned him to her. She was dangerous to him in that respect. He would have to keep his guard up.

Harte hadn't quite reached her when she turned and looked directly at him, as if she had known he was coming. Hell, she probably did know. He scowled faintly, but when she smiled, seemingly happy to see him, his pulse quickened. Dammit, what was it about her that got to him so much?

"Good morning, Mr. Delaney," she greeted him politely while gathering her hair over one shoulder to hold it in place. "I have brought your amulet back to you. I know you rarely take it off."

*Yes, she's right again,* he thought, looking down at the medallion that dangled from Lily's slender fingers. He had put it on after Camillia's death to remind him never to trust another woman. He had the distinct feeling that he would need such a reminder so long as Lily Courtland was around. As he took the chain and looped it over his head, he glanced at the aborigines. Their faces reflected identical smiles.

"Have you decided to help me?" Lily asked, searching his face with anxious eyes.

Harte was careful that his expression revealed nothing. "I think we can come to some kind of agreement."

"Oh, thank you so much. You won't be sorry. I swear it."

Her words came with such quick, genuine relief that Harte felt she couldn't possibly be lying. But could anyone be as innocent and trusting as she appeared to be? Good God, she had blithely boarded a slaver captained by a man as dangerous-looking as Ringer, and now she was ready to join forces with Harte himself—a man she didn't know from the devil. She was either courageous as hell or incredibly naive.

"We're almost to the mouth of the Potomac," he told her. "Once we reach the city, I'll take you and the boys to my house until I can find out something about your brother. There's plenty of room there, and Hannah can see to your needs."

Lily's beautiful topaz eyes seemed to hold him against his will. "Is Hannah your wife?"

Harte hesitated, uncomfortable with the idea that she could discern things about him without his knowledge. "You mean you don't already know? After last night, I figured you'd know everything about me by now."

A tiny furrow marred Lily's smooth brow, and he easily read the hurt in her eyes. She wasn't very good at hiding her feelings. Or was she *very* good at it?

"Please don't make fun of me, Mr. Delaney. I don't know everything about you or anyone else. I sometimes can sense things or see pictures in my head, but I can't control what I see, or when, and often I don't even understand who or what I'm seeing." She stopped for a moment, staring intently at him long enough to make Harte fear that she might perceive his plot against her brother. He breathed easier when she spoke again.

"If I come to your house with you and try to help you with your work, will you help me find Derek?"

"Yes, I definitely will do that," Harte answered, glad she had asked the question in a way that allowed him to answer truthfully. He would certainly do what he could to locate her brother, and then he would capture him for the Federal government. But Lily didn't have to know that.

Lily's apprehension seemed to melt away, and when her lips curved into a soft smile, etching dimples in her cheeks, Harte caught himself staring stupidly at her. Annoyed with himself, he turned and walked away without another word, determined to keep his distance, even though she tempted him more with her soft beauty than any woman he had ever known.

Later that afternoon, after they had weighed anchor in the city of Washington, D.C., Lily looked around the bustling docks near the Navy Yard Bridge, grateful to have her feet planted on solid ground once again. Even the short voyage up the American coast with Harte Delaney on the Union gunboat had been too long, after the dreadful voyage on the *Sea Rover*. Quickly she put thoughts of Ringer and his crew out of her mind. She never wanted to think about any of them again.

Harte was speaking in low tones to a blue-coated officer in charge of the ship. He towered over the smaller man, his black hair shining ebony in the sun. Cold and withdrawn, he suffered deep within his soul—she had sensed it when she held his medallion. She didn't understand why or what had caused his pain, and she probably never would. Harte Delaney kept to himself. She didn't think he would ever confide his feelings to her or to anyone else.

When Harte joined them a few minutes later, he seemed angry. He looked at the Kapirigis, and when he spoke, his voice betrayed irritation. "I sent down some clothes for the boys too. Why didn't they put them on? They can't go traipsing around the city in their loincloths."

"They didn't choose to wear American clothes," Lily answered calmly.

Harte frowned darkly. "Well, that's just too damn bad. Tell them they'll end up in jail walking around half-naked like that."

"I don't have to interpret English for them. I taught them to speak our language when Derek first found them in the bush."

"Well, they haven't said much to me in English."

"They haven't spoken to you because you treat them like domesticated animals, just like the white Australians do. When you treat them better and earn their trust, they'll speak to you."

Anger shadowed Harte's handsome face. "There's a coach waiting on the quay. Come on, we're wasting time."

Lily took the Kapirigis' hands and followed Harte to a large black coach waiting at the foot of the gangplank. She and the boys climbed inside while Harte instructed the driver and then settled into the seat across from them.

"How far is your house?" Lily asked once they had rolled away from the river and turned into a busy thoroughfare. She peered curiously out the window at the small stores lining both sides of the street. She had learned much about America from Derek's letters and was curious to see how the warring Americans lived.

"I live out in Georgetown. Once we get on Pennsylvania Avenue, it's about three miles."

"Is Charleston close by too?" Lily asked.

"No," he answered laconically, then pointed out the window. "We'll be passing the Capitol building soon, if you'd like to see it."

Lily leaned closer to the window in time to see a huge domed structure loom into view. Rows of massive columns lined the impressive facade, but carpenters' scaffolding clung to one side of the building like the skeleton of a giant locust.

"Is that where your president lives? The one who wants to free the colored people of your country?"

"No. President Lincoln lives in the White House. Down that way in President's Park." He pointed down a side street. "We'll be passing it soon. How did you know about his policies?"

*He doesn't trust me,* Lily thought, not looking at him but well aware that he watched her closely and weighed her every word for signs of treachery. He must be a lonely man, she thought, if he looks upon everyone he meets as an enemy. She wanted to ask him about the gallows she had seen in her dreaming. Who had been executed that day? Someone close to Harte Delaney? A friend or relative?

She frowned as a terrible thought occurred to her. Suppose that what she had foreseen was Harte Delaney's own death. She had had a vision of her mother's demise and had lived with that grief for nearly a year before the onset of the fever that took her life. She stared at him in distress, holding her hand to her mouth as a wave of nausea came over her.

"What's wrong?" Harte asked in a concerned voice.

Lily tried to forestall his query. "I have a headache. I get them sometimes after I've had a dreaming."

His light-green eyes briefly delved into hers, but they were quickly veiled with a studied dispassion that made it impossible for her to read his expression. He always seemed so intense and guarded, as if he wore a mask. "Do you always become ill after you experience one of these . . . ah . . . dreamings of yours?" he asked.

"Only when they're of a violent nature, like the one I saw last night."

"You felt it as if you were really there, didn't you?" he asked, still scrutinizing her closely, but giving nothing of himself away.

Lily nodded, wondering if she had been wrong and he might be willing to discuss the dreaming with her.

"Will you tell me how it works, Lily? Do you always have to hold an object to trigger these visions?"

Lily had never really discussed her dreamings with anyone other than her parents and Derek. They had made every effort to protect her from outsiders for fear she would be harmed or ridiculed. She had rarely left Malmora—until her life had been shattered by her father's murder. She felt uncomfortable discussing her visions with Harte Delaney.

"Usually. But I don't always see pictures in my head when I hold objects in my hand. Sometimes I just sense things about people or places."

"Tell me about these pictures. Is it like looking at a photograph?"

"At times it's as if I am the person and experiencing their emotions. Sometimes it's very frightening during a bad dreaming. The one last night was full of pain and horrible fear."

Lily waited for him to respond, but he merely lapsed into silence and turned to stare out the window.

Beside her the Kapirigis were whispering together in their own language about the soldiers filling the streets. There were so many armed military men that Lily couldn't begin to count them. Indeed they seemed a sea of blue as they marched along in their navy-blue uniforms. With so many on their side, surely Harte Delaney's Northern faction would win the American conflict. Or did the South have just as many men willing to fight and die to keep the black man in slavery?

After a long, bumpy ride, the carriage turned into a quiet residential street lined with large brick homes. There was little activity on the sidewalks or on the well-tended lawns. When she stepped out of the carriage in front of the Delaney residence, she saw that it was one of the grandest homes on the shady street, constructed of red brick and rising three stories.

After Harte paid the driver, he ushered Lily and the boys up the brick-paved front walkway beneath huge oak trees so quickly that she realized he didn't want them to be seen by his neighbors; no doubt he was embarrassed by the boys' lack of clothing. The long front veranda adorned with dark-green grillwork, led to the front door, which he quickly opened and allowed them to precede him into the spacious foyer.

"Hannah? Where are you?" he called into the silence of the big house.

Lily tilted her head back to admire the lovely chandelier with its teardrops of cut crystal. Red-velvet chairs were positioned on either side of the front door, and a massive balustraded stair rose at the back of the foyer. She had never been inside such a magnificent home. Her own house at Malmora was comfortable and homey, but its walls were not covered with velvety white wallpaper etched in gold leaf, nor did it sport lush royal-blue-velvet portieres draping the doorways.

"I guess she's back in the kitchen," Harte said, gesturing toward the fine chairs against the wall. "Sit down, if you like. I'll be right back."

Lily watched his progress down the long hall, then turned around to find the Kapirigis admiring their faces in one of the ornate, gold-framed mirrors that flanked the door. She smiled as they practiced jabbing their spears at their own reflections; she was glad to see them happy after the cruel way they had been treated by Ringer's men. When the front door suddenly swung wide, they stepped back in surprise.

A young Negress, perhaps eleven or twelve years old, came into the hallway, her arms piled high with bundles wrapped with brown paper and white string. She was dressed in a plain black dress and a white apron, like the maids Lily had seen in the households of the rich British homeowners of Melbourne. Humming happily to herself, the girl tried to kick the door shut with her foot. Totally unaware of Lily and the boys, she accomplished the task and was able to dump her cumbersome packages on the marble-topped table. Then she looked into the mirror and saw the reflections of the Kapirigis where they stood right behind her.

"AAAAAAA—"

The scream was so high-pitched, Lily felt a shaft of stabbing pain that instantly revived her previously diminishing headache. The girl's big brown eyes rolled back in her head, and she crumpled limply into a heap of black cotton and white organdy. The Kapirigis bent over her curiously, and Harte emerged at a run from the back hallway.

"Good God, what happened to Birdie? I heard her scream all the way out in the back yard."

"The Kapirigis frightened her, but they didn't

mean to," Lily explained quickly, stepping back as Harte bent and patted the girl's cheek.

"Birdie? Can you hear me?" When the poor maid remained as still as death, Harte frowned. "Hannah's nowhere to be found, and now this."

He picked up the young servant and carried her into an adjoining room. Lily and the boys followed him and entered a most luxurious parlor permeated with the clean, pleasant scent of beeswax and furniture oils. Somewhere in the back of her mind an ancient memory flew to the surface, a fleeting glimpse of her grandmother's cozy sitting room in Sussex long before they had sailed off to Australia.

While Harte lowered Birdie to one of the gold-and-white-striped satin sofas, Lily admired the chamber's furnishings. Oval side tables flanked each couch, their well-oiled surfaces polished to a mirrorlike sheen. Blue-and-gold wing chairs were placed before a wide front window, which was draped with blue curtains edged in gold fringe.

"I suppose she'll come around in a minute," Harte was saying. "Birdie's always been timid." His eyes lingered on the spear-toting aborigines. "I can't imagine what frightened her."

Lily knew he was being sarcastic, and she took offense until he grinned slightly. Surprised, Lily smiled back, thinking that now he looked like the man she had dreamed of meeting. But his pleasant expression faded quickly when Birdie moaned and began to stir. Suddenly, before anyone could move, she came to and lurched upright on the sofa, her dark-brown face stark with terror. When she saw Harte, she began a panic-stricken babbling.

"Mister Delaney, call de watch! I done seen painted-up, head-huntin' wildmen in the front hall! Wid white faces and long spears to stick in me!" She looked around wildly, caught sight of the twin terrors she'd been describing, and let out another blood-chilling shriek. The objects of her hysteria grinned at each other and squatted down to watch.

"Calm yourself, Birdie," Harte said curtly. "Nobody's going to hurt you. I brought them here. They're my guests."

"But, suh," Birdie cried, clutching the lapels of his coat in her hands, "they cain't be your guests 'cause they's naked as jaybirds."

At that point, Lily began to find the whole episode amusing, especially Harte's obviously annoyed attempts to soothe the excited girl.

"They're not naked, Birdie," he said impatiently. "They've got on loincloths."

Birdie was not to be placated. "I bets they's gonna cut off our heads and shrink 'em up 'til they's no bigger than apples, just like them shrunked-up heads I seen down on dat African trader ship at the docks." She began to tremble, pressing herself as deep into the couch cushions as she could get. Her eyes widened until they looked almost as round and white as two hen's eggs.

"Birdie, don't be ridiculous," Harte ordered sharply as his maid began to make mournful moaning sounds. "They're just little boys, even younger than you are. Can't you see that? Now where's Hannah? I need her to make up the guest rooms."

"She still down to de market gettin' taters."

"Then I guess you'll have to see to our needs. We're hungry and tired, and we'll want supper right away so we can make an early night of it. Go on now and put on water to heat so Lily can have a bath. Do you hear me?"

Birdie jumped up, pulled on Harte's sleeve, and whispered rather wildly into his ear. Harte frowned blackly and shook his head.

"I'm sorry, Lily, but Birdie's determined to believe the Kapirigis are cannibals. Tell her they aren't, will you?"

Lily couldn't hide her indignation at such an insult to her aboriginal friends.

"Of course they aren't! They're from the Pitjantjatjara tribe of the desert. They hunt kangaroos and crocodiles for food, and the rest of the time they catch lizards or dig up witchetty grubs to eat."

Birdie clapped her hand over her mouth and fled the room without further ado. Harte looked thoroughly disgusted with her.

"She'll be all right. Come on, I'll show you to your rooms myself."

As Lily followed him back into the hall then up the elegant staircase to the second floor, the Kapirigis hung back and spoke together in low tones, discussing the girl they'd frightened, who, they noticed, was now peeking out at them from behind the drapes of the hall door.

"Birdie is a pretty name for the brown woman," Kapi observed in his own language, his large, liquidy black eyes glowing. "She's as pretty as a fluffed-up cockatoo."

Rigi considered his brother's observation for a moment. He nodded. "That's why they call her name Birdie, 'cause she got the same shrill cry of cockatoo when it calls its mate."

"Yes, you are right," Kapi agreed. "And she is mightily afraid of us. She thinks us fierce and savage!"

Rigi grinned with pleasure. "We will throw our spears for her tomorrow, and she will be more impressed with our courage."

Kapi liked that idea. "And we can catch a rabbit and skin its fur, then give it to her as a present. She will like food for her pot. She will like us better then."

"Her skin is brown like ours," Rigi added. "She will be our best friend in this land. She can teach us things about the white people of the United States of America."

"Birdie is a nice name for a nice brown girl," Kapi observed enthusiastically. "See, she is still looking at us. She must like us better already."

Pleased, the boys grinned at each other, then hurried up the steps after Lily and the big white man named Harte, whom Lily had described to them long before they had ever left their home in Australia.

# 5

Hannah Jones trudged up the sidewalk to the back door, still muttering angrily about Birdie's forgetting to purchase the potatoes for tomorrow night's beef stew. Her addle-brained kitchen maid couldn't remember her own name half the time and was certainly more trouble than she was worth.

Still, Birdie was the child of one of Hannah's dearest friends, who still worked back in the big house on the cliffs of Newport. Miz Delaney, Mr. Harte's dear grandmama, had been generous enough to send the girl all the way down to Washington to help Hannah with her work, and Hannah was determined to teach the child how to earn an honest living. Sometimes, however, Birdie Blackmon did try a woman's patience.

When Hannah stepped inside the kitchen door, the first sound she heard was a man's deep baritone voice. Mr. Harte! He had come home earlier than expected!

"Stop babbling and listen to me," he was insisting in a highly vexed voice that Hannah recognized well from his childhood days when she had been his mammy. "They are NOT going to eat you, or anybody else, do you hear me, Birdie? They're only children, can't you see that? There's no reason to be afraid of them."

Hannah's smile disintegrated. What in heaven's name was Mr. Harte talking about? Who might be ready to eat little Birdie?

"Birdie, what in the world's the matter wid you, girl?" she spoke up as she set down her basket of food. She was acutely embarrassed that the troublesome child was causing Mr. Harte grief the moment he returned home, and she continued her sharp scolding with a great deal of feeling. "Now you hush up that whinin' right now, or I'll send you packin' back up to Newport and let Miz Delaney deal with the messes you cause for folks."

Mr. Harte turned around, looking distinctly relieved to see her, and Hannah examined his handsome face affectionately, happy that he was safe at home again. He had gotten himself involved in dangerous work, even before the war had begun, and he was always coming home shot up with some wound or another and exhausted from his reckless life of spying and secrets.

His devil-may-care disregard for his own safety was nearly the death of both Hannah and his dear grandmama, whom Hannah kept informed of his comings and goings. Mr. Harte had not stepped foot in the big house in Newport since his bride had died there, long before the war commenced, and poor Miz Delaney's heart was near broke in two over their estrangement.

"Hannah! Thank God you're here!" Mr. Harte said as Hannah shrugged out of her warm knitted shawl. "I can't get Birdie to listen to reason."

"For shame, Birdie, causing Mr. Harte all this trouble just when he step in the door," Hannah chastised, hands on hips and a frown on her face. The young maid hung her head in shame. "I'm pleased to see you home again and lookin' just fine," Hannah remarked to her young employer, examining him up and down for the bruises and bandages he often sported after his secretive sojourns away from home.

"I've brought home some guests who'll probably be staying here for a while. I don't know how long yet."

Hannah couldn't hide her shock. "Guests, Suh? Here in your house? I don't ever remember you havin' no guests here afore."

"They have nowhere else to go," Harte told her, frowning and tunneling his fingers through his hair. He looked tired and worried, and Hannah decided then and there she would have Birdie pluck clean a turkey tomorrow so she could stuff the bird with Mr. Harte's favorite chestnut dressing.

"I better warn you, though, that my guests are rather different," he continued, frowning slightly. "That's why Birdie's so distraught."

"How they be different?" Hannah asked, glancing at Birdie, who answered her question before Mr. Harte could open his mouth.

"Hannah, dey's carryin' pointed sticks and dey don't wear nothin' but little brown napkins around dey's privates! Dey's gonna boil us up and fix us for stew meat to go wid dose taters you gots, I just knows it!"

Hannah gasped, shocked at Birdie's outrageous remarks. "You quit that crazy talk, girl, y'hear. What's gone and got into you, anyways?"

"In all fairness," Harte interjected with a shake of his head, "they are a bit shocking the first time you see them. So I imagine they gave Birdie a start when she came upon them unexpectedly in the front hall, but they're harmless, I promise. They helped me escape from a very bad situation, so I'd appreciate it if all of you would treat them with respect."

"Have I ever in all my years be showin' disrespect to a Delaney houseguest?" Hannah demanded, highly insulted by his insinuation.

Harte smiled. "No, but you've never had to entertain aborigines before."

Perplexed, Hannah cocked her head. "I don't rightly know what aborigines be, I reckon."

"They're the brown-skinned natives of Australia, and I can warn you that they're a lot less civilized than you are. The two boys are straight out of the bush, but Lily's white."

Hannah's interest in the aborigines faded instantly. "You mean you's plannin' to keep a white girl here in your house, wid you bein' a bachelor? That ain't proper, Mr. Harte. Why, your grandmama will be fit to be tied if she hears you doin' such a disgraceful thing! What'll all your grandmama's friends here in de city think about you?"

Mr. Harte's face hardened, and Hannah was instantly sorry that she had mentioned his grandmama. She had learned to avoid that subject the day Miz Delaney had sent her down to Washington to take care of Mr. Harte.

"You work for me now, not Sarah Delaney," he said in a cold, controlled voice. "Lily Courtland needs my help, and she's going to get it. You know good and well that I don't give a damn what anybody thinks, especially my grandmother's friends."

Despite his reaction, because she was a lifelong, trusted servant, Hannah felt compelled to warn him of the consequences of harboring such guests, especially since he certainly wasn't one to consider what society thought of him. "Now, Mr. Harte, you know there's gonna be a big, bad scandal if any of the folks along here find out you gots a young woman stayin' in your house. You don't want that to happen, do you? Not wid you bein' in the army and bein' a close friend wid the president and all."

"Nothing like that's going to happen because nobody's going to know Lily's here. You and Birdie are not to mention her presence to anyone, do you understand? It's very important that you don't."

Hannah thought that sounded highly irregular and more than a little suspicious, but Mr. Harte was funny about his privacy and he looked plenty annoyed right now. She nodded but could not restrain herself from making one last comment. "But it still ain't right havin' an unmarried lady in a man's house. It just ain't done."

Fortunately, Mr. Harte ignored her final remark as he shrugged on his jacket. Hannah noticed how he winced when he slid his right arm through the sleeve and wondered what he'd done to hurt himself this time. "I've got to get down to the War Department and talk with Pinkerton, but Lily and the boys are going to need bathwater and some supper. They've had a hard time for the last few months, so try to make them feel comfortable, no matter how strange you think they are. I'll be late, so tell them not to wait up for me."

He took his leave, and Hannah gazed after him thoughtfully, anxious now to meet his three houseguests. He'd had a woman in to warm his bed now and again, but just for the space of a night, and Mr. Pinkerton had come for secret meetings in the library, but Mr. Harte had never brought home a little white girl or any of those aborigine kind of boys.

Birdie began to whine pitiably as soon as Hannah turned around to look at her.

"Now you just hush up that silly prattle, girl, and pump up some water to heat for their baths. You're gonna wait on them just like you do for Mr. Harte hisself, so quit all that cringin' and cryin' and git on wid you. But I'll tend to them tonight so I can get a look at the scary wildmen who's makin' you act like a ninny."

Birdie quieted, looking distinctly relieved, and Hannah began setting out a supper of fresh-baked yeast bread, sliced ham and roast beef, and a pitcher of milk on a round silver tray, then climbed the back servant stairs to the carpeted second-floor corridor.

Tapping on the door of the large guest room, she waited until a low voice replied, then turned the knob, not quite sure what she should expect. When she stepped inside, balancing the heavy tray on one palm, all she saw was a little bitty white girl sitting on the upholstered bench at the end of the bed.

The young woman stood up at once, and Hannah was startled to see that she was wearing a pair of men's trousers and a huge white shirt. Even dressed so poorly, with all that golden-blond hair tumbling down her back she was the prettiest little thing that Hannah had seen in a good while.

"How do you do, Miss Lily," Hannah greeted her, carrying the tray forward. "I be Hannah Jones, Mr. Harte's housekeeper, and he told me to bring up some vittles for your supper. Birdie'll be comin' in shortly wid water for your bath."

"Hello, Hannah," Lily said pleasantly, her smile dimpling her cheeks. "My name is Lily Courtland, and these are my friends, the Kapirigis." She pointed toward the fireplace, and Hannah looked quickly in that direction. She stared wide-eyed at the two half-naked little boys squatting in front of the hearth. They did hold spears, the bottom ends resting on the floor, and now Hannah could understand Birdie's reaction—but then they stood and smiled with endearing little gap-toothed grins.

"Why, they be twins, don't they?" she exclaimed in surprise.

"Yes. Please don't be afraid of them. They won't hurt you. They're very worried about the little maid who fainted. They like her very much."

"Birdie be just fine, so don't you worry none 'bout her," Hannah said, which caused the two boys to enter into an excited discourse with one another in some indecipherable language. She set down the tray on the bedside table, then turned her attention to the boys, deciding that what they needed was to be scrubbed down and put into clean britches.

"Goodness me, just look at the two of you," she said, planting her hands on her hips. "Barely a stitch on to keep off the wind, and the weather gettin' colder by the day."

"They've lived in the desert for most of their life, where there was little need for warm clothes," Lily explained quickly, "but I've asked them to wear white men's clothing here and they said they would."

Actually, upon inspecting Lily, Hannah decided she could use a decent outfit herself.

What was Mr. Harte thinking, not providing suitable attire for the poor little things? Sometimes she just couldn't understand the man at all. All he ever thought about was catching spies and outlaws and getting himself hurt. "I'll fetch them some things to wear tomorrow. I have a nephew livin' in a livery stable down aways on D Street, who's just about the same size as these Kapirigis of yours. And I bets you can fit into something of Birdie's 'till Mr. Harte can find you something fine to wear." She walked over to the girl and found her even more petite close up. She patted Lily's arm. "Now you just help yourself to supper and don't worry 'bout a thing. We're gonna takes good care of you and them boys, too, while you is here wid us."

"You're very kind," Lily said. Then she shocked Hannah by taking her hand and holding it tightly. The white girl's eyes closed for an instant, as if she were thinking very hard, and Hannah felt a strange sensation come flying over her, one that caused a shiver to wiggle its way down her spine.

"Don't worry about your daughter," Lily said, opening her odd golden eyes and bestowing a soft smile upon Hannah. "She's had her baby, and both of them are just fine. It's a little girl, and she's healthy and strong."

Hannah's jaw dropped and she began to stutter. "How . . . how . . . ?"

"Please don't be frightened. I just know things sometimes. I told you about the baby because I sensed you were very worried about the birth, it being Julia's first child." She lowered her voice so only Hannah could hear. "The Kapirigis think I'm a witch, but I'm really not."

Hannah stared at her in astonishment, but Lily turned away as the little boys spoke to her in the strangest mishmash of a language that Hannah had ever heard. Lily listened for a moment, then looked back at Hannah.

"They want to know if Birdie would like them better if they wore American clothes. They think she is very pretty, and they're thinking she'd make a good wife for them someday."

"Wife!" Hannah exclaimed, her usual calm control slipping a degree.

"Men of the Pitjantjatjara marry young," Lily told her with a smile.

"Lawsy me," Hannah murmured under her breath, but as the little boys watched her intently with their big, liquidy black eyes, and the white girl presented her with such a beautiful, warm smile, her heart began to melt toward them. *But, my goodness, they're all such strange little things*, she thought. *No wonder Mr. Harte didn't want anyone to know they were in his house.*

"Miss Lily, you's just have your supper in peace while we gets you a hot bath up here and a clean nightshirt to wear to bed. Mr. Harte say he won't be back 'til late, so you can go on to sleep widout a worry 'bout havin' to wait for him."

"Thank you, Hannah."

Hannah went to the door, still a bit shaken by Lily's knowledge of her grandbaby. How could she have known such things? She had even known Julia's name! But if what the girl had told her was true, she could rest easier, free from worry about Julia's well-being. She paused beside the door. There was one way to find out if the girl really knew about Julia's baby.

"Do you know what my daughter be callin' that new baby girl?" she asked, half afraid to hear the answer.

Lily paused in forking up a piece of ham for one of the boys. "She named her Hannah Sue, after you."

Hannah fled the room, her heart thundering in her breast—only last week she had received a letter from Newport in which she had learned that Julia intended to name the child Hannah Sue if it were born a girl.

# 6

At five minutes before ten o'clock that evening, Harte let himself in the front door of his house, crossed the dimly lit foyer, and mounted the carpeted stairs. Pinkerton had been more than intrigued by his account of Lily Courtland and her gift of second sight.

During their lengthy discussion earlier that afternoon, the two of them had concocted a tentative plot to lure Derek Courtland and his ship into a Union trap, while at the same time using Lily's supposed clairvoyance to locate Southern spies in their midst. Harte's orders were to set the operation in motion at once, that same night, if possible.

Tapping his knuckles on the door of the guest room, Harte waited impatiently until the door swung open. One of the aborigines grinned up at him from the doorway.

"Where's Lily?" Harte asked, looking past the boy into the bedchamber.

"She in bed," the youngster said, stepping back to admit him. "She tired."

As the aborigine rejoined his twin brother

on the hearth rug before the crackling fire, Harte crossed the room to the big four-poster bed draped with rose brocaded satin. Lily lay asleep against the pillows, her silky hair spread like a golden cloud over the eyelet-edged white sheets. She wore a plain nightgown of white cotton, and the scooped neckline, much too large for her slender shoulders, had fallen down on one side, baring a good deal of her breast.

Swallowing hard, Harte averted his gaze. The boys were paying him no heed but had resumed some kind of game they were playing with a length of string. Slowly, irresistibly, he returned his attention to the sleeping woman. He just couldn't believe how beautiful she was. She had the kind of face that robbed a man of sleep. Unwillingly, but unable to stop himself, he lifted a curling lock of her hair and caressed the silken strand between his thumb and forefinger.

When the clock suddenly struck the hour with a slow, hollow gong, he guiltily snatched his hand away. Lily opened her eyes, gasping and pushing herself upright when she saw him so close above her.

"I'm sorry if I frightened you. The boys let me in."

"Is anything wrong?" she murmured, looking around nervously and holding the bedclothes against her breasts.

"No," Harte answered, his eyes roaming her face and flowing hair. "I brought home some objects for you to hold, but I guess it can wait until tomorrow. I didn't realize it was so late."

"No, please, I want to help you. I was trying to wait up for you, but Hannah drew me a nice warm bath, and it relaxed me so much that I fell asleep." As she spoke, she reached for a white cotton wrapper lying across the bed and slipped her arms into the wide sleeves. "Have you been able to find out anything about Derek yet?"

Harte was momentarily distracted when she swept back the coverlet and swung a pair of shapely bare legs over the side of the bed. "I've put out feelers for his whereabouts, but it might take some time to locate his ship," he told her. Every word was true, but he felt a twinge of guilt when she presented him with a grateful smile.

"Thank you so much. You don't know what finding my brother means to me."

Harte didn't want to know. He changed the subject. "I see Hannah found you some clean clothes to wear."

"Yes. This gown and robe belong to Birdie. She was very nice to let me borrow them. I hope I'm able to repay your kindness and hospitality."

Again Harte fought an internal battle with a guilty conscience that he had thought he had subjugated and destroyed a long time ago. What the hell was the matter with him? Derek Courtland was an enemy. Be he Lily Courtland's brother or not, the man had sunk dozens of Union vessels and had run the blockade countless more times. Harte had a duty to perform, and he couldn't let his sympathy for one young woman get in his way.

"If you help me identify any Southern spies operating here in Washington, we'll call it even. Let's go and sit close to the fire where it'll be warmer."

The Kapirigis glanced up from their play as Lily sat down near them on a small settee adjacent to the hearth. While she tucked her bare feet beneath her, Harte took a moment to stir up the logs with a poker. When the flames were darting and jumping again, he sat down beside her.

"Are you sure you're up to doing this so soon after last night?" he asked, searching her face for any sign of the headache that had plagued her earlier. "Are you feeling better now?"

"I don't always get the headaches. My dreamings aren't usually as vivid as they were with your medallion."

Certainly not willing to get into a discussion about himself, Harte reached in his coat pocket and retrieved the first object he had brought for Lily to handle. He watched her with wary eyes when he laid the man's evening scarf on the cushion between them.

Lily picked up the long length of white cashmere and slowly caressed the soft fabric between her open palms. Her long, full lashes drifted closed, and she sat perfectly still, as if lost in thought.

"This belongs to a man," she murmured softly, "but I can't quite get a clear picture of his face. The impressions are very dim and disjointed."

Fascinated by her strange ability, Harte watched as she rubbed the cloth with circular motions, her eyes still shut tightly. "He's small of stature and holds himself very erect when he walks. He's married to someone—no, he's not, she's dead now. And he's mourning her. He misses her so much that he doesn't care about living anymore. He wants to die too."

Suddenly she raised the scarf to her face, gently passing the fabric over her cheeks and chin. When she opened her eyes suddenly, Harte was embarrassed to be caught staring at her parted lips. She lowered the scarf apologetically. "I'm sorry. That's all I can tell you about him."

"Did you get any feeling that this man might be working for the South?"

Lily shook her head.

"Do you sense that he can be trusted?"

"Yes."

"He's a courier we use between here and New York City. Lately he's been disappearing for a few days before he reports in for his debriefings. That's when we began to suspect he might be a spy."

"He goes to his wife's grave," Lily spoke up at once, twisting the scarf between her hands. "She's buried near here. In a cemetery enclosed by a high fence—one made of pointed spikes painted a dark-blue color. I can see her clearly there, waiting near her grave for him to come."

"That's the Ferreton Cemetery, I think? But what do you mean, you see her?"

Lily's eyes met his, her lovely face very solemn. "I know you'll probably find this hard to believe, but sometimes I can see apparitions."

"Apparitions? When? In your dreamings?"

"Yes, and sometimes when I'm passing by a graveyard or walking through the halls of an old house. They used to terrify me when I was a little girl, and it's still quite unsettling to see them moving about."

"I should think so," Harte remarked, not at all ready to believe she had actually seen ghosts, but she had described Stephen Harris to a tee, without knowing his name or anything else about him. And Harris was a recent widower.

Harte stared at Lily, realizing in that moment just how important Lily Courtland could be to the war effort if her abilities proved to be real. And more and more, he was beginning to believe it was so.

"What about this?" he asked, handing her a tan leather glove. The instant she touched it, her face grew troubled and her chest began to heave. "There's a dark room . . . there's a candle . . . And there's dynamite," she muttered hoarsely, "dozens of sticks of it, and he's lashing them together with heavy white string.

He's your enemy. He's going to blow up a bridge, one with a curved back."

She sighed heavily, pausing before she continued. "I can't see where it is, but it crosses a wide river, one with a peculiar name—the Patapsco, or something like that—and it runs white with rapids just downstream from a hotel with double porches that are painted yellow and stretch all around the first and second floors. He's going to strap the dynamite to the middle truss, just beneath the planks of the roadbed."

She opened her eyes, but Harte could only stare at her in disbelief. Douglas Minner, the man who owned the glove, was in Harte's own employ, a Federal agent living and working out of Baltimore, not far from the Patapsco River. If what Lily said was true, he had to get up there before Minner could blow the bridge.

"When? Do you know when he's going to do it?"

"No."

Despite her inability to pinpoint the time, the incredible accuracy of her revelations made Harte eager to hear more.

"What about this cigar case?" he said, placing the rectangular gold box into her hands.

Lily held the case flat between her palms and immediately shrugged. "I'm sorry. I get nothing from this at all. That happens more often than you'd think."

"How about this pen?"

As Lily picked up the black writing implement, Harte leaned closer, bracing one arm around her on the back of the sofa. He was absolutely amazed by the things she was telling him. There was no way she could have had this information, not even if she was a well-coached spy. What she was doing did seem like magic, just as she had tried to tell him when they were aboard the ship.

Intrigued, he watched her put the pen against her cheek and wet her lips as she tried to concentrate. Harte's eyes latched onto her full mouth, moist, soft, and pink. Lord help him, he had never felt such strong physical attraction.

Harte forced his gaze away from her lips. He couldn't let himself be tempted. They could not become involved in that way, not ever, especially not after what she had demonstrated tonight. God only knew what else she would dredge up concerning his past if he let her get too close to him.

He realized she was having trouble with the pen too. She leaned her head against the couch cushions and clutched the writing pen tightly.

Lily Courtland was a beauty, one he wasn't yet totally sure he could trust. More important, she was a woman who could divine his innermost secrets by merely touching him. He had to keep her at bay. He was treading on dangerous ground.

"All I can sense is that this pen comes from another country. I think it might be from

France, but I'm not sure. I guess I'm not being much help, am I?"

"You're helping me more than you know."

His gratitude pleased her, he could tell by the way she blushed and lowered her lashes. Again a rush of desire heated his blood. Determinedly, he gave himself a mental shake, trying to remember that she was a virgin.

Not that he was such a saint when it came to women—he had lied, manipulated, even seduced women in order to obtain information, both before the war when he had worked as a detective in Pinkerton's agency and then later when Pinkerton had persuaded him to join the secret service.

No longer was he the carefree young gentleman who attended soirees and fox hunts in Newport. His time in Mexico with Camillia and his role in fighting the Confederates had changed all that, and a hell of a lot of other things as well. Unfortunately, however, he wasn't immune to the brand of charm that Lily Courtland displayed so temptingly. He wondered where she had been in her young life, what she had done and with whom.

"Tell me about yourself, Lily. Were you born in Australia? Do you have any family other than your brother?"

"I was born in England, but my father took us to New South Wales when I was five." She sighed and gazed past the Kapirigis at the leaping flames. "He went there to mine for gold, and he found enough to buy Malmora."

"What's Malmora?"

"That's our cattle station in Victoria, where I grew up. I think you Americans call them ranches. After Mama died, Derek went to sea, but Papa and I stayed and ran it with the help of our hired hands. It's a huge place with thousands of acres, but when Papa started letting the aborigines use it as a sanctuary from the Pacification by Force laws, the other landowners turned on us."

"Is that when the whites can kill the natives?"

She nodded. "Isn't it awful? Papa fought against them, so they shot him. The bank took over Malmora then, and there wasn't anything I could do about it. That's when I decided to find Derek. I was so desperate that I even trusted Ringer to get me to America. You see, Derek's the only one who can get Malmora back."

"I understand," Harte replied, trying not to be swayed by the hopeful look in her eyes. Regardless of her problems, his orders were to catch Derek Courtland and put the *Mamu* out of commission.

When one of the Kapirigis laughed softly, Harte glanced at them, not wanting to discuss her family further for fear she might sense his animosity toward her brother.

"What are they doing with that string?" he asked her in an effort to steer the conversation in a different direction.

"It's a game the aborigines like to play," Lily told him in her soft accent. "They see who can make the most elaborate designs with a length of string. Hold out your hands with your palms facing each other, and I'll show you how it works."

When Harte obeyed, Lily picked up a length of yarn from the floor near the little boys and draped it around his fingers. "First you must wind the string around the outside of your hands like this to get the game started, then your partner separates the strands with his fingers and forms a new design. See—" she plucked two strands and formed them into a simple diamond pattern—"this is an easy one, but the boys can do some of the most incredibly intricate patterns when they start challenging each other." She smiled at Harte. "Why don't you try it? Catch hold of opposite parts of the string and make any pattern you want."

Harte tried to do so, but soon found that his fingers were too large to manipulate the strings without pulling it off Lily's fingers.

"You must be very gentle," she told him, rearranging the yarn, and for the next few moments they took turns working the strings into various designs.

"Now you're showing off," he accused her a moment later when she adroitly fingered the strings into a marvelously complicated star shape.

Lily laughed softly and made the pattern yet more elaborate until Harte stopped her play by lacing his strong fingers through her slender ones, trapping the yarn between their palms.

"You win," he said, smiling.

Lily stiffened as the night wind howled through her consciousness, sweeping out the reality of the cozy chamber and the murmuring voices of the Kapirigis on the floor beside her, *and then the swirling fog parted and she was in the most beautiful place she had ever seen . . . a glade with strange towering trees she had never seen before . . . trees with boughs that whispered when the wind blew through them . . . and a sun-dappled path carpeted with cool green ferns and wild white lilies. . . . She was moving through the lovely place, and then she saw a pool of water . . . dark-blue and calm and still . . . fed by a splashing waterfall cascading from high rocks rising in the distance. . . . More lilies . . . everywhere . . . and the sweetest fragrance . . . honeysuckle. . . . Then suddenly a man rose from the clear water. . . . His back was to her, broad and brown and rippling with muscles. . . . What was he doing? . . . Who was he? . . . Then he turned . . .*

"Harte Delaney," she whispered, her heart caught in her throat.

*. . . And he was smiling at her . . . wading toward her and she realized with alarm that he wore no clothes. . . . Then he stood below her in the water . . . smiling . . . saying words she couldn't hear. . . . Then he was pulling her hand, taking her down into the water with him. . . . She could feel the warmth of the water against her body . . . sighed as the crisp black hair of his chest*

*slid over her bare breasts . . . oh, no, she was naked, too! . . . Then he was locking her body tight against him and his mouth was closing over hers . . .* "Oh, no, no, oh, yes, yes," she murmured as she felt his lips burn like fire against her own *then he was lifting her bodily, and oh, God, his mouth was closing over the hard tip of her breast . . .*

"Oooooh, Harte" she moaned, closing her eyes. She had never felt such wonderful sensations in her life, never knew such pleasure existed . . . *then he was lifting her out, and she felt the softness of the ferns beneath her back and he was smiling tenderly down at her, his lips upon her shoulder and breasts and stomach then against her mouth again with such fierceness that her breath was stolen and her body burned as if she lay on coals of fire and she cried out with pleasure so intense it was almost like pain . . .*

Harte sat transfixed as Lily Courtland violently threw back her head and cried out with uninhibited pleasure, her lips moist and parted, her chest heaving, her nipples erect under the thin white nightgown. He had made love to enough women to recognize a woman captured in the throes of passion. There was no doubt in his mind what Lily was experiencing in her dreaming and that she was doing it with him. It was the most erotic thing he had ever seen a woman do. His eyes fixed on her mouth, he watched her catch her full lower lip in her teeth and move her head from side to side. His blood surged and pumped burning liquid fire through his veins to inflame every fiber of his body.

Suddenly he became aware that the Kapirigis had come up beside him and were leaning over the back of the couch. They watched Lily's slow hip undulations with a great deal of interest.

"Lily having good dreaming this time," one noted to Harte.

"Her not have pain in head after this one," the other added with a sage nod. "Her call for you. Maybe you be man she mate with."

At that incredible remark, Harte jerked his hands from Lily's tight grip, and immediately she opened her eyes, her topaz gaze riveted on his face.

"Oh, Harte, it's so good when we make love," she whispered breathlessly. "I wish you could have been there."

Harte stared at her incredulously, then released a wry laugh. "Yeah, Lily, me too."

"I love you," she murmured in a very low voice, moistening her dry lips, "I always have, since I was a little girl and you began to appear in my dreamings."

Harte froze, shocked by her sudden avowal of love but quick to nip such a thing in the bud. "No, you don't. You've known me just a couple of days. And I don't love you, so don't start thinking I do."

When she looked as hurt as if he had given her a violent shake, he stood and took a few steps across the room. He didn't like this newest development. What the hell was she up to, telling him she loved him? He didn't want her thinking she loved him. He certainly didn't love her. He didn't love anybody, and he didn't want to.

"I've got to be away for a few days," he began hurriedly, but she didn't let him finish.

"Where are you going?" she asked, obviously alarmed.

"To search for the man with the dynamite."

"Take me with you. Maybe I can help you find him."

"I can find him on my own. I'll be back in a few days, and until then Hannah will be here with you."

He hardly looked at her as he turned and left the room, glad to get away from her. He didn't want her to expect that any kind of relationship could ever develop between them, because it couldn't. He wouldn't let it, not with Lily Courtland or any other woman. As he walked toward his bedchamber, he drew his medallion from inside his shirt and held it tightly within his palm to remind him what happened when he got involved with women.

# 7

One day nearly a fortnight after Harte had departed the city for Baltimore, Lily wandered listlessly down the second-floor corridor of his house. At the end of the hall behind the head of the staircase, a long window seat faced the large, walled back yard.

Settling herself among the soft pillows of rose-and-navy plaid, she caught back the sheer draperies and looked down at the lawn just in time to observe the Kapirigis tiptoeing up behind an unsuspecting Birdie, who was pinning wet white bed linens to the clothesline. When the hapless maid heard them and turned around, they held out the rabbit they had painstakingly trapped the previous day.

Unfortunately, they elected to toss the limp carcass at the girl in order to win her regard. Birdie emitted a high-pitched scream that Lily could hear even from inside the house and fled forthwith toward the back door and Hannah's protection, while the two Kapirigis joyously gave chase.

Poor little things, Lily thought, having to

smile at their perseverance. They truly wanted to become friends with Birdie. They had given her all sorts of gifts valuable to them—from captured birds to strung mistletoe berries—but the frightened young maid couldn't seem to get over her initial opinion. Even donning the spotless white shirts and pants that Hannah had given them had not been enough to win Birdie over.

Sighing, Lily looked down at the gown of pink-sprigged white muslin that she wore. Hannah had purchased the garment in a store just down the street, and the dress fit her reasonably well. She wished Harte could see her looking nice—all he had ever seen her wearing was the horribly revealing red dress that Ringer had forced upon her and the men's clothing she had been given aboard the *Integrity*. Perhaps if Harte saw her dressed like a woman, he would consider her worthy of his love.

Thoughts of the cool glade came back, making her shiver all over to think about what would transpire there someday. The things Harte had done to her body in the water were so intimate but felt so wonderful that she just knew he would enjoy them too.

If only he could foresee what lay ahead for them, surely he would fall in love with her. There was no doubt that they were meant to be lovers. Otherwise why would she have seen such an erotic dreaming? She had never seen him making love to her before she had met him in person and touched him. She wanted the dreaming to come true soon. She wanted to feel his hands move over her naked flesh until she writhed and cried out with pleasure.

A warm wave of crimson spread beneath her skin at her own wanton desires, and she wondered when he would come home. Did he miss her and think of her endlessly through the day as she did about him? Would he ever love her as deeply as she loved him?

During her upbringing at Malmora she had often been alone, with no one to talk with except her father and his cattle workers, but now that she had met Harte, she was lonely in a way she had never been before, especially since Harte had asked Lily and the boys to remain at the house and receive no visitors.

Why was he so secretive about himself and his work anyway? Even Hannah didn't seem to know anything about what he thought or did, and Lily had learned that the black housekeeper had been his childhood nurse. Even worse, lately Lily had had an unsettling sense that Harte was hiding something from her about Derek. An awful thought suddenly occurred to her. What if something terrible had happened to her brother? What if he was hurt or the *Mamu* had been sunk by an enemy ship?

Agitated over the possibility that Derek could be in trouble, she rose and paced back and forth in front of the windows. When she paused at the top of the steps with her hand on the newel post, she stared at the closed door of Harte's bedchamber. She had never entered his room, had not attempted to divine anything about his personal life for fear she would see something as violent and frightening as the hanging had been. She squeezed her eyes shut and goose bumps spread over her arms. The dreaming of the medallion had been so vivid.

For long moments she stood still, debating whether or not she should enter Harte's private domain. Would she be sorry if she divined something that caused her pain? But she wanted to know if he was all right, if he knew something about Derek that he wasn't telling her.

After glancing guiltily down the stairwell, she opened the door and stepped into the large chamber. The decor was decidedly masculine. The massive tester bed was carved from very dark teak and hung with slate-gray-and-black paisley brocaded silk. There were few personal effects in sight—no pictures of family, no articles for grooming, no books or newspapers. Everything was as orderly and neat as if no one had ever been there or touched anything.

She walked over to a small desk half hidden in a window alcove, hoping to discover some possession of Harte's, an object that only he would have handled. All she found was a spotless white blotter and an ornate ink bottle with matching gold pens. She picked up the pens but could sense nothing except that Harte had never written with either of them.

Moving to the armoire in the corner, she opened the doors, ashamed to be snooping in Harte's private belongings but unable to stop herself. Three sets of navy-blue military uniforms hung neatly inside, the epaulettes decorated with silver insignia, obviously the sign of some kind of rank in the American army. She wondered if he ever wore the well-tailored garb as she fingered a sleeve adorned with fine gold braid. Again, no sensations swept over her, and she got no sense of Harte Delaney at all. He hadn't worn them, she realized.

Disappointed, she gently closed the doors and turned back to let her gaze circle the room. Perhaps she would be able to see things about Harte only when she held the medallion. It had always been that way with Derek; she had to touch him or hold one of his possessions to trigger a dreaming about him.

As she moved to the foot of the bed, her thoughts returned to Harte. When he played the string game with her, he had been smiling and relaxed, the way she had seen him in her childhood dreamings. Now her visions were very different. She thought of his mouth upon her bare skin, so warm and insistent, and the way his hands had moved over her body and slowly up her thigh to caress her most sensitive places. Even now, days later, the memory caused her limbs to tremble and her loins to burn, and she grasped the bedpost for support.

The moment her fingers closed around the carved wood, she felt the dark roar coming and the sunny room fading and the sound of the Kapirigis yelling to one another outside dissolved *And she was in the bed hung with gray and black, and Harte was standing to one side . . . and there were other people in the room . . . Hannah and a man in a black robe . . . Who was it? . . . "Dearly Beloved," he said, and Lily knew it was a marriage ceremony. . . . She was marrying Harte . . . but his face was cold and hard and angry . . . and her heart was breaking . . .*

Lily opened her eyes. Chest heaving, heart thudding, she stared at the empty bed. They were to be married someday, here in this very room, but the dreaming had been filled with ill will and terrible anger. She swallowed hard and pressed her palms against her hot cheeks, remembering with unsettling clarity the way Harte had looked at her—with stone-cold loathing. Why? Why?

"Well, there you are, I've been looking all over the house for you," an unfamiliar female voice said from close behind her. Lily jumped in surprise and whirled around, shocked to find a young woman she had never seen before standing in the doorway.

"Oh, dear, I startled you, didn't I?"

The smiling stranger strode forth eagerly. Her hair was coppery red, caught up at the crown by pearl-encrusted barrettes that left wispy tendrils to frame her delicately formed face. She wore a skirt of deep burgundy and a white shirtwaist pleated in the front and fastened at the throat with a black-satin bow. An engraved gold watch was pinned to her breast.

"You're Lily Courtland, aren't you? Well, I'm just delighted to make your acquaintance. I'm Harte's sister, Cassandra Delaney, but I truly prefer to be called Cassie. I dropped by this afternoon to visit with Hannah and see if Harte was still alive, since he never deigns to let any of us know, and that's when she told me that you were staying here. I must tell you that I was surprised that Harte actually was social enough to invite a houseguest, but I do hope we'll get to know each other well while he's away. Where is he, anyway?" The girl then beamed a most engaging smile.

"Why, he's in Baltimore, I think," Lily replied, a bit taken aback by the young woman's forthright, be it nonstop, manner of speaking. "How do you do? I didn't know Harte had a sister."

"Oh, I'm not surprised. Half the time, he doesn't claim kin to anybody in the family."

Lily considered that remark odd, to say the least, but further conversation was interrupted as the Kapirigis came barreling through the door, then skidded to a stop at the sight of Cassandra Delaney.

Cassandra shifted her silver-blue gaze to the children. Her bright smile appeared again.

"And you two must be the little aborigines that Hannah was telling me about a moment ago. Well, I must tell you that this is the most exciting thing to happen to me in a very long time! I just can't wait to hear all about your life in Australia. I've studied your country quite extensively and am well acquainted with its culture and history as a penal colony, but there's very little written in the textbooks on the aboriginal peoples, I'm afraid."

Cassandra returned her attention to Lily. "Do you think your friends here would teach me their language? Hannah says it's quite strange to listen to, but I'm rather good with foreign tongues because I've done a lot of traveling around the world. I've learned to speak French, Spanish, and Italian, and I'm in the process of learning Russian from one of the officers at the embassy here in Washington. You see, I have this facility for linguistics. I guess it just comes more easily for me than for other people." Just as suddenly as she had appeared out of nowhere, she changed the subject. "What on earth is that odd L-shaped instrument he's got there in his belt? I don't believe I've ever seen anything like that before. Is it a weapon?"

Lily felt breathless just listening to Cassandra's rapid-fire questions. "It's a boomerang. The aborigines use them for hunting."

"Oh, I see. Would you mind asking your friends if they'd please let me hold it in my hands and examine its construction? Or do they speak English?"

"You can see it," one of the boys said, removing the weapon from his belt.

"Why, thank you, and aren't you the nicest little gentleman?" Cassandra said, smiling and taking the proffered boomerang. She turned it over in her hands as if mightily intrigued with the unusual shape. "Oh, I really must take this to the Institution and let my colleagues examine the design. They'll be as fascinated as I am, I assure you. Lily, you will accompany there as soon as I can arrange a visit, won't you?"

"Institution?" Lily repeated, feeling slightly overwhelmed by the young lady's effervescence, almost as if she were being swept along on a tide of exuberance without her consent.

Cassandra laughed. "Oh, I'm sorry; of course, you wouldn't know what I'm talking about. The Smithsonian Institution is located here in Washington. The professors there study all sorts of scientific inventions and natural phenomena. I'm living there now and working as Doctor Joseph's assistant. He has been to your country on several occasions, so you'll probably enjoy talking with him." She smiled again as she gestured toward the stairwell. "I guess I'm forgetting my manners, but I have a tendency to do that when I'm excited about studying something as interesting as this boomerang. Please come down and have tea with me. Hannah's probably had time to bring the tray into the parlor by now. I especially want you to tell me all about your gift."

"My gift?" Lily repeated, as she and the Kapirigis followed Cassandra down the steps and into the formal parlor beside the front door. She took a seat next to Harte's sister on the white-and-gold sofa in front of a large bay window overlooking the street.

The talkative red-haired girl had been intently examining the Kapirigis' boomerang, but now she looked up at Lily. "Hannah says you have the second sight. You do, don't you?" Before Lily could answer, she shook her head. "If you do, you're so lucky. She said you touched her and knew her daughter had given birth and what she'd named the child. Why don't you take my hand now and see if you see anything interesting about me?"

Lily couldn't believe her ears. Most people didn't want her to touch them after they found out what she could do. Even Harte had seemed to avoid bodily contact with her once he had found out. Somehow she had a feeling Cassandra wasn't like other people.

"Go ahead, Lily, take my hand. Don't worry, I've done this kind of experiment before with other clairvoyants. I think it's a wonderful thing. I'd give anything if I'd been born with such an ability."

"Clairvoyants? I've never heard of that word."

"It just means people who can see things without using their senses."

"I never knew what to call it. The aborigines

thought I was a witch, and so did most of the other people who knew about it."

"That's ridiculous. I consider myself a scientist, and I can tell you that although we aren't sure yet why or how such things occur, we know that it has nothing whatsoever to do with the devil and witchcraft and such. All through history people have believed such superstitious nonsense, but nowadays we're much more enlightened."

"Really?" Lily said, very interested in Cassandra's observations. All her life she had been trying to explain how she saw the things she did, but no one had been able to tell her.

"Oh, yes. Doctor Joseph has interviewed six different people with abilities similar to yours, and the one thing we've found that they have in common is that they've each suffered severe head injuries at some time in their life, usually when they were little children." She leaned forward intently, her silver-blue eyes searching Lily's face. "Did you hurt your head when you were a child, Lily? In a fall, perhaps, or in some other kind of accident?"

Lily was astonished. "Why, yes. I don't remember it, but my mother told me that I fell out of the hayloft and lay like dead for nearly thirty-six hours."

"You see? Doctor Joseph's beginning to suspect that such cranial injuries cause the brain to swell or become dysfunctional in some way that makes the initial tendencies more acute, but no one really knows. The second sight may just be a gift from God or a genetic trait that one inherits from one's forebears. Did your mother have it?"

"Yes, and my grandmother. My brother does, too, but his is quite different from mine."

"There. You see? You fit into both of Doctor Joseph's theories."

Lily was fascinated. Cassandra seemed so sure of herself and her knowledge. The American girl had studied with educated men and met other people who were like Lily, something Lily herself had not done. Lily wanted to hear more about them.

"Please, won't you touch me and see if you can divine something?" Cassandra went on eagerly.

Lily smiled. "I'll try, but I'll warn you, just like I did your brother, that sometimes nothing happens at all."

"I suppose Harte's already got you working for the government, hasn't he?"

Without thinking, Lily nodded. Then she remembered belatedly that Harte had sworn her to secrecy. On the other hand, Cassandra was his sister. There would be little harm in discussing it with her. "I've been able to tell him a few things, but I really have no control over what I see."

"Well, let's try anyway. Here, take my hand like you did with Hannah."

Lily closed her hand around the girl's slender fingers and immediately knew that Cassandra wore small wire-rimmed spectacles.

She saw Cassandra bending over some sort of odd cylinder affixed to a stand.

"Several days ago, on Tuesday, I think, you were working in a laboratory and you accidentally sat down on your eyeglasses and cracked the left lens."

Cassandra gasped in shock, then bubbled over with a delighted laugh. "That's right. I'm nearsighted. I meant to get my glasses fixed, but I forgot all about their being broken."

Cassandra's genuine warmth and goodwill readily communicated itself to Lily, but suddenly she sensed something else quite different.

"I also see a white rose, very lovely and sweet-smelling. It's lying against something soft and dark, black velvet, I think," she said softly. "But I don't understand what it means. Do you?"

A faintly startled expression appeared momentarily on Cassandra's face, only to disappear at once behind another quick smile. "White roses are my favorite flowers," she admitted, withdrawing her hand. "I guess that's why you saw one."

"We will show Miss Cassandra how to throw the boomerang and make it return to her," one of the Kapirigis said suddenly to Cassandra.

"Wonderful!" Cassandra accepted excitedly. "Let's go out in the back yard and let me try right this moment! Tell me about their language, Lily! Can you speak it?"

"Yes. I learned to speak with the Pitjantjatjara when I was little."

"That's supposed to be the easiest way to learn other languages, you know, when you're still a child. I do hope you'll come to the Institution with me and meet Doctor Joseph. He's traveled all over the world to study native cultures—in Africa and in the Amazon and lots of other places—but Australia is his favorite. He'd love to interview you and the boys. Perhaps he could even do an installment about you in the monthly periodical."

"What's that?"

"It's a magazine that tells about the studies being conducted at the Institution." Cassandra suddenly shook her head. "You really have no idea how interesting you are, do you?"

"I guess not," Lily admitted. "I've always felt very different. Most people who found out what I could do were afraid to touch me, so my parents kept me apart from them. We lived out in the bush, away from the townspeople."

"Well, I'm not afraid of you. Actually, you're very lucky to have such a gift. Come, let's go outside and throw this gadget. Are they actually able to bring down their prey with this? What kind of animals do they hunt in Australia? I've heard tell of the kangaroos that live there. Do they really carry their young in a pocket formed in their hides?"

As they made their way toward the rear lawn, Lily answered all of Cassandra's questions, but Cassandra was always ready with more, some of which Lily could not answer.

Even so, she liked Harte Delaney's sister very much. If they could become friends, the wait for Harte to fall in love with her wouldn't be so bad. And perhaps the talkative girl would tell her more about Harte's background, especially about the gold medallion.

# 8

"Are you sure Harte won't mind if we go into the city with you?" Lily asked Cassandra a few days later as they shared a hired conveyance, rattling through the bustling streets of Washington.

Obviously unconcerned, Cassandra shrugged. "Who knows what he'll say? Harte's always so unpredictable about everything. Actually he should be glad there's someone willing to show you around, since he up and left you alone the minute you arrived at his house. There's no telling when he might decide to show his face around here again, so there's no harm in letting you meet my friends at the Institution. I'll bet Harte didn't even tell you where he was going, did he?"

Even though Cassandra's question seemed innocent enough, Lily was hesitant to answer. Lily had a strong feeling that Harte wouldn't want anybody to know where he was or what he was doing, not even his sister. "He didn't say much. Do you think he'll return soon?"

"I daresay he will—now that's he's got you

and your gift to help him with his spying," Cassandra answered offhandedly. "Ever since he became a detective, he's been downright obsessed with his work." She peered out the window at the passing shops. "We should be reaching the Castle any moment now."

"The Castle?"

"That's what we call the Smithsonian. The place is absolutely magnificent. You'll see. The building's constructed to resemble an Italian Romanesque castle, twelfth century, if I remember correctly. A man named James Renwick designed it about twenty years ago, and it's got just about everything that we need for our scientific studies—all sorts of laboratories and lecture halls—it's my favorite place in the whole world."

Beaming happily, Cassandra chattered on about the subject which was obviously very dear to her heart. "Doctor Joseph's the secretary and director. He and his family live on the second floor. I've been staying with them since the war started. I'd live at Harte's house if he'd let me, but he won't. He's always off on some kind of secret mission somewhere anyway. Even before the war broke out, when he was a Pinkerton agent, he was always getting himself in dangerous scrapes, getting shot or beaten up by a bunch of criminals." She paused and looked closely at Lily. "Actually, I shouldn't be discussing Harte's work with anyone, not even you, because Harte says Confederate spies are lurking all around us here in the city. But I know I can trust you because he's got you working for him, doesn't he?"

Lily nodded uncertainly, and Cassandra continued her animated discourse about her beloved Institution. Lily listened dutifully, but outside she could hear the Kapirigis' voices now and then from the driver's perch, upon which they had begged to ride. As they drove down the wide length of Pennsylvania Avenue, the domed Capitol building appeared in the distance and shone brightly in the early-afternoon sun.

They passed a strange obelisk that was still under construction, and Cassandra told her the monument was to honor George Washington, the first president of the United States. As they continued past the peculiarly shaped structure, Lily decided the American people must have loved Washington very much; after all, they had named the entire city after him.

Soon other massive government buildings bloomed before them, but again Lily was amazed at the throngs of blue-coated soldiers everywhere—every one armed with a long rifle and ready for action, in every street and lane, marching in cadence or pushing caissons of artillery. Others rode cavalry horses and wore long swords attached to their belts with yellow sashes, and Lily wondered what color uniforms the army of the Southern states wore.

"There are so many soldiers," she murmured, half to herself. "Does the South have as many?"

For the first time Cassandra looked pensive. "No, but they fight with great passion to preserve their beliefs." She paused to look at Lily. "My other brother fights for the Confederacy, you know."

Lily couldn't hide her surprise. "I didn't know you had any brothers besides Harte."

"Yes. Stuart's a year younger than Harte. I haven't seen him since the war started; none of us have. He's a superb horseman, so he may ride with a cavalry unit. I think he might be out west somewhere."

"You mean he and Harte are fighting on opposing sides?" Lily asked, finding such a thing hard to comprehend.

Cassandra nodded sadly. "It's not just our family, either. The war has split a lot of families apart. You see, my father was born in Newport, Rhode Island, but my mother, Charlotte Harte, came from one of the oldest families in Virginia. The Hartes can trace their lineage all the way back to Jamestown, which was the first permanent British settlement in North America. That's where they got Harte's name, from my mother's branch of the family."

"How did your parents meet?" Lily asked, pleased that Cassandra was so open with the details of Harte's family. She had a feeling she would never get such information out of him.

"Papa came to Richmond on one of his

ships—his family owns a shipping firm out of Newport and a publishing house in Baltimore, too—and Mama said she fell in love with him the first time she saw him, in the receiving line of the governor's ball. She came north to live with him, but when he died before the war started, she took Stuart and me home to live at Twin Pines, her plantation house on the James River."

"Harte didn't go with you?"

For the first time since they'd met, Cassandra seemed reluctant to answer one of Lily's questions. "Well, that's a long story, but I'll just say that my mother and my grandmother never got along with each other. Mama and Papa lived with Grandmother Delaney at the Delaney mansion called The Oaks, and when Harte was born, Grandmother decided she wanted him to become her heir. She groomed him to take over all the Delaney enterprises from the time he was old enough to walk."

Cassandra sighed and shook her head. "When Mama decided to take us back to Virginia, Grandmother had already enrolled Harte in a military academy. Mama didn't want to leave him behind, but she didn't have much choice in the matter. Grandmother can be very willful. Stuart and I were young when we went to Twin Pines, so we're really close friends but neither of us ever got to know Harte very well. Harte and I have become a bit closer since I came here to study after Mama died two years ago. Well, at least he tolerates me. I don't believe anyone knows him well, because he likes to keep to himself. I don't think he ever truly forgave Mama for going off and leaving him the way she did. And now he's estranged from Grandmother too."

"Really? Why?"

"I don't know for sure, but it has something to do with Harte's wife."

Lily stiffened. The idea that Harte Delaney might have a wife had never occurred to her. If he already had a wife, how could they marry? A hard knot began to form in her chest, and she bit back her distress, appalled at the sick disappointment in the pit of her stomach.

"He's married?" she forced herself to ask. "He didn't tell me he had a wife."

Cassandra darted a quick look at her. "Oh, he's not anymore. They got married about ten years ago when he was really young. They hadn't been wed long when the girl died in some sort of accident up at Newport. Her name was Camillia, I think, and apparently Harte blames Grandmother Delaney for her death. There was quite a scandal about it all, but Grandmother has always had enough money to hush up anything that hurts the Delaney name. Nobody ever talks about it—not even Hannah, and she'll tell me anything else I want to know. She keeps in touch with Grandmother too, I know that for a fact. She tells her how Harte's doing because he won't see her or talk to her."

"How awful," Lily murmured, but now she knew Camillia was the girl she had seen when she held Harte's medallion—the dark-haired one in the yellow dress. Despite the fact that she was relieved that Harte was no longer married, her heart ached for the pain he must have suffered when his bride had died. His family life was so scarred and bitter. No wonder he held himself aloof from people! But Cassandra didn't seem to have been affected. Lily suddenly wondered why.

"How do you get along with your Grandmother Delaney, Cassie?"

"I hardly know her. She didn't care much for me, I guess. She invited Stuart up to The Oaks once, though, to have his portrait done for her gallery. I think he might have met Harte's wife while he was there. Anyway, for the most part, Harte's the only one Grandmother Delaney ever had anything to do with."

Cassandra averted her gaze, but Lily heard a thread of vulnerability in Cassandra's words that made her think perhaps she was a little hurt by her grandmother's indifference. Again, she felt a wave of pity for the Delaneys, but she had no time to ask any other questions.

The carriage slowed to a stop. "Here we are, Lily! This is the Smithsonian Institution," Cassandra cried, smiling again and explaining its history as she descended to the street. "An Englishman named Smithson left a grant to start a place of learning in America, and the story is that he was the illegitimate son of some kind of lord named Northumberland, or something like that, and when Smithson made his wealth, he wanted to use his money to build a place where his name would live on forever, long after the Northumberland name had been forgotten. He never set foot on American soil, but his wish came true, for here's this splendid legacy of learning named for him. Someday I intend to leave my mark on science too."

When Lily followed her from the coach before the impressive facade of the Smithsonian Institution, she stared in awe at the turrets and crenellated corner towers, which did indeed resemble those of a medieval castle. Long rows of arched windows lined both the first and the second floors, but her attention was diverted from the magnificent edifice as the boys jumped down from the high seat—Kapi carrying a spear and Rigi holding a boomerang.

Cassandra hurried ahead of them, leading the way through the arched stone portal, and Lily followed more slowly with the boys, curious as to what she would find inside. Just past a pair of immense doors made of heavy oak panels, Cassandra called out to a man who was passing through the vast entrance hall.

"Robert! Come, let me introduce you to my friends."

The man changed his course at once, smiling as if very pleased to see them, especially Cassandra.

"This is Miss Lily Courtland, and the little ones here are Kapi and Rigi." She draped her arms around the boys' shoulders. "Lily, this is my good friend Robert Jennings. He's quite a brilliant scientist, and at the moment he's interested in learning how to forecast the weather. His ideas are fascinating."

"I'm very pleased to meet you, Miss Courtland. Perhaps you'll let me show you my weather invention before you leave."

"We'll come by your laboratory later," Cassandra answered for Lily, "but right now we don't have time. Doctor Joseph's expecting us upstairs in his office, and we're already late. Do you know if he's there?"

"I believe he's working on one of his electromagnetic experiments."

"Oh, good. I've been wanting to assist him on that project. Thanks, Robert. We'll try to drop by your office later."

Robert Jennings bowed courteously to Lily, and she smiled back, thinking him an extremely pleasant man, before following Cassandra, whose patent leather pumps made loud clicking sounds as she crossed the white marble-tiled floor with her brisk, energetic walk. The Kapirigis kept close beside Lily, staring with awe at the displays of animal skeletons in glass cases along the walls.

After passing through several intersecting corridors, Cassandra stopped before a door set with a panel of smoked gray glass. Smiling at Lily, she tapped her knuckle against the window. A voice from inside called for them to enter, and when they opened the door, a stout, serious-looking man dressed in a black frock coat and vest was sitting on a high stool behind a counter covered with all sorts of gadgets connected by wires to peculiar-looking cylinders and scopes.

"Cassie, my dear! Come in, please. So good to see you again. I suppose these are the interesting young people you've been telling me about."

The elderly man smiled kindly at Lily, and when he shook her hand a picture welled up in her head of the timid-looking professor embracing an elderly, gray-haired woman. His wife, Lily sensed, and they were kissing each other as passionately as Harte Delaney had kissed her in her dreaming about the beautiful glade. The memory of Harte's holding her naked body against him in the warm, clear water sent a flood of heated color to her face.

"So you're our little clairvoyant, are you?" the professor was saying. "I certainly won't pressure you, my dear, but I do hope you'll agree to participate in one of our experiments while you're here today. You have a great gift, but a mysterious one that few of us understand."

"My mother always said those of us who had the dreamings were cursed and blessed at the same time."

"I can imagine it would seem that way at times." Doctor Joseph peered at her over the top of his bifocal glasses, his keen eyes full of kindness and understanding. Lily liked him at once.

"And these are the aboriginal twins," he remarked, examining the Kapirigis with the same benign interest. "I suspect they would enjoy seeing our Australian room. We have some very interesting artifacts, but I'm sure they will be able to enlighten us a great deal about the authenticity of our exhibit. We are certainly honored to have them here, I must say."

The two little boys grinned with pleasure.

"They've brought their boomerang along to show you. It's simply amazing how they can toss it so far, then make it return to them," Cassandra interjected eagerly, "I tried it myself and couldn't get it to work, but they say it's quite deadly to their prey."

"Indeed? How very interesting. I do hope they'll demonstrate the technique for me. Before I forget, Cassie, Thaddeus was here earlier today asking about you. He wants you to come to the demonstration of his new balloon."

"Oh, how exciting! I hope he'll be able to take me up soon. Have you ever seen an observation balloon, Lily? They're absolutely huge and filled with heated air to keep them aloft. Thaddeus formed a balloon corps at the beginning of the war and had great success in directing cannon fire from so high in the sky."

Lily shook her head, amazed to hear there was such a thing, but the hot-air balloons were only one of the marvelous inventions that she observed throughout the morning as she followed Cassandra around the halls of the Smithsonian Institution. She met many of Cassandra's friends and colleagues, observed all sorts of intriguing experiments, and was highly impressed with Cassandra's ability to converse about electromagnets and paleontology and archaeology with such wise and studied men.

Even though she found everything around her fascinating, the things she had learned from Cassandra about Harte never left her mind. Especially concerning his dead wife named Camillia. Who had she been? What had happened to her? Was she the reason he didn't want to love another woman? She was determined to know. She decided that she would ask him when he returned, because, whether he knew it yet or not, he was going to fall in love with her, and they were going to be married. There could be no mistake about it.

Anxious to make sure that Lily had not started off on her own to find her brother, Harte swung down from the saddle and left his horse to be looked after by the stable boy. Although he hadn't liked leaving Lily alone at his house, his journey to Baltimore had been worth the time and effort. Thanks to Lily, Federal agents had captured Douglas Minner before he had a chance to blow up the bridge.

Harte no longer harbored any doubt that

Lily could be an extremely effective weapon for the Union, and now his primary concern was keeping her out of Confederate hands. Together with Allan Pinkerton, he had come up with a well-laid plan designed to maintain Lily's help in identifying enemy agents and at the same time bring Derek Courtland to justice.

Striding up the brick path toward the kitchen, he thrust away the vague sense of betrayal that tried to flicker into life in his thoughts. He was a soldier; he had a duty to perform. Lily's brother had single-handedly done more to help the Confederate war effort than most of the South's best generals. Lily knew a war was being waged, and the fact that she had landed so fortuitously in Harte's lap was not his fault. Besides, she would be able to find her brother and tell him about their father's death. That's what she had asked Harte to do for her, and he would see it done.

When he opened the back door and entered the house, Hannah looked up from her task of rolling out a piecrust on the kitchen table.

"So you've done come home at last," she said, wiping her hands on her apron. "Miss Lily's been asking for you near ever' day."

"Where is she?" Harte asked, glancing toward the front of the house. "I need to talk with her."

"She's outside wid Miss Cassie and those little Kapirigi boys."

"Cassie's here?" Harte asked, his brow darkening with a frown. Since his younger sister had moved to Washington, she had shown a provoking tendency to drop by his house for a visit at her whim, usually without notification or permission.

"Oh, yes. Miss Cassie's been callin' ever' afternoon. I declare, those two girls just took to each other like flies to spilled molasses. Cassie's already took dem down to that big castle place of hers to meet her friends—"

"What?" Harte exclaimed angrily. "I didn't want anyone to know Lily and the boys were staying here! I told you that, dammit!"

Hannah puffed up her immense bosom and put her hands on her wide hips, looking mightily offended. "I am just the housekeeper here, Mr. Harte. I shore cain't tell Miss Lily and Miss Cassie what they's can or cain't do. Anyways, Miss Lily got real restless here all alone."

"I should have known that Cassie'd show up and cause trouble," Harte muttered under his breath. "Well, where are they now?"

"Out in de shed."

"The garden shed? What the hell are they doing there?"

"I don't rightly know, Mr. Harte, but I think dem aborigine boys are showin' Miss Cassie something she wants to know 'bout."

At least they hadn't run off to the city again, Harte thought, feeling disgruntled with the lot of them as he took the path around the side of the house and through the rose garden to the small shed that had been built against the brick wall. There were no windows, and the door was closed. What in the devil could the four of them be doing inside?

Harte walked closer and put his ear against the door. He could hear the low murmur of conversation inside. Shaking his head, he jerked open the door and found the two young women sitting cross-legged on the ground with their skirts gathered around them. The Kapirigis squatted on their haunches on the other side of the girls.

All four looked up at Harte, but the elongated rectangle of sunlight from the open door fell upon Lily. She greeted his unexpected appearance with a radiant smile of welcome that only an angel could possess. Harte immediately felt an overwhelming rush of relief and pleasure at seeing her again, then berated himself for his own reaction.

His sister's acknowledgement of his presence, on the other hand, was an impatient gesture to shut the door and a highly irritated command: "Well, come in and close the door, Harte. Kapi and Rigi are right in the middle of their ceremony."

Harte had to duck his head to negotiate the low doorway. When he had gotten in, he crouched down beside Lily and examined her appearance. She wore an apricot-silk dress, one he assumed Cassie had gotten somewhere for her. The pastel color warmed Lily's skin to a soft peach glow and made him want to caress it with his fingertips.

"Thanks to you," he whispered to her, "we got the man you described before he could blow the bridge."

"I'm glad," she answered softly. "Have you learned anything of Derek's whereabouts?"

"Shhh, Harte," Cassandra said, glaring at them. "You're ruining the boys' concentration. They're demonstrating how the Pitjantjatjara do their sacred paintings. They have secret holy places where they paint pictures of animals and birds, and of the Mamu—that means 'evil spirit' in their language—but they're a bit afraid to show me what the Mamu looks like. See, there on the wall? They've painted pictures of kangaroos—they call them *malu*—and crocodiles, and all sorts of interesting things."

Harte looked up at the ceiling and found it covered with the same strange, elongated white figures that he had seen in the Kapirigis' cave by the river. He realized that the Kapirigis had on their loincloths again and had repainted their faces white—no doubt at Cassandra's insistence—and he hoped fervently that Birdie wouldn't show up and let loose one of her bloodcurdling shrieks.

"I told them they could have this shed for their rituals. You don't mind, do you, Harte?" Cassie continued in a low tone. "They really shouldn't be denied their cultural dignity. Look, they've made black paint out of the coal, and I got them the white paint from the art supplies at the Institution. In the desert they make it from grinding up the leaves of some plant indigenous to Australia, but that's unavailable here in the United States."

"Is that so?" Harte said, as he crossed his long legs and leaned back against the wall, wondering why on earth Cassandra cared so much about such trivial things.

The aborigines went back to their painting, with Cassandra watching intently. Kapi lifted a blue-sprigged white china bowl—one that Harte suddenly recognized as the antique sugar bowl off his own dining room hutch. To Harte's surprise, the boy took a small portion of the thin white paint into his mouth, pressed his palm flat against the wall, and then, with a sound that was inordinately impolite, spewed the paint out of his mouth onto the back of his hand and the wall around it, thus leaving a handprint on the wall in a primitive kind of stencil.

Harte had to grin at the absurdity of the whole scene. "Why don't you try that, Cassie? I bet you could make a nice design spitting on the wall like that."

His sister glared at him. "Quit making fun of them, or they won't demonstrate their customs to us. We're not really supposed to be watching them do these spirit paintings because it's taboo, but Lily persuaded them to let me observe just this once in the name of science. If you'll just watch and listen and quit being so critical, you'll find it fascinating."

"Sorry," Harte muttered, but he wasn't nearly as fascinated with the crude drawings that Kapi and Rigi were making on the wall as he was with the way Lily looked in her new dress. During the last three weeks away from her, he had begun to believe he had imagined how beautiful she was, but he hadn't. She was exquisite—there was no better word to describe her. He found himself fighting another urge to trace his forefinger down her elegant cheek to see if it could possibly be as soft as it looked in the dim light. He shook himself, determined to remember how important she was to his work. As long as she was working for him, he had to keep his hands off her.

"I understand that you went into Washington," he murmured softly so as not to disturb his sister, who was closely monitoring the aboriginal artwork. A great deal of loud spitting and spattering was being emitted at the other side of the shed.

"We went to the Castle, where Cassandra lives, a few days ago," she answered hesitantly. "Are you angry that we left the house?"

If he had been at first, he wasn't when Lily gazed up at him out of worried amber-gold eyes. "No. I just don't want anything bad to happen to you before we can find your brother. You've been through a lot already."

"I can't tell you how grateful I am that you're

willing to help me find Derek," she said with such sincerity that Harte shifted uncomfortably.

*What's the matter with me?* he thought furiously. How many times had he lied to women and set up elaborate traps in order to succeed in his missions? Lily was an innocent, that was true—but Derek Courtland wasn't. He had to keep telling himself that.

"I'm the one who should be grateful to you," he said, glad he could find something honest to say. "But I need to talk to you alone. I think I've come up with a way to locate your brother."

"Oh, that's wonderful," Lily whispered, her face filled with joy. "Tell me, quick."

"Let's go inside so we can have some privacy."

"May I come too?" Cassandra asked quickly from the other side of the shed, readily revealing that she'd been eavesdropping on their low conversation.

"This is between Lily and me," Harte said, perturbed that his sister had ingratiated herself to Lily while he was gone. Cassandra did not know how to hold her tongue and had proved it more than once. He never told her anything.

Harte helped Lily to her feet and walked her to the house so they could talk in his office. He had to be extremely careful; otherwise she might sense his plot to capture her brother, and all his plans would go awry.

"Would you like Hannah to bring us some tea or coffee?" he asked solicitously after she was seated across from him at his desk.

"No, thank you. Please tell me about Derek. Do you know if he's all right? I've been so worried about him," she said, sitting on the edge of the chair and eagerly awaiting his reply.

Even after her harrowing ordeal with Ringer and his crew, she hadn't learned to distrust people, Harte realized. She was looking at him now out of her huge amber eyes, and Harte was appalled at how much he wanted to take her in her arms, to comfort her and tell her everything was going to be all right. But such reassurances would only be lies. At the moment he was her very worst enemy, whether she knew it yet or not.

Damn her eyes! He'd better get a hold on himself and not let her get to him. Derek Courtland's capture was too important to the North. It was time to proceed with the plan.

"Please tell me where he is. Can I go to him?"

"I'm sorry, I still don't know his exact whereabouts," he answered. When her face fell, he proceeded slowly, feeling guilty as hell. "But I've had an idea that I think might work, if you're willing to go along with me on a short voyage."

"Where?"

"From what I've found out from our intelligence sources, your brother sails his ship from port to port, so it's very difficult for anyone to predict where he'll go next. But we've heard on good authority that he's set up headquarters somewhere near Nassau. Perhaps if we put out the word that you're looking for him, maybe even send a letter to Nassau in your handwriting, he'll come looking for you. Of course, we can't expect him to sail up the Potomac, because he's wanted by the Federal government. But I can take you to Bermuda—that's a British colony and I've heard he frequently goes there."

"What is Bermuda?"

"It's a chain of islands about six hundred miles from here. It's a neutral port, so it would be safe for him to weigh anchor there."

Lily hesitated, a delicate frown marring her forehead. "You work for the Federal government," she said, watching him closely. "Won't you arrest him if he goes there?"

"No," Harte lied without a change of expression. "I'll be on medical furlough because of my arm. You can trust me, Lily."

Lily was immediately apologetic. "Forgive me for doubting you, but I felt I had to ask. I hope you're not offended."

Harte felt like a louse for exploiting her naiveté, but didn't show it. "I understand. Do you want to try it? I can't guarantee it'll work. He may not come to Bermuda at all, but I think he might."

Lily looked down at her lap, and Harte watched her moisten her lips with her tongue. She had a habit of doing that, and he had a habit of being affected by it. He swallowed hard, realizing how easy it would be to reach out and pull her into his arms. She would let him, he knew it. She had already told him she loved him. She wanted him, and she was obviously as attracted to him as he was to her.

But it would be better to keep his hands off her until Derek was in his control; she might sense what he was really up to. After that, he wouldn't have to worry about it anymore because she would hate his guts. And that was probably the best thing for both of them.

"Will you be with me?" she asked, blushing prettily as if highly embarrassed to be asking such a question.

He would have to be with her all the time, of course. That's the reason he had chosen Bermuda over other sites. He owned a house there. "If you want me to, I will."

She raised eyes that shone like precious topaz set ablaze. "Yes," she said. "I want us to be together."

Harte was almost undone by the way she was looking at him, and he knew how close he was to ruining everything. He stood abruptly.

"All right," he said, his tone strictly business. "I'll arrange passage as soon as I can. We should be able to sail in a day or two. Do you want the boys to come with us?"

"Yes. They'll want to return to Australia with Derek and me."

"Fine. I'll let you know as soon as the arrangements are complete."

Harte left the room quickly, realizing he had

better learn to keep his distance from her. Lord help him, he wasn't sure he could do it. He was glad Lily wanted to take the Kapirigis with them. Two chaperones with sharp spears prone to following Lily's every footstep might be the answer to the problem. He wanted her so much, he wasn't even sure that spears would provide enough discouragement.

# 9

A week later Lily stood beside the Kapirigis at the port railing of the *Baltimore Star,* a sleek schooner owned by the Delaney Shipping Line. The short voyage to Bermuda had been uneventful, with calm seas and fair weather. Earlier that morning the coral-pink beaches of the British colony had appeared on the horizon, and now they had dropped anchor in Hamilton Harbor.

Turning slightly toward the stern, she watched surreptitiously as Harte spoke with Rodney Terrance, the bearded young captain of the ship. Although Harte had been courteous and respectful, he had openly avoided her and left her to spend her days with the boys. Not once had he approached her cabin or joined her for a meal. Only occasionally did he stop to speak with her or the boys when they wandered up on deck to take the fresh air. He had spent all his time with the captain and the crew, all of whom seemed to be old friends of his.

Cassandra had begged to come with them,

but Harte had refused even to consider the idea. He didn't trust his own sister, and now his actions indicated that he didn't trust Lily either. She had made a mistake of revealing her love for him. Now he acted as if she didn't exist. But he was meant to hold her and kiss her—she had seen them together in a dreaming. But when? And where? How long would she have to wait?

During the last few days, when she'd had little to do but think, she had begun to believe that Harte was afraid she would sense his innermost secrets through her visions. Lily smiled to herself. If only he knew! Now that they had met, she saw nothing but erotic glimpses of them together, naked and making love, scenes that made her skin ripple with gooseflesh even now, at the thought of the things Harte was going to do to her.

"The boat's being lowered now, Lily. Has the crew collected your baggage?"

Harte had come up quietly behind her, and Lily turned, half expecting the cold, guarded look that had been on his face the entire voyage. To her surprise, however, he was smiling—his wonderful eyes were as warm and green as the water sweeping in to the shore. Her knees went weak.

"Yes," she murmured, hoping that he would be forced to spend more time with her after they disembarked.

"Bermuda is very beautiful," he said, turning his gaze to the blue-shadowed hills that rose behind the beach. "I think you'll like it. I always find it hard to leave."

"You've been here before?" Lily asked. She suddenly realized how little she knew about him despite the dreamings she had experienced for so long.

Harte didn't look at her, and she felt that he wasn't comfortable answering questions about himself. Why was he so withdrawn?

"I own a house here, over there at the distant end of the bay." He gestured toward a spot far away, high in the hills above the sea. Lily shielded her eyes against the glare but failed to detect any rooftops in the dense vegetation above the sandy, coral-pink beaches.

"You'll be comfortable there. It's quiet and peaceful, and the view is breathtaking."

"You *are* coming with us, aren't you?" she asked. Something in the way he had spoken alarmed her.

Harte gave a faint smile. "Of course. I promised you I would, didn't I? The launch is ready for us. Come along, and I'll help you down the ladder."

When he took her elbow and led her toward the starboard loading rail, Lily immediately felt better. Perhaps now that they had reached Bermuda, they would become closer. Perhaps he would learn to trust her and would talk to her more openly.

Moments later she sat in the gently bobbing longboat and watched him help the Kapirigis down into place. Both settled on the seat beside her, talking excitedly in their own tongue and pointing at the dozens of boats anchored in the crowded harbor. Harte climbed in and found a seat in the stern, and after several minutes of steady rowing by the six burly seamen, the bottom scraped against the sand on a deserted stretch of beach.

Harte stepped over the side the moment they landed and made his way toward a tall man who awaited him at the top of the beach. Lily wondered who the stranger was. One of the oarsmen helped her out of the boat, and while their meager luggage and Harte's lone satchel were transferred to the shore, the Kapirigis jumped into the water and splashed through the gentle waves to examine a crab that was scuttling through the shallows. Without further ado, the launch was heaved back through the incoming waves toward the *Baltimore Star*.

Glad for the wide-brimmed straw hat that Cassandra had provided for the trip, Lily looked up at the town built at the base of the low hills edging the curved beach. They had landed a good ways from Hamilton's busy wharf area, but Lily could see that the place was larger than she had first assumed. The houses were made of limestone in a simple square construction and were picturesque in pastel pink, yellow, and blue. They decorated the sides of the hills like those she had read about in her books of fairy tales when she was a child at Malmora.

Soon Harte rejoined her and led her with him toward the road. The man he had met on the beach was gone. "I've hired a buggy from an old friend to drive up to the house."

"Did he have any word about Derek?" she asked quickly, suddenly realizing that Derek might already be in Hamilton if it was indeed one of his ports of call.

"No, but don't be discouraged. He'll come eventually. All we have to do is be patient and wait for him."

Harte was an important man in the Union army, Lily realized. How long would he would be able to stay with her before he was ordered to return home? Even if he did stay, Derek would probably insist that she and the Kapirigis return to Australia with him. She wasn't sure she wanted to do that, not now that she had found Harte.

"What if it takes weeks or months?" she asked, afraid to hear his answer.

"Once the word gets out that you're here, I think he'll come at once."

"Will the ship wait for us?" she asked, watching the oarsmen propel the longboat over the smooth water toward the moored schooner.

"It'll anchor here for several days while the crew unloads the holds. The *Baltimore Star* has done a steady business with the Hamilton merchants for years, since before the war started. After Captain Terrance is finished here, he'll sail her on to St. George, on the other side of the island, and pick up a return shipment of goods."

Lily considered his answer as he led her to the road, where a sleek black horse and a bay mare were hitched to an open buggy bedecked with gay yellow fringe. Harte helped her up onto the driver's seat and joined her there, while the Kapirigis scrambled onto the rear, where they could ride with their bare feet dangling off the luggage hold.

Harte slapped the reins, and the horses began the ascent of the winding road that meandered away from the town and inland through tall palm trees. Even the muffled thud of hooves against the packed sand seemed loud in the peaceful afternoon.

"I guess you're pretty exhausted," Harte said suddenly, giving her a sidelong glance.

"I'm glad to finally be here. Did your friend have any idea when Derek might show up?"

"You're very eager to see him, aren't you?"

"Oh, yes. He's been gone for nearly three years. He's all I have left now that Papa's gone."

Harte kept his eyes on the road ahead. "Apparently he docks in Hamilton whenever he's in the area. I've left word on the waterfront as to where he can find you."

He lapsed into a thoughtful silence, and Lily took advantage of the lull in their conversation to admire the tropical surroundings. The narrow path they followed often disappeared between palms that speckled them with dancing, dappling shade and then snaked out onto the edge of low cliffs that presented breathtaking glimpses of the turquoise-tinted sea.

Flowers bloomed everywhere, vibrant scarlets and golds and purples, and sweet-smelling red bougainvillea wound through the undergrowth beneath the majestic palms, whose ragged fronds rustled in the constant breeze from the roaring ocean waves below the cliffs. Lily welcomed the warmth and sunshine and peaceful quiet. It was the most beautiful place she had ever seen.

By the time they rounded the far side of the bay, Lily could see the roof of Harte's house. A few minutes later she discerned the warm, pale apricot of the limestone walls. As they came out of the trees, she saw the long lawn of verdant grass that swept up to the front of the small house perched on a low bluff overlooking a pale-pink beach. In the distance she could barely make out the rooftops of Hamilton and the ships dotting its harbor.

"It's so beautiful here," she said breathlessly. "No wonder Cassie wanted to come with us."

"Cassie's never been here," Harte said. "None of my family has. I won this place in a card game a long time ago."

"Why would anyone wager ownership of such a beautiful home?" Lily wondered, thinking she surely would never have made such a bet if she had been lucky enough to possess the apricot house on the edge of the sea.

"Actually, Randolph was glad to have a reason to return to England, but I daresay his family wasn't too pleased with him. This land has been in their family since the seventeenth century, when George Stellar landed here on his way to Jamestown. Ironically, there were a few of my own ancestors on that same ship. The fabled Hartes of Virginia—my mother's holy family."

Lily easily detected the sarcasm in his last words, and she knew then that Harte had been hurt deeply when his mother had left him behind and taken his brother and sister back to Virginia to support the South. He still ached inside, she thought sadly, even though so many years had passed. To divert his thoughts from his mother's desertion, Lily quickly changed the subject. "Did the British settle Bermuda with convicts the way they did in Australia?"

"No, only landed gentry stepped ashore to claim their lands. But Georgia was originally a penal colony. It's one of the states that seceded from the Union. It's a member of the Confederacy now."

By the time the two horses had taken them to the front door of the house, a freckle-faced young woman dressed in a scoop-necked white blouse and a full white skirt had stepped off the stoop to greet them. Her white-blond hair was braided into a queue down her back, and she was holding the hand of a little boy who looked about eight years old. His hair was a darker shade of blond, and he had even more freckles than the woman. As Harte reined the horses to a stop, the boy grinned widely and darted around the back of the buggy to get a better look at the Kapirigis.

"Hello, Lucie," Harte said to the young woman, climbing out and lifting Lily down beside him. "Please allow me to introduce my guest, Miss Lily Courtland."

"How do you do, miss?" The girl smiled and dropped a small curtsy.

Lily nodded in acknowledgement, wondering who she was and if she lived in the house with Harte.

"And this is Kapi and Rigi," Harte continued, as the two aborigines jumped to the ground and silently eyed the white boy. "They'll need a room of their own."

"Hello, Kapi and Rigi," Lucie said, smiling at the boy with the freckles. "This is my son, Bobbie. He'll be willin' to show you around, I expect. He's about your age, it seems."

"There be two of you, and you look just the same," Bobbie decreed with a tilt of his fair head, looking from one boy to the other in a close examination. "Wanna see the beach?"

"Yes," Kapi said.

"Me, too," Rigi chimed in.

In response, Bobbie took off across the yard at breakneck speed without uttering a word, obviously proud of his fleetness of foot. The two aborigines lit out after him, clearly determined not to be bested. Lily had a feeling that this race might be the first of many such duels of strength and skill.

"I trust everything has been all right since the last time I was here?" Harte was asking Lucie. "Have you and your family been well?"

"Yes, sir. It's been an awful long time since you've come over for a stay. We heard about the war goin' on in America and figured you was caught up in it in some way or other."

"That's right, but I plan to stay longer this time. How's Barnabus and the baby?"

"The husband's just fine, sir. He's been workin' in the distillery factory for a time now, and little Tommie's going on five years old."

"Is that right? Doesn't seem possible." Harte shook his head, then glanced at Lily. "Lily, why don't you let Lucie show you up to your room? You can take a nap and freshen up. I have some things to attend to, but I'll join you for supper on the upper veranda, if you like."

"Will you be gone long?" Lily asked, absurdly afraid that he was going to go back to the ship and sail away without her. As silly as her fear seemed, she was beginning to feel a curious sense of dread. Something was wrong about the place, about Harte being there. She felt it, but she didn't know what it was.

"I'm just going to put the horses up and take a look around the place. You'll have plenty of time to rest and relax. I know you're tired."

Lily watched him lead the horses off down the lane to a separate stable made from the same apricot-tinted limestone. She *was* tired, she realized, as she trailed Lucie through the open front door. The thick stone walls kept the interior of the house cool and dim. Everything was bright and clean, the walls freshly whitewashed and the simple windows undraped. The furniture was sparse, the spacious rooms airy and uncluttered. She had a feeling that the residents of Bermuda rarely stayed inside their homes, instead enjoying the outdoors where they could be surrounded by the beauty of the island.

"Please come this way," the soft-spoken maid said, leading her up a narrow flight of stone stairs at one side of the small foyer. "I'm sure Mr. Delaney would want me to put you in one of the rooms overlooking the sea."

"Does he bring people here often?" Lily asked, trying to make her question seem casual. More specifically, of course, she was wondering if he had brought any other women to this private paradise of his, and who they were, and if he had loved any of them.

"No, ma'am," Lucie answered, opening a door at the top of the steps. "He's never brought nobody else here, not as long as I been takin' care of this house. And I been workin' for Mr. Delaney for near seven years now. He always just come by himself and spend his time walkin' down there on the beach for hours and hours."

"Do you live here too?"

"No, ma'am. Me and Barnabus and the boys

have us a little place about two miles down the road. I only come here through the day to keep the place clean and ready in case Mr. Delaney do come. Then I cook and clean when he's here."

As she spoke, she stood back, and Lily preceded her into a cool, spacious bedchamber. Doors opened onto a stone balcony overlooking the ocean, and sheer white drapes billowed in, carrying the salty tang of the ocean breeze.

"If you be needin' anything else, just come find me," Lucie said, with her easy smile. "I'll be fixin' you up a nice supper before I go back home tonight. There are a few things that might fit you folded up there in the wicker chest. I keep them here in case I need a change of clothes for some reason or another. It's very warm here through the days, and you'll be hot in dresses such as that one," she added, gesturing at Lily's long-sleeved dress.

"Thank you, Lucie."

The girl left, and Lily stepped out onto the balcony and rested her hands against the wide wall. The sun-warmed stone felt good beneath her palms, and she laughed to herself when she saw the Kapirigis still chasing the swift-footed Bobbie at least a mile down the beach. *They already like it here,* she thought, gazing out at the vast horizon where the dark-blue ocean met the azure blue of the sky. She wondered if Derek would sail into sight soon. Sighing, she turned, reentered the bedchamber and lay down on the large white iron bed, relaxing into the soft feather mattress. Her last conscious thoughts were how very good the crisp white sheets felt, how wonderful the sea breeze smelled. Then she fell asleep, her dreams as tranquil as the untroubled ocean below her windows.

# 10

"Well, Lily, what do you think? Is Moon Cove to your liking?" Harte asked later that evening as he poured red wine into her glass. He leaned back against the blue-striped cushions of the wicker chair in which he sat, near Lily's bedchamber doors on the upstairs patio. Throughout their evening repast, she had been unusually somber. Harte wanted to know why.

"Being here is like visiting paradise," she murmured from her seat atop the low wall. She kept her eyes on the beach below the house.

Harte was pleased. He loved Moon Cove and always had, but since he had obtained the property, he had hoarded the pleasure of its beauty for himself. Moon Cove was his own personal sanctuary. He came here when he needed to rest his mind and relax. He had never brought anyone else here, not until now. Inexplicably, he had wanted Lily to share with him the beauty of the shining sea, the shimmering sun, and the impossibly blue sky. But something was clearly bothering her.

"What are you looking at?" he asked at length.

"The Kapirigis have built a *wiltja* down the beach a ways. I can see their fire from here."

"What's a *wiltja*?"

"It's a hut made from brush and grass. The Pitjantjatjaras build them for shelter."

Harte smiled. "There's a perfectly good bedroom here for them to use, right next to yours."

"They miss their own ways. They asked if they could live on the beach while we're here, and I said yes."

"All right," Harte agreed. After another long, heavy silence, he attempted conversation again. "You're very quiet tonight. Is something wrong?"

"I didn't think you wanted to talk with me," she answered, still not looking at him.

So she had noticed his attempts to keep a safe distance between them while they were aboard the ship. He had left her alone with the twins for companionship, but certainly not because he had wanted to. His plot to capture Courtland was risky, and the details had to be handled with care. Lily's brother was no fool. Derek Courtland had shown his craftiness and quick thinking countless times when evading Federal gunboats that pursued the *Mamu*. He wouldn't walk blindly into a trap, not even if he thought his little sister was in trouble. But he might get careless. Harte was counting on that.

"That's not true," he said lightly, taking a sip of his wine. "I'm happy to converse with you. What would you like to discuss?"

"You."

"I'm afraid that subject's a bit boring. Can you think of something else?"

At that, Lily turned and looked straight at him. Her eyes glowed slightly in the light filtering out from the bedchambers behind them like rich, molten gold. "I'm beginning to get a strange feeling that everything isn't as it should be," she said, not taking her intense gaze off his face. "Are you hiding something from me? Something about Derek? Is he all right?"

Harte tensed with dread and tried not to show it. "As far as I know," he answered truthfully, "your brother's fine. Lily, don't you trust me anymore?"

Lily returned her gaze to the dark ocean. Her chest rose and fell in a deep, forlorn sigh. "I'd like to know you better, but you're always so guarded and distant."

Harte set his goblet on the glass-topped table beside his chair. "I'm a private person, Lily. I always have been. Don't be insulted that I prefer not to talk about myself. It has nothing to do with you."

"Cassie says you don't trust anyone, that you won't let anyone into your life. Especially women. Is that true?"

"Cassie has no idea what I think or how I feel about anything."

"Why not? She's your sister."

"We're not as close as you and Derek are. We were brought up in different homes," he said in a curt tone meant to discourage any further talk of his family. He picked up Lily's untouched glass and carried it to where she sat on the stone balustrade. "Here—you haven't touched your wine."

Lily didn't answer, nor did she pick up the goblet he placed on the wall beside her. Harte sat down, silently watching the wind from the beach gently toy with the silky blonde curls cascading down her back. She wore island attire: a low-necked white blouse and a white skirt that was embroidered with green and red thread around the bottom. She looked more beautiful than any of the native women. The neckline dipped low, hinting at full, soft curves, and Harte decided instantly that he needed to put more distance between himself and this tempting woman. *A couple of miles and a barbed wire fence might be enough,* he thought dryly. Shifting uncomfortably, he tossed down the remainder of his wine and returned to the table to pour himself more.

"I think you're afraid to get near me," she accused suddenly, making Harte freeze in the process of lifting the bottle.

She was right, but Harte made sure she didn't know that. "Why would I be afraid of you, Lily?" he asked nonchalantly as he refilled his goblet.

"Because if I touch you I might be able to divine some of the secrets you try so hard to hide from everyone. That's what scares you, isn't it?"

Harte was immediately wary. She was so close to the truth! He sipped his wine, trying to decide the best way to answer. She was sensing his reticence with her, but he didn't think she realized that his secret concerned her brother. Not yet, anyway. The moment she did, she would leave, and he couldn't let her do that. He needed to throw her off, give her another reason for his avoidance of her. And he could provide a different rationale for his behavior—one that was true.

"Maybe it's something really simple, like I want to make love to you more than any woman I've ever seen, but I know I can't, so I keep my distance."

Faint surprise flickered over her face, then she looked down at her lap. He had embarrassed her, he realized, but that was good. Maybe it would keep her away from him. She was so young and lovely, her expressions so easy to read. She hadn't yet learned to hide her feelings from others. She was innocent, sheltered by her family until a few months ago. She had no idea how cruel and unfair life was—especially in his world of spies and lies, where deception was the reality.

"Why can't you?"

Her sudden question startled him. He had expected maidenly indignation, not a demand to explain himself. He chose his reply cautiously. "Because I'm not going to take advantage of a young, unprotected girl who saved my life."

"Even if she loves you and wants to be taken advantage of?"

The corner of Harte's mouth lifted in a faint smile. "Not even if she *thinks* she's in love with me."

Lily remained quiet for a few moments. "I did see us making love together when we were playing the string game." She paused. Their eyes locked. "It was wonderful and right for us to be together that way. I know how it's going to feel when you touch me, and I want to feel it. I want you to share it with me."

Her blatant invitation was the last thing Harte had expected, but he wasn't immune to the sensual promise in her low, husky words. His eyes lingered on her mouth. She had the most desirable mouth ever created. He took a deep breath. Things were getting entirely out of hand.

"Good God, Lily, what are you trying to do?" He stood up and moved to a spot along the wall, several yards away from her. "I don't love you, Lily, and I don't intend to marry, and I'm not going to use a young, inexperienced woman like you for my pleasure, then just walk away. You shouldn't want that either, not with me or any other man."

"There isn't any other man for me," she said flatly.

Harte said nothing. He should leave while he still could, he thought. He should take a long walk on the beach. Better yet, a swim in the cold ocean might put out the fire smoldering in his loins.

"You're going to make love to me eventually. I saw it in my dreaming. You might as well just get it over with."

Harte turned disbelieving eyes on her. Then he laughed at the absurdity of her remarks. "You're certainly being practical about losing your virtue to a man who'll never be able to love you, much less marry you."

"All my virtue will get me is a high price on the Damascus slave block. And you *are* going to marry me. I saw that, too."

Harte frowned. Lily was hard to reason with but, God help him, he was weakening. He had better beat a hasty retreat before it was too late. "I think this has gone far enough. I'm going to bed before we do something we'll both regret."

"I won't know your secrets, if that's what you're worried about," Lily said calmly, moving closer to him. "The dreamings have changed since I met you. Now all I see when I touch you is the two of us together in some beautiful place. You smile at me and pull me into the water with you . . ."

With that, Harte's willpower and better judgment began to crumble around the edges. She was so close now, she smelled so good, she looked so beautiful. He wanted her in a way that was almost frightening, especially to him, a man who prided himself on his control. He reached out and touched her cheek, startled by the way she melted instantly into his arms.

Lily clung to him, pressed her cheek against his chest, locked her arms tightly around his waist, and Harte's blood ran rampant with need, thundering through his veins, surging, throbbing in his heart and brain and temples, until all he could hear was the beating of his heart. He lost all grasp of caution, didn't care about Derek Courtland or his capture, cared only about holding Lily's warm, willing body close against his own.

"I don't love you, Lily, you have to understand that," he muttered hoarsely as his mouth came down over hers. Her lips quivered, but she tasted every bit as soft and sweet as he had known she would. Her response was trembling and tentative at first, the timid kisses of a woman inexperienced in love, but soon she became unabashedly eager, demanding more from him as she opened her lips and met his exploring tongue.

Harte's passion leapt out of bounds, igniting with a need he had had never felt before in his life, and he realized he was losing all control as he surrendered his senses to the smooth softness of her skin, the silken texture of her flowing hair, the sweetness of her mouth.

Lily moaned as his kisses lengthened and grew more aggressive, exploring her throat and breasts, and even that low sound of desire inflamed him. Holding her tightly against him, he pressed her backward upon the wall and sank to his knees at her side, his mouth hungrily tasting the slender column of her throat where her pulse throbbed with deep, impassioned breathing. She cried out, her fingers clutching his hair, and he knew he should stop now before it went further, but he couldn't, God help him, he couldn't.

Using the last vestiges of his willpower, Harte pulled back. "Lily, I don't want to do this to you . . ."

"Please . . ." she breathed, her lips parted. She pulled his head down and stopped his protests with a kiss.

Harte was lost, no longer able to deny himself what she was offering to him so willingly. Groaning, he swept her up and carried her to the bed, standing over her and staring down at her with intense, eager anticipation as he ripped off his clothes. He came down on top of her, capturing her wrists and holding them on either side of her head.

"You can still say no and I'll stop," he whispered, his lips moving against Lily's mouth, though he was not really sure if he could stop.

"Don't stop," Lily whispered, but her heart was thudding so hard that she felt as if she might faint. Despite her inviting words and her eagerness to experience Harte Delaney's lovemaking, now that the moment was at hand, she felt afraid—but not enough to pull away. She wanted to know what it was to give herself to Harte Delaney. She wanted to feel her body respond to the man she loved. It was meant to be, this night, no matter what Harte said. There was no fighting it. If she was to lose her virtue, she wanted it to be with Harte.

Closing her eyes, she lay in a trembling state of arousal as he began to unlace the ribbons holding together the front of her blouse. His calloused palm smoothed lightly over her bare midriff, then took her breath away as he molded it over her naked breast, coaxing her nipples erect. Gasping, she felt his face against her flesh, his lips pressing warmly against her flat stomach. She squeezed her eyes tighter, then widened them in shock as his warm tongue flicked against the hard tip of her breast and sent a flaming arrow of fire deep inside her womanly core.

"Aaaah, stop," she moaned incoherently, as his hands moved over her flesh, softly, gently, but then he paused . . . "I mean, *don't* stop . . . please don't stop . . ."

Somewhere outside her whirling passions, she heard him laugh softly. Then he was exploring her body again, his mouth and fingers touching everywhere with slow and thorough reverence, sampling every inch of her flesh. Then his lips found hers and ended the low gasping sounds she heard herself making.

Lily slid her arms around his neck as he ventured beneath her skirt, unfastening buttons, pulling garments away, touching her bare leg at the knee, then sliding upward to her inner thigh and beyond, until she felt she would surely not be able to bear the pleasure he was bringing to her with the tender caresses of his fingertips. She squirmed and arched up to meet this gentle probing, but his mouth attacked hers again, hot and hungry, willing her to respond, making her forget everything but him and the exquisite feelings exploding inside her body, bringing her off the bed with panting exertion, her fingers clutching the bedclothes as she was wracked by one exquisite wave of sensation after another.

"Now you know how love feels," he whispered, his voice so hoarse that Lily could barely understand him. She could only nod weakly, still experiencing starbursts of indescribable pleasure as he rose above her, big and strong and masculine.

"It will hurt this first time," he whispered against her cheek, then captured her mouth with relentless kisses as he came down into her, groaning aloud as he molded himself to her body. Lily moaned, felt him inside her, felt the initial stab of pain, but she only wanted him to stay a part of her. She wanted to hold him tightly, his body so warm and hard, his skin smooth, his muscles rippling beneath her palms. She did love him. They were destined for each other, even if he didn't know it yet, even if they were lovers instead of husband and wife, even if it were only for this one time. She smiled when he cried out with uninhibited pleasure, and for the first time in her life she felt totally complete.

Some time later, when their passion had

cooled and Lily lay curled in Harte's arms, Harte stared up at the billowing white curtains that draped the bed, shocked at his own shattering response to the woman in his arms. Feelings he didn't want, or need, crowded his mind, but she had given herself so freely, so eagerly, and it had been so good for him. Now what the hell was he going to do? She had avowed her love sweetly and innocently, but how would she feel when she found out he was using her to capture her brother?

"I know you didn't want to do this," she whispered softly a moment later, her long, silky lashes downcast, her lips moving against his chest. "But I want you to know that I'm not sorry it happened, even if it never happens again."

Harte smiled at her endearing admission. He tightened his arms around her. "I have a feeling it's going to happen again . . . fairly soon."

Obviously pleased by his remark, Lily lifted her head and rested her chin in her palm. She studied Harte's face. "Did you like it, too?"

Harte laughed. "You aren't acting much like a deflowered virgin."

"I've waited a long time for this moment, but I was afraid you didn't really want me. I know you've probably been with lots of other women."

"How do you know that?"

"Because Cassie told me, and," she hesitated, then shyly lowered her eyes, "because I don't think any woman could resist a man like you."

A wave of unbelievable tenderness swept over Harte. He rolled over on his side, pulling Lily close against his chest. His fingers tangled in her hair, and he brought her lips to his in a gentle kiss. Instantly his body was aflame again with wild, uncontrollable desire, passion taken to nearly unbearable heights when she kissed him back as if she couldn't stop. The guilt he had been feeling about capturing her brother faded, and he lost himself to her body, like warm velvet beneath his touch, the long strands of silky hair wrapping them together. The wonder of making love to Lily was a new kind of joy, a fulfillment of pleasure he had never felt before.

# 11

Lily awoke to the delicious sensation of Harte's lips pressing against her bare back. She smiled dreamily and murmured with pleasure until he turned her over and found her mouth. Though more than thorough, the kiss turned out to be much too brief.

"Time for breakfast," he said cheerfully, handing her a cup of coffee from the tray on the bedside table. "I've been up for hours and Lucie's made breakfast and gone back home, but I didn't wake you because I knew you had good reason to be exhausted." Harte grinned at her. He sat down at the foot of the bed and leaned back with one arm propped idly on his knee.

Lily held the sheet around her, blushing at the way he was openly admiring her bare shoulders and tousled hair. Now, with daylight streaming in the window and the sheer organdy curtains billowing wildly in the sea-fresh air, the long night of lovemaking seemed like a dream, a wonderful experience too good to be real. On top of that, she felt at a disadvantage with Harte fully dressed in a spotless white shirt and brown riding breeches.

"You shouldn't have let me sleep so late," she said, sipping the steaming aromatic brew. The tray held several oranges and a bunch of purple grapes, but she found herself more hungry for Harte's kisses than for any kind of morning fare. She wondered if he would want her again now that he'd had her all through the night, or if men tired of a woman after making love to her. "Or maybe you should have stayed in bed with me."

Harte gave her a slow smile. "I was highly tempted, believe me, but we'll be up late tonight, too, I suspect, and we have things to do today."

*He does want me again,* she thought, very pleased. "What do we have to do today?"

"Get dressed and I'll show you. And wear something that's easy to get off. I've already got the horses saddled and ready. You do ride?"

"Derek taught me when I was four years old. Where are we going?"

"You'll see. I'll wait for you downstairs."

He was gone before she could say more, and she leaned back against the pillows, realizing how happy she felt. And he was different too. Ever since they had come to Moon Cove, his mood had been lighter, his frown less evident. She hoped she had something to do with the change in him. She wanted him to be happy, to forget his worries and the problems of the war, at least for a little while.

Already missing him, she hurried to the bowl and pitcher and hastily performed her morning ablutions, then picked up one of the simple cotton skirts and tops Lucie had left for her. She quickly donned the cool garments and stepped into the matching white sandals.

When she ran down the outside stairs that descended from the double verandas overlooking the sea, she found him waiting with the horses. He came to meet her, and Lily forgot everything else when he took her in his arms, lifting her off her feet and kissing her until she was flushed and breathless.

"You look beautiful. Come, let's get you mounted."

He gave her a boost into the saddle, then swung agilely onto his own horse. Lily followed as he walked his mount across the grassy lawn to a steep, twisting path that led down to the beach. She hadn't ridden since she had been forced off Malmora, and it felt good to be astride a horse, even though her body was still slightly tender from her lengthy initiation into lovemaking.

The sun was high and warmed the top of her bare head, and when they reached the long expanse of lovely pink sand, she shielded her eyes and looked down the beach toward the Kapirigis' *wiltja.* She couldn't see the boys anywhere, but when she looked back, Harte was cantering down the beach in the opposite direction. She turned the mare's head after him, knowing that in that moment, she would have followed him to the end of the earth if he had asked her to.

Happier than she had ever been, she rode slowly along the splendid beach. The ocean was a pure turquoise color that took her breath away, the waves calm and quiet except where they crashed upon a series of low rock cliffs that jutted out into the bay. She thought of Derek and realized with some guilt that she was no longer sure she wanted to return to Australia and Malmora. She wanted to be a part of Harte Delaney's life. She had waited so long to find him.

Smiling to herself, she pressed her heels against the horse's flanks and cantered faster, reveling in the wind that tossed her loosened hair, completely unmindful of the way it tangled down her back. She felt totally free, and she liked it. Ahead of her, Harte had turned his horse into the palm trees, and when she entered the dense foliage after him, she looked around with delight, thinking the island had to be the most beautiful place in existence. As she followed the sandy trail edged with emerald-green ground ferns and violet-flowered vines, she knew she had been there before, somewhere, sometime.

By the time Harte brought them out into the glade with the deep-blue, tranquil pool, she realized that the scene was the one from her dreaming. Harte had disappeared behind a cluster of palms, and just past him she could see the high rocks with the splashing waterfall. She smiled again, her body anticipating what was about to happen.

By the time her mare had picked her way along the bank, Harte had already dismounted and disrobed. As he dove naked into the water, she slid from her saddle and stood on the bank. When he emerged from the dark-blue water, his back was to her, the fine strong muscles rippling as he reached up to push his hair back from his forehead. Then he turned and Lily felt the strange sense of unreality that always came over her when she relived a vision in the flesh.

Harte was coming toward her now, smiling, his teeth white against his tanned face. This time, however, she felt no shock or embarrassment as she had when she had held his hands during the string game. Today, she quickly slid her blouse down her arms and pushed her skirt down over her hips, eager to join him in the clear, warm water.

"Why are you smiling?" he asked, but his green eyes glowed as he regarded her nakedness with unveiled intensity.

"Because I know exactly what's going to happen next."

"So do I," he murmured, reaching up and pulling her down into the water. Lily slid her arms around his neck and pressed against his chest. She closed her eyes. "This is what I saw when we played the string game. That's when

I knew we were truly meant to be together. I've been waiting for you to bring me here."

"I knew I was missing something good, but I never dreamed it was this good," he murmured, holding her waist and lifting her up until his mouth found her breasts. Lily locked her arms tighter around his neck, her legs around his waist as he took them deeper into the pool, kissing her throat and chin along the way. Their wet bodies slid together, slick and warm, but his mouth felt hot against her skin. He continued to hold her tightly, stroking her, arousing her, just as he had done in the dreaming, but this time she could feel every tingling sensation, every caress of his mouth, the clean scent of his hair, the taste of his sun-browned skin, and she was lost to him and the way he could make her feel.

She hardly knew how he got her back on the bank, barely felt the soft ferns beneath her back. Their legs were tangled together half in the water, then he was atop her, rising up like a sun-bronzed god, just as she had seen in the dreaming, but so much better, so tenderly. And now it was real, with the splashing of the waterfall behind them, with his impassioned breathing in her ear. He was saying her name as he made love to her, whispering endearments, and such joy filled her, pure, warm joy, and she knew she loved him so desperately it was almost painful.

"Tell me, Lily, what do we do next?" he

asked against her mouth, then gave a low, sensuous laugh.

"I'll show you," she said through the kiss, pushing him onto his back and straddling him. She moaned as he entered her, throwing back her head and closing her eyes to savor the feeling of him becoming a part of her. She rocked slowly, her fingers curled around the hard muscles of his shoulders, and when his palm closed gently over her breast, she cried out with pleasure and leaned forward, her long hair brushing his chest. He rolled back on top of her, his fingers tangled in her hair, taking her into the water again and holding her tightly. Slowly he moved into her, swirling the water around them, until they clung to each other, their breath mingled, fast and panting, gripping each other until the fulfillment came with swift, hard release, rocketing through them both and finally leaving them weak and satiated.

"Did you really see all of this?" Harte asked when he could speak again, still holding her close against him in the pool.

Weakly, Lily laid her cheek on his shoulder and nodded.

"No wonder you were so determined that you loved me," he murmured. "Dare I hope that you've seen other moments like this one?"

"Dozens," she sighed contentedly. "Hundreds."

"Hundreds?" He laughed.

Lily bit her lip. "Do you love me yet? The way I love you?"

Instead of answering, he kissed her, and Lily felt sorrow expand in her chest, making her heart hurt. He still couldn't say he loved her, even now that she had given him everything she had to give. "When Derek comes, he'll want me to go home with him," she said, wanting him to ask her to stay.

"I don't want to talk about Derek," he said, pulling her out into the deeper water. "Come, let's swim out to the falls."

Lily shivered, feeling uneasy. She sensed something when Harte said Derek's name, something bad, something frightening, but now it was fading as he drew her into his arms again. He kissed her, and she thought only of him and the lovely things he was doing to her beneath the water.

# 12

Harte drowsed in sleepy serenity, his arms looped idly around Lily's soft, sun-warmed body. In the past few weeks, they had spent so much time in the glade of white lilies that he had finally strung a hammock between two palm trees near the bank, where the shadows were deep and cool. The sun bore down in the middle of the sapphire-shaded pool beside them, glittering on the water like white diamonds, and the net cradle in which they lay with limbs intimately entwined swayed slightly in the ocean breeze.

Comfortable and more at ease than he had been in more years than he could count, Harte liked the way she felt cuddled against his chest. For nearly six weeks now, they had been together at Moon Cove, laughing and playing in the surf with the Kapirigis and Bobbie until Harte felt as carefree as a boy again. More so, in fact, since his grandmother had seen fit to cart him off to the sterile confines of a military boarding school at the age of eight.

At the thought of Sarah Delaney, a rush of

bitterness blighted his contentment. Hell, during his youth in Newport the only time he had been able to act like a child was when his grandmother wasn't around. When Cassandra and Stuart were playing tag on the lawns overlooking the sea, Harte had been in his grandmother's office studying the different kinds of ships sailing in the Delaney fleet.

He had never even built sand castles on the beach until he and Lily did it a couple of weeks ago. It had been on Christmas Day, and Lily had molded the wet sand into a small house, then fetched a palm frond for a Christmas tree. She had said it was the house in which they would live when he gave in and decided to marry her.

Harte smiled to himself, remembering how aroused he had become watching her stretch and bend this way and that as she sat on her knees in the surf. She was intent upon forming the walls and chimney of their future home, her thin white shift clinging provocatively to every inch of her slim curves. He sent the boys away to hunt for shells so he could make love to her. Her skin tasted warm from the sunshine and salty from the sea, and their lovemaking was gentle and tender and even better than the time before, but that was the way it always was with Lily.

In truth, time had seemed to stand still since they had come to Bermuda, the clock waiting patiently for his arm to heal and for them to fall deeply in love before it began to tick again. And he was beginning to fear it might be happening to him, just as Lily's dreamings had predicted. He had become disillusioned with love so long ago and at such an early age, but now Lily, with her guileless beauty and genuine passion had brought back a taste of goodness and innocence into his jaded existence. She was good for him.

"Close your eyes, Harte," she whispered softly, her lips nibbling at the side of his throat.

"They are closed," he murmured lethargically, tightening his grip around her waist when she attempted to squirm out of his grasp.

She laughed at his possessiveness. "Let me go. I'll be right back. I want to show you something I can do, but you can't look until I tell you. Promise?"

"Promise," he answered with a little smile, reluctantly releasing her, then stretching out on his back and lacing his palms under his head. He could hear the Kapirigis shouting to little Bobbie somewhere near the waterfall. He wondered what Lily was doing as he swung gently in the hammock waiting for her to reveal her surprise.

Though he hadn't realized the extent of his fatigue, he knew now that he had desperately needed to get away from the war and the constant mental strain of the subterfuge and danger of his work. Other than a short medical leave now and then to heal his body, he hadn't been out of the States since Sumter had been fired upon to start the war. He hadn't felt so rested and refreshed in years, both physically and mentally, as he did now.

As the days went by and his feelings for Lily grew stronger, he became increasingly disenchanted with his plot to capture Derek Courtland. When he had so callously planned to use Lily as bait, he hadn't expected that she would become so special to him. He had used plenty of other women in his life without getting attached to them. But Lily was different. She wasn't a double agent, she wasn't the enemy, and she trusted him implicitly.

Even now that they were lovers, she still demanded nothing from him, though he knew she wanted more. She had been honest about that too. She wanted him to love her and marry her. But he would never do that. She would accept that in time.

"You can look now!"

Lily's voice floated faintly to him from a good distance away, and her endearing desire to surprise him brought another indulgent smile to his face. She could be so sweet at times, so childlike, but she wasn't a young girl anymore. Lily Courtland was an extremely desirable woman who gave herself with such eager abandon that she took Harte's breath away. Even now, he wanted her back in his arms so he touch her and feel her flesh quiver beneath his lips. Aroused at the mere thought of it, he sat up and glanced around the sun-dappled glen. She wasn't in the water, where he had expected her to be.

Frowning, he stood and put his hands on his hips while he scanned the thick growth of wild Easter lilies along the bank. Across the water, beside the waterfall, he caught sight of the three little boys, sitting on a flat rock, their necks craning upward toward the high boulders that overlooked the pool. Harte followed their gaze. His heart stood still.

Lily had climbed to the top of the cliff and was poised next to the point at which the swift-flowing stream gushed over the rocks and rained furiously down into the deep water. Harte's muscles turned to stone, and he could not move. Dear God, she was standing so close to the edge. Writhing serpents of fear slithered alive inside him.

Camillia had fallen to her death from a similar precipice. Although he hadn't been at The Oaks the day she had taken her life, he had visualized the gory scene in his mind a thousand times—how she must have looked when she stepped out into midair and spiraled like a lifeless rag doll, to die broken and bleeding on the jagged rocks rising out of the sea.

"Watch this, Harte," Lily called merrily, waving at him from her high perch. The children clapped with excitement, and to Harte's absolute horror, Lily stepped forward to the edge of the rocks.

"No! Lily, don't . . ." Harte tried to shout,

but his words were choked and hoarse as she suddenly leapt off the cliff.

Frozen with dread, Harte watched her plummet toward the dark-blue pool at the base of the falls, executing a perfect swan dive until she slipped with scarcely a splash into the water. His heart expanded until it seemed to fill his entire chest, all the guilt he had suffered over his wife's suicide crashing over him in towering waves of pain and remorse.

Terrified, he waited with bated breath the eternity that it took Lily to resurface. When she did, laughing and calling his name, anger came swiftly—irrational, uncontrollable, roaring through his mind like a runaway locomotive, so hard and fast and brutal that he couldn't stop it.

"Derek taught me to do that," she called to him as she swam closer and stood up in the waist-deep water. Harte sloshed out fully clothed to meet her, and her proud words faltered as he suddenly jerked her up off her feet, his fingers digging painfully into her slender shoulders.

"Dammit, what are you trying to do? Kill yourself? What a goddamn stupid thing to do!"

Locked in unreasoning fury, Harte shook her hard, his features twisted in such rage that Lily's face drained of color. Even when her eyes met his, filled with shock and confusion, he couldn't control himself. He wanted to shake her senseless, over and over, until she realized the irresponsibility of her actions. Instead, he pushed her away from him, turned blindly, and strode furiously back to the beach.

Past midnight that same evening, Lily sat on the wall of the seaside patio, looking out into the darkness of the ocean. Hours had passed since Harte had stalked off without a word of explanation, and he had not come back. What if he didn't? What would she do if he had left her for good?

The two of them had never had an argument before, not about anything, and she shuddered when she remembered how angry he had looked and how hard he had gripped her. He was such a huge man and so strong; for the first time since they had met, his physical strength had frightened her.

What in heaven's name had made him explode like that? She couldn't understand what had gone so wrong, but she missed him. They had been together constantly since their arrival at Moon Cove, and he had changed so much, touching her with his smiles and whispers of love. Now, without him, she felt adrift.

"Don't be sad," Kapi said from his seat next to his brother on the wall near her. "The green-eyed one come back soon."

Lily tried to force a smile. "I know."

Rigi came then and laid his small brown hand on Lily's shoulder. "You come live in *wiltja* with the Kapirigis. We not yell at you. We love you."

For the first time, tears burned hotly behind Lily's eyelids. She had neglected the Kapirigis since she had met Harte Delaney. She had thought only of him and how much she loved him, and she shouldn't have. The boys were far away from their home and much too young to understand the love between a man and a woman.

"I will come visit your *wiltja* soon, Rigi, I promise," she murmured, hugging him close. The minute Kapi saw her embracing his brother, he came scampering over for similar treatment. Lily gathered him close as well, then bit her lip when ragged emotions flooded over her again. The children felt so little and warm, and they smelled of the sea. "I need to stay here tonight and find out what's bothering Harte. You understand, don't you? He's very upset with me."

"He not like you dive in water," Kapi said, with a knowing look.

"Better not do that any more times," Rigi added solemnly.

Lily had to smile, but as she hugged them again, she heard Harte's deep voice call her name from somewhere in the house.

"There he is now," she whispered quickly. "I'm sorry, but I have to talk with him alone. You don't mind, do you?"

"Kapirigis not let him hurt Lily," Kapi growled fiercely, jerking his trusty boomerang from his belt and glaring toward the door.

"He didn't hurt me, and he's not going to.

Now you and Rigi run along to bed. Tomorrow I'll come to your *wiltja* and hunt for shells with you, I promise."

"Bobbie, too?" Rigi asked.

When Lily nodded, the twins smiled at each other in obvious delight, then ran swiftly across the stone patio and disappeared down the steps that led to the beach.

"Lily, answer me! Where are you?"

Lily didn't respond but fidgeted nervously until Harte loomed in the doorway of her bedchamber. She grew still and waited for him to speak, not sure what to say or how to act.

"I owe you an apology," he said in a subdued voice.

Although she was relieved that he was no longer angry, Lily was troubled by the unprovoked violence he had displayed toward her. She had seen another side of him, one she didn't like. She wanted to understand why he had acted the way he had.

"Tell me why you were so upset. Was it because of the dive? The rocks aren't that high, and you know I'm a good swimmer."

Harte moved a little way down the wall from her and stared at the ocean swells crashing against the beach. Long moments passed, but just when Lily had decided he wasn't going to answer, he began to speak.

"My wife died in a fall from a cliff." His voice was barely audible above the sound of the surf. "When I saw you up so high, it brought it all back. I overreacted. I'm sorry."

"Her name was Camillia, wasn't it? She's the woman I saw when I held your medallion, the one with the yellow dress."

"She's dead. That part of my life is over and done with."

His voice was low and tortured, and Lily felt a surge of jealousy sear her heart to think that he still grieved so for the other woman. She gazed at his chiseled profile and the stiff set of his shoulders. "I don't think it's over and done with, or you wouldn't have gotten so angry today."

Harte frowned, but he didn't look at her. "Just let it go, Lily. It does no good to talk about it. I'm sorry about today. It won't happen again."

"You must have loved her very much to still grieve for her after all this time. That's why you don't want to marry me, isn't it?"

"I never loved her, not the way you think."

Lily couldn't hide her shock. She shook her head in confusion. "I don't understand."

Harte kept his eyes locked upon the darkness. "I was only eighteen when I met her. Pinkerton had already recruited me as a detective and sent me into Mexico to infiltrate a band of outlaws. They called themselves *comancheros* and ran guns over the Texas border to the Comanches."

Lily had heard of the American Indians who rode horses and shot bows and arrows, but she knew little else about them and she didn't want to. She only wanted Harte to tell her about Camillia.

"To make a long story short, I became one of them and was feeding information to Pinkerton through Camillia's father. He ran a cantina on the Rio Grande. That's where I met her. She was young, too, only sixteen. We became friends, then lovers, and through her I got involved with some Mexican revolutionaries fighting against the Santa Anna government."

Harte paused momentarily, and even though his face showed no trace of emotion, Lily realized how hard it was for him to talk about his past. She wondered if he had always been able to control his feelings by force of will. "I got caught riding with the Juaristas in a battle near Veracruz, and they kept me in irons in one of their filthy jails for months before they decided to hang me."

A muscle twitched in his cheek as he gritted his teeth. "That's what you were seeing when you held my medallion. Somehow I got lucky, and the noose slipped before it could kill me. I guess it just wasn't my time to die. The soldiers left me for dead, but Camillia and her father cut me down and hid me in their cellar."

Lily saw his fists clench, and his voice grew tighter, hard-edged. "When the soldiers found out I was alive, they came looking for me. Camillia and Juan wouldn't tell them where I was, so they raped her right in front of her father and then shot him in the head."

Lily gasped in horror, beginning to understand just how terrible the demons haunting Harte's past really were. He had gone through so much pain and suffering, as a small boy, as a young man, all his life. No wonder he couldn't trust anyone. Her heart ached for him.

Agitated, Harte took a few steps down the patio, then braced his palms on the wall. "We had to get out of there, so I took Camillia and crossed the border. She had no kin left, nowhere to go, and she was in love with me. So I married her." He shrugged. "I shouldn't have. She'd probably be alive if I hadn't."

When he continued, his voice roughened with anger. "I took her home to meet my dear grandmother, but Sarah hated Camillia from the moment she walked through the door. You see, a Mexican peasant girl wasn't good enough to be a member of the great Delaney dynasty, and Sarah made sure Camillia knew it."

Harte sighed. "So what did I do? I went back to work for Pinkerton and left Camillia in my grandmother's tender care. I figured Sarah would turn her into a suitable wife while I was gone, but the truth was, I really didn't give a damn as long as I got to do exactly what I wanted."

There was a short pause. "I was in Texas riding with the *comancheros* when Camillia killed herself. Grandmother called it an accident, of course, but I know what it really was. I didn't even know she was dead until three months after it happened, when Pinkerton finally got word to me in El Paso."

"Oh, dear God," Lily whispered, going to him and putting her arms around his waist. She laid her cheek against his back, wanting desperately to console him. "I'm so sorry, Harte. You've suffered so much. But you can't blame yourself for what Camillia did."

"Yes, I can. Grandmother drove her to take her life—there's no doubt in my mind about that—but I let it happen. We're both at fault."

Suddenly he turned and pulled Lily tightly against him.

"Lily, listen to me," he said gruffly. "If Derek does come here, I don't want you to go back to Australia with him. I want you to stay with me. I want to take you back to the States. Tell me you'll go with me."

Lily smiled, relieved to learn that he wanted her to be with him. He had not mentioned their future before, not once.

"You told me you liked being alone," she whispered, wanting desperately for him to tell her he loved her. "That you didn't like having people in your life."

"I want you."

Lily's lips trembled, but she had to ask the question. "But do you love me?"

*He's not going to say it,* she thought, *and he never will.* Why was it so hard for him to say the words? Because of Camillia and what had happened to her?

"I want us to be together like we have been here at Moon Cove. Isn't that enough?"

Lily squeezed her eyes shut, disappointment flooding over her. It had to be enough if she wanted to be with him, and she did. She couldn't imagine just sailing away and never seeing him again. "I want to be with you, wherever you are."

Harte's embrace tightened, and his mouth sought hers eagerly. Lily met his kiss, and for the first time in her life, Lily doubted her dreamings of their marriage. But she couldn't deny her feelings for him. She loved him more than anything in the world. She wanted to erase the painful memories of Camillia that caused such guilt and agony in his heart. She wanted to make him happy.

# 13

Derek Courtland propped a high-topped black boot against the slanted trunk of a palm tree and focused his brass field glasses on the coral-tinted house that lay a good mile or more down the beach. If the loose-tongued drunk he had plied with liquor at the Sea Star Saloon the night before could be believed, an American businessman named Delaney owned the house. Apparently, the man had sailed into Hamilton Harbor nearly two months ago on the merchant schooner *Baltimore Star.*

Furthermore, Derek had learned that a young lady had accompanied Delaney, one who answered Derek's little sister's description. Since their arrival, the American had occasionally appeared on the docks to speak with the crew of his ship, but the girl had not been seen again. Derek had a strong feeling that the woman living in the house he now watched was Lily, but he sure as the devil wasn't stupid enough to walk up and knock on the door in order to find out for certain.

When his first mate had showed up at Derek's lodgings in Nassau with Lily's letter, he had been astonished to discover that she was in Bermuda instead of safe at home on Malmora with his father. There was no doubt, however, that the small, neat handwriting was hers. The minute he held her brief note bidding him to come to her, the strange sixth sense that ran in his family began to trigger all sorts of warning signals. He knew at once that she was in trouble and needed him.

Derek hadn't seen a vision or had a premonition, but he rarely did. Lily was the one who could predict the future, not Derek. His mental powers manifested themselves in other ways, but his intuition told him now that he had better set sail on the *Mamu* without delay. Now that he was so close, he was eager to see Lily again. He hadn't been home to Australia in three long years, and he had missed his family.

As he watched the wide veranda of the limestone villa, a woman suddenly came into sight. Derek sharpened his attention, then a slow smile spread over his face. He recognized his sister's flowing, honey-blond hair. She was wearing a dress, though, which surprised him. Lily had favored men's shirts and trousers since she was old enough to climb into the saddle. But the girl he saw now was Lily, there was no doubt about it.

Almost at once, however, a tall, powerfully built man joined her at the wall overlooking the sea. Was that Delaney? Derek wondered, watching as he walked up behind Lily and pulled her back against his chest in a proprietary fashion. When he began to nuzzle the side of her throat, Derek frowned with disapproval. Who the hell was this man? And why was Lily letting him be so familiar with her when she had never shown an interest in any other men?

He watched them sit down on the terrace wall and saw how the man touched her continually—stroking her hair, caressing her cheek. Often he would take her hand and kiss it, then steal another kiss from her lips, and Lily acted as if she enjoyed everything he did. Whatever the relationship between them, she certainly wasn't being held against her will, nor was she being mistreated. The man treated her with loving respect, but Derek still didn't like the situation. Something was wrong. But what?

When an object whacked loudly against the tree trunk inches from his head, making the bark fly, Derek dropped to his knees and drew his pistol. He scanned the bushes behind him for his attacker but found no one in sight. On the ground nearby, however, he saw a small red boomerang stuck in the sand. Instantly, Derek knew who his stalkers were.

"Kapi! Rigi!" he called, grinning and rising to his feet. "Come out where I can see you! It's me, Derek!"

Two little black heads popped up from the thick fronds of a palmetto tree a few yards away, and the aboriginal twins came running, glad smiles wreathing their faces. Derek caught one small wriggling boy in each arm, laughing as he swung them around. The Kapirigis squealed and hung on for dear life until Derek wrestled them down on their backs and held them there.

"You sneaky little crocodiles! What do you mean, tossing a boomerang at my head?"

"We not know it you, Captain Derek," Kapi said, giggling and trying to squirm free from under Derek's large palm.

"Where the *Mamu*?" Rigi demanded, sitting up and retrieving his beloved boomerang. "We want go home."

"She's well hidden on the other side of the island. I can't believe Lily brought you two little rascals with her. What's she doing here anyway? And who's the man up there kissing her every chance he gets?"

"He be the man of her dreamings."

"Lily's fabled green-eyed man? Well, I'll be damned. She finally found him, did she?" Smiling, Derek remembered how he had laughed when Lily had described in detail her future husband—at the age of six.

"He like her, and she like him."

"Yeah, I noticed. Are they married?"

"They share same bed. We peek in window one time and see them." The twins grinned sheepishly.

At that bit of enlightenment, Derek's scowl darkened. "Then they'd better be married, by

God." He looked back at the Kapirigis. "Can I trust him?"

"He help us escape from bad men."

"What bad men?"

"Men on ship who take us for slaves. Lily too."

"What do you mean?" Derek asked, but as the little twins told him the tale of the voyage aboard the *Sea Rover,* his anger began to build, followed closely by a very real concern. Lily would never have set off for Melbourne by herself, much less for America, unless something was dreadfully wrong.

"Now, listen, boys. Go on back to the house and bring Lily down to me. Don't tell her I'm here. And make sure the man doesn't come with her. Got it?"

The Kapirigis nodded in unison, then sprinted up the beach toward the house, their flying feet kicking up sand and leaving a double trail behind them. Not long after they joined Lily and Delaney on the veranda, the American rose and entered the house. Derek smiled in satisfaction as the two little boys took Lily's hands and began pulling her down the path to the beach. He waited behind a giant palm until she had almost reached him.

"Hey! Sis!"

His voice was barely perceptible over the crash of the waves, but Lily heard it. She turned at once and, shielding her eyes against the bright sun, after a moment discovered his position in the thick vegetation. She looked at first shocked, then overjoyed. Derek laughed as she picked up her skirts and ran toward him, throwing herself bodily into his arms like she always had when he came home from the sea.

"Oh, Derek, you've finally come!" she cried breathlessly. "It's been so long since I've seen you!"

"Long enough for you to grow up," Derek said, holding her at arm's length and examining her face. She was tanned a becoming peach tint, and the sun had brought out a few freckles on her slim nose. "I wasn't sure it was you when I saw the dress."

Lily laughed, the same sweetly infectious sound he remembered from their childhood. She had followed him around like a little puppy when he had lived and worked on their family's cattle station. He had missed her, and Malmora, more than he had realized.

"And you've grown hair all over your face," she teased as she reached up to touch his short-cropped black beard. "Now you look just like a pirate."

Her remark was closer to the truth than she knew, but there would be time to tell her about his own endeavors after he found out what had brought her so far from home. "Who's the man you're with? What's he to you?"

Lily's expression softened, and her eyes grew warm. Derek had seen plenty of women in love—not a few of them with him. He knew the look well. Lily loved the tall American, whoever he was.

"His name is Harte Delaney. Come on! We've been waiting for you for weeks now. That's why Harte brought me here to Moon Cove—to find you." Eagerly she took his hand in an effort to pull him out of the cover of the trees.

Derek resisted. "Wait a minute, Lily. I'm a wanted man in the Northern states. This could be a Union trap."

"Oh, no, it isn't. I promise. Harte works for the War Department in Washington, but he gave me his word that he won't bother you. He'd never break it. Oh, Derek, you're going to like him. He's so handsome."

Derek grinned. "I doubt if that'll make much impression on me. Where did you meet him?"

"I'll tell you everything once we get up to the house. Come on, please. Harte's the only one out here, except for the Kapirigis and me. You're perfectly safe, I swear it."

"No, Lily. Let's talk here first. I want to hear about Father. Is he well?"

A stricken expression came into Lily's eyes, and she squeezed his hand. "That's why I had to come find you, Derek. Papa's been killed."

Derek's face reflected his shock. "Father's dead?" Grief hit him as hard as a fist, and he shook his head, not wanting to believe her. "When? What happened? Was he in an accident?"

"No. Strassman's men shot him."

Reeling under the impact of this news, Derek clenched his teeth and fought desperately to regain his composure. For a few minutes, it was all too much for him. He couldn't speak. Then, "My God, I can't believe it. Why, for God's sake? Strassman's quarrel was with me, not Father. Father never hurt a soul."

"Some squatters found gold on Malmora, out in the hills. You know the place—where the aborigines have their sacred ceremonies in the caves, near where Pike's Creek crosses the gully. Strassman demanded that Papa sell him the land, and when Papa refused, Strassman had him shot. I can't prove it, but I know he did. Rebecca thinks so too."

"So Becky's still married to Strassman?" Derek asked, unable to hide his disgust.

"Yes, but she still loves you. She told me she did."

"Not enough to keep her from marrying that bastard for his money."

"She regrets that now. He never lets her go anywhere without sending his hired hands to accompany her, and she hates the way he treats the aborigines."

"Strassman and his men are all a bunch of murdering swine, every damn one of them," Derek muttered, but his thoughts went back to his father. *How can he be dead?* he thought, his chest growing so heavy he found it hard to breathe. He would never see him again. Damn Strassman to hell!

"It was all so awful, Derek. After Papa's funeral, they began to harass me too. They'd come at night and shoot the livestock. They killed all our dogs, even Shep. I was afraid they were going to kill me, and I didn't know what to do or where to go. So I finally rode into Melbourne and bought passage."

"The Kapirigis told me what happened with Ringer. God, Lily, you were lucky to get away from them alive."

"I know. I wouldn't have if it hadn't been for Harte. He rescued us, then took us to his house, and now he's helped me find you. I owe so much to him."

Derek put his arm around her. "I'm just glad you're safe. I'm here now. We'll go back to Malmora. If Strassman killed Father, I'll make sure he pays for it."

Lily bit her lip and looked down. "I don't know if I want to go back. I love Harte, Derek. He's the one in my dreamings. I knew him the minute I saw him."

"The man with the green eyes," Derek murmured, but the more Lily spoke about Delaney the better Derek felt about the man's motives. Delaney had certainly treated his sister with kindness, and he had risked his life to deliver her from evil men. Even so, when Lily finally persuaded Derek to go up to the house to meet the man she loved, the instincts he had inherited from his grandmother screamed for him to get out while he still could and take Lily with him.

* * *

Harte finished the last statement in his letter to Pinkerton and waved the parchment back and forth to dry the ink. The secret agents from the *Baltimore Star* whom he had placed in Hamilton and across the island in the town of St. George had obtained more than enough information from Confederate blockade runners swilling tankards of ale in the taverns. The South was in serious trouble—running short on food, supplies, and ammunition.

Apparently, it wouldn't be long before Richmond either fell or was starved into submission. Perhaps he wouldn't be required to imprison Lily's brother after all. If the war ended before Derek Courtland showed up, Harte wouldn't have to arrest him and Lily wouldn't be hurt. More and more Harte hoped that would be the outcome.

Sealing the envelope and slipping it into his coat pocket, he rose and flexed his injured arm. The bullet wound was nearly healed; he had full use of the arm again. Glad that he was finished with his work and able to rejoin Lily for the walk on the beach he had promised her earlier that afternoon, he left his desk and went in search of her. He didn't have far to go. The moment he stepped into the airy front parlor, Lily came running in from the seaside veranda. He opened his arms to her, smiling at her eagerness to press herself close into his embrace.

"Harte, guess what?"

"What?"

Lily beamed up at him, obviously delighted by her latest discovery.

"Derek's here!" she cried happily. "He came up from the beach while you were in your office."

Harte stiffened warily, but tried to hide his reaction from Lily's smiling eyes. He looked past her toward the veranda. How could Courtland possibly have slipped through the network of men watching the house and the road? Their orders had been to intercept him before Lily even found out he was on the island.

"He is?" he replied cautiously. "Where?"

"Out on the porch. He's very anxious to meet you. I've been telling him how wonderful you are, of course. And Harte, he's going home to deal with Strassman. Isn't that good news?"

Harte forced a smile as she eagerly grasped his hand and led him outside, but he was at a loss as to how to take Courtland into custody now that Lily had seen him. He didn't want to arrest him in front of her, but what other choice did he have, dammit, now that his men had let Courtland through?

Outside on the patio, Derek Courtland sat at the glass-topped table. He stood as Lily brought Harte forward to meet him. Harte estimated that the notorious Australian blockade runner stood well over six feet, perhaps an inch or so shy of Harte's own six foot four. His black hair was shaggy and long enough to be tied at the nape with a ribbon. His features were strong and masculine, his nose slightly aquiline, his jaw square and shadowed by a close-cropped black beard. His eyes were as black as night and watched Harte's every move as if he already knew he couldn't trust him. He wore a single six-shooter strapped to his hip.

"Here he is at last, Derek. This is Harte Delaney. I'm so happy the two of you finally get to meet."

Derek Courtland proffered an open palm. As Harte gripped his hand firmly, their gazes locked in silent appraisal. Harte thought he saw something flare in the other man's dark eyes, but Derek smiled, his teeth very white and even in contrast to his dark beard.

"So you're Lily's green-eyed man," he said in a distinct Australian brogue much more pronounced than Lily's. "My sister tells me that you've been taking good care of her. I owe you a debt of gratitude for that. She's lucky you showed up when you did."

"I'm the lucky one," Harte answered carefully. He had the distinct feeling that Derek Courtland knew how to take care of himself better than most and was more than adept with the weapon in his gold-studded black-leather holster. He was glad his own derringer was strapped in his shoulder harness, within easy reach.

Lily beamed happily and slipped her hand through Harte's arm. "Come and sit down. Lucie left dinner ready to serve before she went home, and Derek and I have so much to talk about."

Extremely on edge, Harte sat down across from the captain of the *Mamu.* Lily brought out three plates of broasted chicken and sweet potatoes, but Harte said little except to answer a question now and then, preferring to listen to Derek and Lily talk about their cattle station in Australia.

During the course of the evening, as the sun lowered and painted the sky with muted swirls of blue, violet, and mauve, Harte realized how much Lily adored her older brother. *God help me,* he thought, half sick inside, *she'll hate me if I arrest Derek.* But he had no choice; he was under direct orders to do just that. But he'd be damned if he'd do the deed right before Lily's eyes.

"Lily, you've been up since sunrise," he remarked much later, long after darkness had fallen and he'd seen Lily stifle several yawns. "Why don't you go on up to bed? Let your brother and me smoke a cigar and get to know each other better."

Lily seemed so pleased at the prospect that Harte was wracked with guilt.

"All right. I am tired. I do hope the two of you will become good friends. Derek, how long can you stay?"

"Not very long. I want to return to Malmora as soon as possible."

Lily bent and gave both men a swift kiss on

the cheek then moved into the house and out of sight. Neither man said anything at first.

"Would you like a cheroot? They're Cuban, the best there is," Harte offered, removing a flat gold case from his vest pocket. He snapped it open and held it out toward his guest.

Derek chose one of the narrow, square-tipped cigars and lit it on the flame of the candle lantern that flickered on the table between them.

"So you've come here to arrest me, have you?" Derek said quietly.

Shocked, Harte stopped in the act of puffing his cigar to flame.

Derek grinned. "I knew the moment we shook hands."

"Don't tell me?" Harte said, leaning back in his chair. "You've got it too?"

"Sis senses things stronger than I do, but I do have my own special instincts. One of which happens to be that I always know when I meet up with an enemy."

Harte considered whether or not to pull his gun. He decided not to. "It's nothing personal, you understand. I'm just trying to put an end to the war, and you're prolonging the fighting each time you bring in a shipload of guns and food to a Southern port."

"Aren't you a bit concerned as to what Lily's going to think about all this? Or have you just been using her to get to me? I really wouldn't like that at all, Mr. Delaney."

"I was, at first," Harte admitted with some

reluctance, "but she's a hard woman to resist. I've grown fond of her, and I have no desire to see her get hurt. Perhaps you sensed that about me too?"

Derek smiled, holding the slim cigar idly between his fingers. "Lily's always been very innocent. My family and I sheltered and protected her since she was a little girl. Therefore, she's very easy to love and very easy to hurt. I think she's going to be devastated if you turn me in. You'll lose her. Are you willing to risk that?"

Harte frowned. "I'm a soldier under orders. I don't have a choice. As a man and the captain of your own ship, I suspect you understand that."

"And would your orders be compromised if you and I came to some kind of mutual terms that would make for a more pleasant outcome to this predicament that you've gotten us into? Both for you and Lily, and for me?"

"I could be court-martialed for letting you go."

"Not if no one ever found out."

Harte leaned back and considered Derek Courtland's suggestion. Lily's brother had surprised him. He was not the greedy privateer Harte had envisioned. Courtland was well educated, well spoken, and—most important—Lily's only living kin.

"I love my sister, Delaney, and I know her well. If she finds out you set her up to get to me, it'll take her a long time to forgive you, if she ever does. A fate that you probably deserve, but one that she doesn't. I don't like to think of the hurt and disillusionment she'll suffer when she finds out what you've been doing to her."

Derek was right, and Harte knew it. "All right, Courtland, I'm listening. What do you have in mind?"

"I have no undying loyalty to the Confederate cause. In fact, I think slavery ought to be abolished. I grew up disgusted with the way the white man enslaves the aborigines of my country. I took the *Mamu* through your blockade because it's made me very rich, very fast, and because I knew people have been starving in the streets of Richmond and Charleston since you mates up North started strangling off their supply lines."

Derek paused, leaning back and releasing a cloud of blue smoke into the air before he continued. "Both of us know the war's not going to last much longer, and now I've got a pressing reason to go home. I won't be bothering you anymore, so why break my sister's heart and ruin your future with her just to bring me in?"

Harte grinned at his calm audacity, but at the same time he knew every word Courtland said was true. "And I suppose you'd be willing to give me your word as a gentleman not to fight against the Union in the future?"

"I'm afraid the word 'gentleman' doesn't often apply to one engaged in my livelihood. But I'll give my word of honor on the happiness of my only sister, and she does mean a hell of a lot to me, you can believe that."

Harte stared at him thoughtfully. "You've got a deal, Courtland, for Lily's sake. But I will say this much. If you break your word, if you lift a finger to help the South's war effort, I'll come after you with everything I've got."

"Indeed you would, and I wouldn't blame you."

"When do you leave?"

"Now."

"Lily will be upset."

"Tell her I couldn't stay but not to worry about me. I'd feel better about leaving her with you if I knew your intentions toward her."

"I'll take good care of her."

"Do you intend to marry her?"

Harte steadfastly met his gaze. "No. I'm not the kind of man who'd make a good husband."

To his surprise, Derek smiled. "Lily's dreamings say you'll marry her, and Lily's dreamings always come true. Otherwise, I wouldn't think of leaving her here alone with a man who doesn't want to wed her. But, to use your own words from a moment ago, if you do hurt her or abuse her in any way, I'll come after you with everything I've got."

"Indeed you would, and I wouldn't blame you."

The two men studied each other for another moment. Then Derek stood and crushed out his cigar. Harte watched him walk slowly across the patio and down the steps until he was swallowed by the night. Oddly enough, Harte felt no remorse over his decision to let Courtland go. No one would be hurt by Derek's freedom, and now Lily would have no reason to hate him.

Sitting alone in the darkness, he took his time with his cigar before rising and making his way upstairs. He found Lily waiting for him in bed, soft and naked and beautiful, and he quickly disrobed and joined her under the sheets.

"Isn't Derek wonderful?" she whispered against his neck. "Do you like him?"

"Yes," he said truthfully. Then he sighed because he knew how disappointed she would be that her brother had already left and without even a good-bye.

"Tomorrow we'll have more time to talk," she was saying as he kissed her forehead and let his hand roam the silken flesh of her back to cup her hip.

"Derek's gone, sweetheart," he told her softly and felt her tense in his arms.

Lily pulled away slightly. "Gone? Where? Why?"

"He thinks it's dangerous to stay here, and he's anxious to return to Australia."

"But why didn't he say good-bye?" she said, pushing herself onto her knees. She sobbed, a pitiable sound that twisted Harte's heart. "How could he just leave me again after being away for so long?"

"He knew I would take care of you," he whispered, pulling her down against his chest when she began to weep. He held her close, sorry for her pain but realizing how much more grief she would have felt if he had thrown her brother in jail. For the first time since the war had started, he had ignored his duty. That was hard for him to accept, even if it did mean keeping Lily's affection.

# 14

As Harte slapped the reins and the horses trotted away from the house on Moon Cove, Lily and the Kapirigis waved a last good-bye to Lucie while little Bobbie chased along the buggy, crying his heart out because his friends were going off without him.

Regret filled Lily's heart, for she had grown to love the house on the sea as much as Harte did. The breezy bedchamber and the warm stone patio had become their own special place. She would remember it forever as the place where Harte had first made love to her. Alone together in the apricot house that was buffeted by sea winds and kissed by the sun, it hadn't mattered as much that Harte couldn't say he loved her or that he didn't want to marry her.

Would their newfound pleasure in each other be so idyllic once they arrived in Washington and Harte returned to his secret and dangerous work? Would he still want her then, in a city full of beautiful American women that he could have? In her heart there was an awful, icy fear that he wouldn't. Even worse, she had an uncanny sensation that something horrible was about to happen.

"We'll come back here often, I promise," Harte said softly, giving her fingers a comforting squeeze. His gentle understanding helped to soothe her uneasiness, and she leaned her head against his broad shoulder, wanting to believe every assurance he uttered. Perhaps nothing would change when they got back home. Perhaps with Cassandra's help, she would teach Harte how to give love as well as receive it. Perhaps they could become a real family.

"I'm looking forward to seeing Cassie again, aren't you?" she said aloud, realizing that she had missed Harte's friendly, energetic sister.

"Actually, I haven't thought much about her, one way or the other."

Lily pondered Harte's answer, thinking how strange and cold Harte's family was. Being with Derek had made her realize how much she loved and missed her own brother, but it had also brought back all the hurt and grief of her father's death. They had been a close family for so many years, and now there were only the two of them. How long would their separation last this time?

Harte, on the other hand, seemed unaffected by any blood ties or family loyalty. He and Cassie seemed more like casual acquaintances than brother and sister, and Lily wondered how he could be content with such an isolated life. He seemed to embrace his solitary existence like some sort of shield, always pushing other people away before they could get too close to him. Would he push her away someday, too, as he apparently did everyone else? Or could she, in time, help him learn to love and trust again? She would try her best and hope that someday they would be wed in his house, just as she had foreseen.

The weather was warm and pleasant, and even the Kapirigis were quiet and introspective on the drive into Hamilton. They were as disappointed by Derek's hasty departure as Lily had been. Lily sighed to herself, trying not to contemplate the troubles lying ahead of them. Instead, she said her silent farewells to the wild lilies growing alongside the winding road and the fringed palm boughs dancing in the breeze. She gazed for a long moment at the unique azure of the sea where it met the sky and tried to memorize everything about Bermuda—the sights, the smells, the sounds that had made up the happiest days of her life.

By the time they reached the beach, where the launch waited to transport them to the ship, Lily had resigned herself to her fate. As they were rowed toward the *Baltimore Star*, she listened to Harte tease the Kapirigis about having to wear shoes again once they reached Georgetown and then smiled at their dismayed faces. Not until she was hoisted aboard the vessel did she realize that something was amiss on the ship.

"What are they doing?" she asked Harte, looking back into the stern, where a knot of sailors were gathered. When Harte didn't answer, she looked up at him and was immediately alarmed by the expression on his face. "Harte? What is it? Has something happened?"

"I don't know," he told her, but the strange tone in his voice betrayed him. He did know. She felt it, and a horrible fear rose swiftly in her chest until it caught in her throat and choked off her breath.

"Harte, please," she cried, clutching his arm. "Tell me what's wrong."

"Lily, take the Kapirigis and go belowdecks to your cabin. I'll explain this to you later."

Lily frowned as Harte sent the Kapirigis on ahead with their satchels, but she lingered where she was and watched the soldiers, instinctively aware that something momentous was happening. A moment later, she saw Derek. He stood in the midst of the armed sailors, his hands bound behind him.

"Oh, my God, Harte, they've got Derek!"

"Wait, Lily . . ." Harte began, but he didn't stop her when she ran down the deck toward her brother. The soldiers parted for her, and she threw her arms around Derek's waist.

"Derek, what's happening? What are they doing to you?"

"I suppose I got a bit careless when I left last night," Derek answered in a low voice, but his eyes watched Harte as he approached them.

"This is a mistake," Lily cried desperately. She turned frantically to Harte. "Tell them to let him go. You promised me he wouldn't be arrested. Please, Harte, explain it to them. They don't understand that we made an agreement."

No one said anything for a moment, but when Harte's eyes met hers, Lily knew the truth. Everything he had told her had been lies.

"I can't believe you would do this to me," she managed somehow, but her throat was so tight with shock and grief that she strangled on her words.

"Should we take the prisoner on down to the brig, Major Delaney?" the first officer asked tentatively. "Or do you want to question him first?"

Lily looked at Harte, praying that she would wake up and find that the knife he had just thrust so deep in her heart was nothing but a terrible, ghastly nightmare. She wanted to wake up and find herself safe in Harte's arms in the pink house beside the sea. But she couldn't wake up. All she could do was listen to Harte's orders.

"Take him below for now. I'll talk to him later."

As the sailors led Derek off toward the companionway, Lily attempted to follow, but Harte's fingers closed around her arm.

"Lily, I know how you must feel right now," he said in such a subdued voice that she could barely hear him, "but I can't release him now that he's already in custody. I did let him go last night, but now I have no choice but to hold him."

Lily looked up at him, her eyes burning with unshed tears. "You gave me your word."

"Try to understand my position, Lily."

"You lied to me. You used me against my own brother." Her voice caught as the full brunt of his betrayal hit her, and she didn't give him time to answer. Her heart torn in shreds, she turned and fled belowdecks to her cabin, not sure she could bear the pain of what Harte had done to her.

Harte waited until they were well out to sea before he dared to go below and face Lily's wrath. The betrayed look in her eyes would not leave his mind, but he had no easy answers to assuage her hurt and certainly no excuses that would make her feel better. He had betrayed her. He had tricked her. He had used her.

When he reached her cabin, he hesitated again, dreading the coming confrontation. He knocked lightly, but there was no answer. Taking a deep, fortifying breath, he turned the knob and entered. Lily lay on the bed, and he walked across the dimly lit cabin and gazed down at her. Her face was ravaged by weeping, and he felt sick, knowing he was the cause of her suffering. When she looked up at him, every fiber in his body strained toward her.

"I'm sorry, Lily."

"Then let Derek go."

Harte sat down on the bunk, and she inched away, watching him with a distrustful look he hadn't seen before. "I'm going to try my best to get him released, but I can't make you any promises."

"I couldn't believe them if you did."

Harte's brows came together in a frown, but what she said was true. He had grown so used to using lies and deceptions that his word had become only a tool to get what he wanted. Deep inside, he felt disgust at himself and what he had become. He had used Lily just as he had so many others, but oh, God, this time what an awful price he was going to have to pay.

"I don't blame you for being angry, but you have to remember that Derek is guilty of crimes against the United States. He's not an innocent man."

Lily's eyes met his, full of fear. "If they find him guilty, they'll hang him, won't they?"

He hesitated, not wanting to tell her that her fears were well-founded. "I'll do what I can, I swear," he said instead, then swallowed hard as her tears brimmed over and began to roll down her cheeks. "Lily, we've been happy together. Don't let this destroy everything . . ."

"You've destroyed what we had," she whispered, rolling over and sobbing into her pillow.

Harte sighed, wanting to put his arms around her and comfort her. But it was too soon. Once they got back to Washington, once she had had time to think, she could relent. He let himself out of the cabin quietly, ready to talk to Derek now. If he would swear himself out of the war and promise to return to Australia, the court would probably be lenient. That was Derek's only chance, and Harte's only hope to gain Lily's forgiveness.

# 15

Cassandra Delaney bunched her watered-silk skirt up in her fists, impatiently swept the deep-pink fabric aside, then stepped down from the hired hack onto the driveway of her eldest brother's Georgetown estate. She had only just been informed that morning that Harte had returned home from Bermuda, and almost a week ago, at that. As usual, he hadn't even had the courtesy to notify her of his arrival back in town.

Pushing open the spiked black iron gate, she hurried up the walkway toward the porch, then came to an abrupt stop when an acorn glanced off her new pink tulle and velvet bonnet. When a second nut bounced off her shoulder, she turned her head and peered up into the spreading branches of the oak tree that shaded the front windows. From the tree limb just above her, she saw the Kapirigis' little faces peering down at her. They giggled mischievously, their small teeth shining against their dark skin.

"Kapi! Rigi! You little imps! Come down

here right now and tell me what you're doing back at Harte's house! Why aren't you on your way to Australia?"

Obediently, the twins shimmied down the trunk, carrying their weapons with them. When they stood before her, bundled in winter clothes but still wearing identically irreverent gap-toothed grins, Cassandra had to laugh. She hugged them close, delighted to see them again. "I've missed you two! And so has Dr. Joseph and everyone down at the Institution! But why have you come back to Washington? Is Lily here with you?"

"Yes, but she not like the green-eyed one no more," Kapi told her, his face growing sober. He shook his head sorrowfully.

"She cry much. He frown and say real bad words," Rigi added somberly. "Is not good 'round here no more. And we is sad 'cause Birdie's gone off to live at a new port."

Perplexed, Cassandra frowned. Then she realized where the maid had probably gone. She smiled. "You must mean Newport. That's the town up in Rhode Island where my Grandmother Delaney lives. Birdie's family still works for her, so I suppose Birdie's gone up to visit her mother." She glanced toward the front door. "Is Harte here today?"

"No. Lily be in house, but he go do work. He stay gone much. We stay in tree so he not growl at us like speared crocodile."

Cassandra considered the Kapirigis' revelations for a moment. Then she pulled apart the drawstring of her velvet bag and dug inside for her coin purse. "Here, darlings, take this penny and run down to the corner mercantile for some licorice drops while I go inside and talk with Lily."

Delighted to oblige, the two boys took the money and raced each other to the gate. Still astounded by the unexpected turn of events, Cassandra climbed the steps and admitted herself to the entrance hall. Why on earth would Harte have brought Lily back with him? What was he up to now?

There was no one in the foyer, so she moved past the staircase and slid open the doors to the rear parlor. She found Lily alone in the room, sitting in the cushioned rocker beside the hearth.

"Lily? I can't believe you've come back. I thought you'd be on your way home by now."

At the sight of Cassandra, Lily came to her feet and hurried to embrace her. "Oh, Cassie, I'm so glad you're here," Lily said, her voice heavy with unhappiness. "Everything's in such a mess."

"What on earth has Harte done now?" Cassandra demanded as she unpinned her hat and slipped out of her fur-lined pink silk cape. Intently examining Lily's distraught face, she seated herself on the sofa and drew Lily down beside her.

"I found out why Harte really took me in and offered to help me find Derek," Lily said in a low, tormented voice. "I still can't believe he could be so deceitful."

Cassandra gave a sniff of disdain. "Well, he can be, and he's good at it. Harte's been a Pinkerton detective for years now, and believe me, he's got lying down to an art. What did he do to you?"

"It was all a plot from the beginning. The only reason Harte took me to Bermuda was to lure Derek there so the secret service could capture him."

"He didn't get him, did he?" Cassandra asked quickly.

"Yes. He had Derek arrested."

"Oh, no!" Cassandra gasped, truly appalled. "How could he do that to you?"

"He says he didn't want to. He says he's only doing his duty."

"Yes, he would say that. Where's Derek right now? What did Harte do with him?"

"I don't know for sure. Derek came back with us aboard the *Baltimore Star*, but after we landed here, he was transferred to a prison ship. I don't know where they took him, but Harte says they'll try him for treason."

"Oh, my Lord, Lily. This is just terrible."

Lily nodded miserably. "Harte promised me he'd intervene on Derek's behalf, but Cassie, I'm so scared they'll hang him. And it'll be all my fault for sending for him."

"No, it's not your fault. My brother engineered this, not you." Cassandra patted Lily's hand in an attempt to console her. "Harte's a powerful man in Washington, Lily. He's one of the president's bodyguards, for heaven's sake. He knows Mr. Lincoln well. He should be able to persuade the court to be lenient. Maybe he can even get a presidential pardon."

Cassandra frowned as Lily dabbed a handkerchief at the tears of worry welling up in her eyes. She put a comforting arm around the other woman's shoulders. "Everything's going to be all right, Lily. I'll talk to Harte too, and maybe some of my friends down at the Smithsonian can put in a good word for you and Derek. The fact that both of you are Australians might make a difference, you know. And you have helped Harte with his secret service work, haven't you? That ought to hold you in good stead with Pinkerton and the military judges."

Lily nodded, but when she suddenly shut her eyes and tightened her grip on Cassandra's hand, Cassandra realized at once that Lily was entering into another one of her strange dreamings. She watched warily for a moment or two, then Lily opened her eyes again.

"Did you have a vision?" Cassie asked, and an inexplicable shiver undulated down her spine.

"I saw a long-stemmed white rose lying on black velvet again," Lily said, shaking her head in bewilderment. "I sense it nearly every time I touch you. Isn't that strange? I just can't understand why it's always the same image."

Cassandra knew why. She quickly changed the subject. "Listen to me, Lily. Everything's going to be all right. I'll talk to Harte for you and try to persuade him to let Derek go. Did they get the *Mamu,* too?"

"How did you know Derek's ship was called the *Mamu*?" Lily asked in surprise.

Cassandra hesitated. "I don't know. You or Harte must have mentioned the name to me at some time or other. Or perhaps the Kapirigis did. Was the ship captured?"

"No. Derek's too smart for that. He left the ship anchored in a safe place while he came on his own to see me. He was going to sail back to Melbourne, but Harte's men caught him before he could get away."

"What about you, Lily?" Cassandra asked sympathetically. "I guess you must hate Harte now after what he's done to you."

"Everything's different between us," Lily admitted softly. "I can't stop being angry with him. Every morning when I wake up and think about what he did to me, I get sick to my stomach. Sometimes I really get quite ill and queasy."

"Well, that sounds like morning sickness to me. If you were married, I'd think you were with child," Cassandra murmured absently, barely noticing how Lily paled at that suggestion. "But I suppose all you need is some fresh air. Come on, Lily, get your cloak, and I'll take you and the Kapirigis for a drive down Pennsylvania Avenue. It's really quite pleasant for early February. I've a hired hack waiting outside, and I have several more errands to run for the professor. You'll feel better once you get out of this stuffy house, I know you will. And try not to worry too much about Derek. You have friends here too, and we'll all do everything we can to get him released."

While Lily went to fetch her wrap, Cassandra's mind worked furiously to concoct a plot that would accomplish the difficult task of freeing Derek Courtland. Cassandra did have important contacts who could help her, both in Washington and elsewhere. As soon as she had questioned Lily further on the subject, she would choose a plan and set the wheels in motion.

When Harte returned home late that evening, the house lay shrouded in the same melancholy silence as earlier in the day when he had left for the War Department. He hung his coat and hat on the carved coatrack beside the door and gazed up at the second-floor landing where one of the gas lamps burned at low flame.

God help him, he missed Lily. She had kept herself away from him for nearly a fortnight now. They hardly spoke to each other. Unfortunately, he had grown accustomed to having her curled up warm and soft in his arms in bed at night. He wasn't used to being denied the woman he wanted, and he didn't like it.

He climbed the stairs and looked in on the Kapirigis. There they were, cuddled together in the large four-poster bed they shared. He wondered when they had begun to use the mattress instead of pulling blankets down onto the floor and sleeping under the bed. Maybe they were finally on their way to becoming civilized. Or perhaps the cold weather outside had driven them up off the floor. Quietly, he shut their door and walked toward his own room at the front of the house. He stopped with his hand on the doorknob and looked across the hall at Lily's bedchamber.

His intention had been to give her time to cool off so she could forgive him. The idea had sounded good at the time, but he hadn't expected her to stay furious for so long. Of course, she had good reason to be, but she loved him and always had, and that worked to his advantage. She was a sensual woman; she no doubt missed their lovemaking as much as he did. Perhaps the time had come for him to insist that she relent and come back to his bed. She knew he was doing everything he could for Derek. Hell, Derek understood that Harte had done what he'd had to do. Why couldn't Lily?

He started to knock, then changed his mind. Instead, he turned the knob and opened the door. Lily sat at her dressing table, but when she saw him she half-rose and turned, still clutching her silver-backed hairbrush.

"I was afraid I might wake you," he said, affected not a little when he saw how the candlelight shone through her sheer gown, giving him a veiled glimpse of the lush curves of her slender body.

"Do you have news about Derek's release?" she asked at once.

"I'm still working on it," he replied as he shut the door. A twinge of guilt coursed through him. In truth, he didn't want Derek free until the war was over, and neither did anyone else in the Federal government. Courtland's incarceration would be a demoralizing blow to the Southern cities that expected to receive supplies from his blockade runs. Not many other ship captains were as reckless or as successful as Derek Courtland and the *Mamu*, and now that Wilmington had been closed with the capture of Fort Fisher, even fewer would get through the blockade.

When Lily turned her back to him, Harte moved up behind her and lightly placed his hands on her shoulders. Her muscles grew tense beneath his palms, and he began to gently knead them.

"Don't do this to me, sweetheart," he whispered close to her ear. "I want you back in my arms. I want to make love to you. I miss you."

Beneath his fingers he felt her shiver. Harte smiled to himself. Her hair lay in loose curls down her back, and he drew it to one side, luxuriating in its thick, silken softness. He pressed his lips to her temple, her sweet perfume intoxicating his senses until he came close to losing control. He wanted her so much, his hands trembled, and she was so close, so warm.

"I had to do it, Lily. You know I did. I didn't want to hurt you, I swear. I'll get him out as soon as I can, I promise you."

In the ornately framed mirror, she watched his face intently and listened to his softly uttered words, her huge eyes reflecting topaz fire in the candlelight. She wanted to give in, he could see it clearly, and his heart beat faster until his body burned with the blood racing through his veins.

Slowly, cautiously, he slid her robe off her shoulders, watching her in the glass as it fell onto the bench behind her. She shut her eyes, her tongue darting out to moisten her mouth. She wasn't going to stop him. He pushed down the strap of her nightgown and kissed her bare shoulder. She swallowed hard. When he slid both palms beneath the thin fabric and cupped the soft fullness of her breasts, she moaned and let her head fall against his chest.

"Please, Harte, don't," Lily murmured weakly, trying hard to be strong, but when he was so near to her, when he touched her, she couldn't think straight, couldn't remember the lies he had told her. Her chest began to heave as he fingered the tips of her breasts, and when his other hand closed around her waist, clamping her back tightly against his own aroused body, she began to melt, inside and out, her heart, her body, her mind.

"Don't . . ." she gasped breathlessly, but her

denial lacked any real conviction, and Harte paid it no heed. He turned her in one swift motion, his lips coming down hard and eager, hungry, hot and determined to bring down any kind of barrier she might try to prop between them.

All conscious thought dipped and righted, and she knew he was seducing her against her will, knew it and hated herself for not stopping it, but she couldn't. She still loved him. She always had, and she couldn't stop her body's response to his touch, not even after what he had done to her brother.

"Oh, God, I want you," he whispered against her mouth. Then he was lifting her against him, taking her to the bed, where he swept back the covers. He lowered her there against the pillows, then came down on top of her, and Lily could no longer fight her need to be with him. Her arms encircled his neck, her breathing became harsh and irregular against his mouth as he kissed her over and over, sending her senses whirling with a crazy vertigo that robbed her of all conscious thought. She sank into a world of only touch and sensation, of lips and caresses and murmured words of desire.

When their clothes were heaped on the floor, he came against her, their flesh sliding together, and she clung to him as their bodies became one and he made her his all over again. Afterward when she lay in his arms, there were no words to say. She wept until she fell asleep again and forgot his lies and treachery, and her weakness for his touch.

# 16

*"Pooooli,"* Cassandra repeated, dutifully pursing her lips and trying to get the Pitjantjatjara pronunciation exactly right.

Kapi sat cross-legged in front of her chair. He leaned forward, took her face between his small hands, and held it so she would watch while he repeated the word, his mouth open wide to show how the tip of his tongue curled up to the roof of his mouth to make a completely different kind of L sound. *"Puli,"* he said again. "It mean 'rocks.' "

Rigi grinned at his brother's language instruction. "You say *'puli'* good, Miss Cassie."

"Thank you very much, Rigi," Cassandra said, obviously pleased. "Tell me again how to say 'fly.' "

*"Punpunpa,"* the boys chimed together.

Lily turned away, wondering why Cassandra wanted to learn how to speak the Pitjantjatjara dialect. In truth, *"punpunpa"* meant "waving away a housefly," and she doubted if Cassandra would ever have need to converse on that subject. She walked to the front window and stared out at the deserted street. She had never been so unhappy. She wanted to run away, but she couldn't. She had nowhere to go. Everyone she cared for was in America—Derek, the Kapirigis, Cassandra, and most of all, Harte.

Sighing, she sank down on the tufted-velvet cushions of the windowseat. Harte was trying to get Derek transferred to Washington so Lily could at least visit him. She was grateful for his efforts, but that didn't negate the fact that if it hadn't been for Harte's deceit, Derek wouldn't be suffering in a jail cell anywhere. She couldn't forget how easily he had lied to her, used her to further his own ends, with no thought for her feelings. She wondered if he truly did love her the way she loved him. Sometimes she wondered if he could really love anyone.

He came to her often, and tried to act as if nothing were wrong, but they hadn't made love since the night he had robbed her of her willpower and made her forget his treachery. She was weak when she was around him. Perhaps she should wait elsewhere for Derek to be released. Cassandra had already invited her to stay in her dormitory room at the Castle.

Pain cut into her like a slashing saber at the idea of leaving Harte's house. The idea of returning home to Australia no longer gave her any pleasure. She liked living in America. She wanted to be with Harte, despite all their problems.

Her eyes sharpened when she saw Harte ride into sight at the end of the street. As always, her heart thumped wildly in her breast. When he dismounted at the front hitching rail and strode up the sidewalk toward the house, she stood waiting with the awful feeling of half-dread and half-excitement that was now so familiar to her.

"Lily! Where are you?" he called as soon as the front door opened. Cassandra and the boys looked up from their vocabulary lesson when he appeared on the threshold.

"Hello, Cassie. I'm sorry, boys, but I need to speak with Lily alone. I'm afraid it's urgent. Would you mind waiting in the dining room for a moment?"

"What is it?" Cassandra asked, rising quickly.

"Please, Cassie, just do as I ask."

"All right, but I'm getting sick and tired of being treated like a child who can't be trusted," Cassandra complained as she trailed the little boys into the adjoining room.

Harte waited for them to pull the sliding doors together behind them. Then he crossed the room and took hold of both Lily's hands. She strove to remain unaffected by the feel of his long tanned fingers closing tightly around hers and by the intense, solemn look in his beloved green eyes, but she couldn't. She was torn by the urge to lay her head against his chest and let him hold her. She wanted to give up her anger and believe any lie he chose to tell her.

"Lily, I know you're still angry and disappointed with me. And I know I deserve it. But please set your feelings aside for a few minutes. I desperately need your help."

As he drew her down beside him, Lily frowned. Something was wrong, something important and serious enough to worry Harte, who sometimes seemed to have no feelings or remorse about anything he said or did.

"Is it Derek?" she asked, suddenly afraid for her brother. "They're not going to hang him, are they?" Her throat dried up and closed until she couldn't swallow.

Harte shook his head. "No. He's fine. I'm still working on his release. But right now I'm going to tell you something that's top secret. No one knows this but Pinkerton and myself. Please, Lily, swear to me that you won't repeat this information to anyone. I'm going out on a limb to tell you."

"I won't tell anyone," she said, sobered by the gravity of his demeanor. "What is it? Are you in danger?"

"No. The president is."

"Mr. Lincoln? How?"

Harte took a folded piece of parchment out of his breast pocket. "We've stumbled upon a Confederate plan to kidnap the president. One of the plotters was a Federal agent and an informant of mine, but he wasn't allowed into the inner sanctum of the conspirators. He did get his hands on this, however." He held up the paper. "It's a coded message from one of the major Southern spies here in Washington. We've been trying to catch him for nearly two years now, but he's been too clever. Whoever it is must have high contacts here in the government, so it's imperative that we get him."

"And you want me to see if I can tell you who he is, don't you? The way I did before we went to Bermuda?"

Harte gazed deep into her eyes. "Lily, you have every right not to help me with this, but I can't tell you how important it is to capture this person. He is responsible for irreparable damage to our cause. He has sent out information that has gotten our soldiers ambushed and killed. He's dangerous."

"Why do they want to kidnap the president?"

"We think they intend to take him to Richmond and hold him there. The South is low on manpower, because we've captured so many of their soldiers. They intend to exchange the president for the prisoners of war that we're holding so they can return to their units and resume the Confederate fight."

Lily stared coldly at him. "Men like Derek?"

"Yes." Harte remained silent for a moment. "Will you do it, Lily? Just this one time. Please. I'll not ask you again, I swear."

"I'll do it, but only if Derek is brought here to Washington so I can see him."

Harte nodded. "All right. I'm sure Pinkerton will agree to that in order to gain your help. I'll do everything in my power to get it done, Lily. You must trust me this time."

Lily wasn't sure that she could believe him. His handsome face was as closed and unreadable as ever, but she had little choice except to help him. "All right."

Obviously relieved, Harte handed her the paper. Lily took it in her hands, not looking at the printed letters that covered its surface. She rubbed it lightly between her palms, closing her eyes and trying to concentrate. Almost at once she saw the long-stemmed white rose on a bed of black, and she knew with sinking heart that Cassandra was the Confederate agent whom Harte so desperately wanted to capture and imprison. God help them all, Cassandra was working against her own brother.

A great desolation rolled over Lily's heart, and she opened her eyes and gazed despondently at Harte. *What an awful thing,* she thought. *What terrible betrayals this American war is bringing upon families and friends.* Harte's mistrust of his family had been founded in truth after all. His jaded, cynical outlook, which she had tried so desperately to soften, would only be bolstered.

And what about Cassandra? Her only friend in America. Lovely, intelligent Cassandra, who had comforted her so many times since she had come back to Washington. How could Lily identify Cassandra as a traitor and see her punished?

"I'm sorry. I don't see anything," she said, quickly handing the paper back to Harte. She avoided his measured scrutiny.

"Are you sure, Lily? You had a strange look on your face for a moment, as if you had sensed something."

"No, I didn't. I'm very sorry, Harte." Lily looked at him, at his tanned face, at the veiled pain always in his eyes, and she couldn't stop the deluge of emotion that rushed up from within her. She put her arms around his neck and felt her heart break for him. "Oh, Harte, I'm sorry you've suffered so much. I wish I could stop all the pain you've had in your life. I wish I could just make everyone good and kind and truthful for you—"

Harte's arms tightened around her. "Lily, what is it? Why are you so upset? I didn't mean for this to bother you so much," he whispered against her ear.

But Lily was upset. She felt full to the brim with despair, her heart like lead, and she wanted to go far away from the treachery and betrayal and lies and deceit she had found since she had left Malmora.

"Hold me," was all she could say. "I don't want us to fight anymore. I don't want us to be apart anymore. I can't bear this pain inside me, Harte, not for another minute."

"I'm so sorry for hurting you, Lily," he murmured, stroking her hair. "I won't ever do it again. I promise you."

Lily wept against his shoulder, tears of anguish that had been pent up for much too long. Desperately, she clung to him because she loved him and because he had never known anything but betrayal from those he loved.

From the adjoining dining room, Cassandra listened at the closed sliding doors with single-minded concentration while the boys sat at the table and practiced drawing English letters on their slates. Harte had said he had something important to ask Lily; it probably concerned one of Cassandra's agents. She could hear only the faint murmur of their voices, not what they were saying. At one point, it sounded as though Lily was crying. What on earth had happened?

Putting her hands on her slim hips, she looked around helplessly, trying to figure out if there was a better place from which to eavesdrop on the parlor. They were sitting in the windowseat, but with the windows closed there was no way she could hear better from outside the house.

Her attention perked up when Harte's voice came nearer. She listened intently until she heard the front door close. He was gone. Perhaps she could persuade Lily to tell her what had Harte in such a stew. Sliding open the doors, she saw that Lily still sat by the bay window. She had her handkerchief out and was drying her cheeks.

"Lily, darling, what is it? Is Harte in trouble?"

"Oh, Cassie," was all Lily said, but with such pathos that Cassandra was taken aback. She crossed the room, afraid now that Lily's manner did not bode well for Derek Courtland.

"Oh, Lily, have you gotten bad news about your brother?"

Lily shook her head.

Cassandra sat down, wanting to take her hand and comfort her, but afraid, as always, that Lily might divine more about Cassandra's affairs than she wanted her to know.

"Harte gave me a letter written by a Confederate spy. He said there was a plot to kidnap the president and that he needed to identify the person responsible. I saw a white rose on a black background, Cassie, the same rose I see every time I touch you or one of your possessions."

Cassandra could not move a muscle. Lily had spoken quietly, almost tonelessly, but the expression in her amber eyes was awful to behold. She knew, Cassandra realized. Denying her involvement with the South would be pointless.

"I knew it was only a matter of time before you found out," she admitted unwillingly. "I took a chance of being discovered every time I was around you."

"Harte's your brother, Cassie, your own flesh and blood. How could you work against him like this?"

"You hate me, don't you?"

Sighing heavily, Lily shook her head. "No, I don't hate you. I just don't understand why you and Harte are the way you are. Why you hurt each other, why you lie and use other people . . ."

"You and Derek are close. You had a normal life back in Australia with your parents. Harte and I didn't have that. Our family has been split into two separate camps for as long as I can remember. Mother was completely, totally Southern-born and -bred. She took Stuart and me home with her when we were little and taught us to love Virginia and all that the South stands for. Twin Pines plantation has been in our family for two hundred years. You love Malmora the same way, don't you? Surely you can understand why I do the things I do."

"But the South enslaves the Negroes. That's wrong. You must know it is."

"Of course I know it, but that's how it has always been. It's the Southern way of life. Not all of us treat the slaves badly. We treat our people well. We clothe them and feed them. They're like children, like Kapi and Rigi. They don't want to be free."

"The Kapirigis would die if they weren't free. People with black skin aren't children, Cassie. They have hearts and brains and feelings just like we do."

Cassandra knew Lily could never understand the Southern viewpoint. It was complicated and convoluted, even to her. "Are you going to tell Harte about me?"

"I don't know what to do."

"If you tell him, he'll have me thrown in jail just like he did Derek."

"If you had told me he'd do that to you a month ago, I wouldn't have believed him capable of it," Lily murmured wearily. "But now I'm not sure. All I know is that I don't want Harte hurt anymore, and he could die because of what you're doing. When I first met Harte, the day he helped the Kapirigis and me escape from Ringer and his men, he was nearly killed because Ringer got a message from an informant in Richmond. You sent it, didn't you, Cassie? You found out where he was going and why, and you sent men to intercept him. Oh, Lord, how can you live with yourself? Harte's your brother!"

Cassandra felt guilt rise up to inflame her conscience, but she suppressed it, as she always did. "It's war. Harte does what he has to, and I do what I have to. I told them he wasn't to be harmed. I wanted him taken to Twin Pines and held prisoner there where he couldn't hurt us anymore. His missions were extremely effective against us, and I wanted to stop him."

"I think this war's a terrible thing. I don't see how your country can ever be the same again, regardless of who wins or who loses. I hope my country never, ever has to fight against itself like this. It's horrible. Families fighting their own families!"

"Lily, please, you can't tell Harte about me. Listen to me. I can help you get Derek out of prison. I've been working on it with the agents in my network ever since you told me he'd been taken. I know you probably won't believe me, but it's true. Derek's a hero to our cause.

He has run the blockade and brought in food to Southern ports where women and children are starving because of what Harte and his men are doing."

When Lily just looked grieved beyond words, she continued quickly, afraid of what might happen if Lily made the wrong decision. "Harte can't let him go while the war's going on, no matter what he tells you. Derek and the *Mamu* hold out hope for the people in our occupied cities. When they hear he's been detained, their morale will suffer. That's why I want to get him out so badly."

Cassandra took hold of Lily's shoulders urgently. "I can do it, Lily, I know I can. We've already found out that Derek's being transferred to the Old Penitentiary here in Washington. There's a guard there who can be bribed. If you'll help me, we can free Derek without hurting anyone. He'll be able to return to Australia, if he wants to. And so will you. Harte has used you too. Can't you see that? This is your chance to pay him back."

Lily bit her lip. "You've never been in love, have you, Cassie?"

"What's that got to do with anything?"

"You haven't really loved deeply, or you'd understand how I feel about Harte."

"Please Lily, I can get Derek out. I know it. And if you want, I'll leave Washington and work somewhere else where Harte won't be affected. I can go to Baltimore or New York."

"Tell me what you intend to do to get Derek out and let me think about it for a while."

Relieved, Cassandra began to set forth the plan she had discussed with her Confederate colleagues in the city. They had rescued prisoners before, and she had no doubt that Derek Courtland's escape could be arranged as well. At the moment, however, she must convince Lily not to turn her in, no matter what she had to say or do to accomplish that goal.

# 17

Derek Courtland considered his cell in the Old Penitentiary more than comfortable. He'd spent the last three weeks holed up in cramped quarters aboard a prison ship anchored in New York harbor, and these new accommodations on the grounds of the Washington Arsenal seemed close to luxurious.

From his seat at a small wooden desk, he could look out into the three-acre prison yard and watch the sun rise over the twenty-foot-high brick wall that separated the inmates from the outside world. The narrow cot provided by his jailors was made up with fresh, clean-smelling linens and, surprisingly enough, it was of an acceptable length to tolerate his six foot three-inch frame.

Exceedingly better conditions than he had been forced to suffer during some of the darker moments of his life, he thought, and the fact that he had been transferred to the Federal capital after facing a military tribunal on the charge of treason boded well for him. Perhaps his sister had been working diligently for leniency.

Lily had been distraught over his capture the last time he had seen her, but from what he had seen of her relationship with Harte Delaney at Moon Cove, she wouldn't have to work too hard to get her way with the man. Delaney was obviously smitten with her, and the American agent had powerful connections in Lincoln's government.

The clank of the lock brought him to his feet, and he was surprised to see the object of his conjectures materialize in the doorway of his cellblock. Derek came to his feet as his visitor crossed the floor and stood just outside the iron bars.

"Hello, Courtland," Harte Delaney said, glancing briefly at the empty holding pens on either side of Derek's cell. "I see you've been given private quarters. Are you being treated all right?"

"I have no complaints yet, but if you've come to release me, I'm certainly willing to go."

Delaney mirrored Derek's grin of challenge. "I let you escape once, and you got yourself captured the same night. I'm afraid I'm not in a position to give you a second chance."

Derek lifted a shoulder in a small shrug. "Well, sit down, anyway, mate, and tell me about my sister. Is she well?"

"Yes. She's here in the city, awaiting permission to visit you."

"Good. I trust she's still angry as hell at you for putting me here."

"Yeah, afraid so."

Delaney dragged a wooden chair from beside the door and sat down. Derek stretched out on his bunk and waited for Delaney to reveal the purpose of his visit.

"She wants me to let you go, of course," Delaney continued, propping his booted foot on his opposite knee, "and I told her I'd try to get you released. Unfortunately, that's a lie. You've been a thorn in our side too long for us to let you out, at least while the war's still going on."

"You flatter me."

"Lily won't understand that reasoning, and as long as you're languishing in here, she's not going to forgive me for using her to lure you to Bermuda."

Derek leaned back against the wall and gazed thoughtfully at Delaney. "And I suspect you want me to smooth things over between you and Lily?"

"She doesn't believe I let you go the night before your capture. As a matter of fact, she no longer believes anything I say."

"Should she?"

"No, but then I've never pretended to be anything I'm not. She's known from the day we met what kind of man I am, and she chose to overlook my shortcomings."

"My sister's more naive than most girls her age, Delaney. Probably because she's been overprotected for so long. Her special gifts are frightening to the more ignorant of the world, and we didn't want her hurt or humiliated. In hindsight, that might have been a mistake, I don't know, but I'm sure not convinced that you're the man she needs."

"I'm the worst kind of man for her, and we both know it. On the other hand, she's in love with me."

"You said you didn't love her. Have you changed your mind about that?"

"I've come here asking for your help to win her back, haven't I?"

Derek considered Delaney's response, but he strongly sensed that Delaney loved Lily, so he accepted the man's evasive answer at face value. "If I help you with Lily, what do I get in return?"

"The military tribunal you faced in New York has found you guilty of treason and sentenced you to hang. They really had little choice, considering the enormity of your crimes against the Union, but I'm pretty sure I can pull enough strings to get your punishment commuted to banishment. If I do, you'll have to agree to return home to Australia once the war ends and never set foot on American soil again." He paused briefly. "The South can't hold out much longer against us anyway, so chances are you'll be in jail only a few months, or even less. Columbia in South Carolina's about to fall, and Charleston's sure to go down next."

"God help the Confederacy," Derek muttered, thinking of his brave friends still in

Charleston, determined to fight to the death for a cause that Derek had realized was doomed from the beginning.

"God has chosen to preserve the Union, it seems," Delaney pointed out calmly, "and the South's damn lucky that Lincoln has no intention of crushing them for their treason. He intends to try to bring the Confederate states back into the Union with dignity. That ought to ease your mind a bit."

"That won't be an easy task," Derek said, but he was a pragmatic man. His life was at stake. "So I talk to Lily for you, then all I have to do is sit here in this cell until the war ends, be that tomorrow or three years from now. After that, I go free, but I can never come back to the United States."

"That's right, providing I have enough influence to pull the deal off with my superiors in the War Department."

"I really don't have much bloody choice, now do I, Delaney? But I do want Lily to be happy, and since she thinks you're the green-eyed man she's always dreamed about, I have a feeling you're probably the only one she'll settle for."

"You don't have to worry about her happiness. You can rest easy on that. I'll treat her well, and I'll take good care of her. Once we get over this misunderstanding about you, we'll be all right again."

"When can I see her?"

"It'll probably take me a few days to arrange

permission for her to visit you," Delaney told him, rising and proffering his palm through the bars. "Take care of yourself, Courtland. If you need anything, send word and I'll try to get it in to you."

Derek watched the big American rap on the outer door and exit the cellblock, more than relieved by the new development in his plight. Despite his reservations about the man's intentions toward his sister, he felt Harte Delaney would be true to his word. He would make every effort to get Derek's sentence suspended, and Derek felt certain that Delaney would marry Lily in time. The instant that their palms had touched in the farewell handshake, Derek had gotten the distinct sense that the poor man would be miserable as long as Lily remained angry with him.

Later that evening, Derek watched through the bars as a short, squat jailor named Gus Whalen hung the heavy metal key to Derek's cell on a nail just inside the outer door, then left the cellblock to assume his duty at the desk in the prison corridor.

Pretending to be asleep, Derek lay still, making every effort to hide his excitement. For the last three days he had been waiting for the guard to leave him alone with the key. He rose and moved silently to a spot in his barred cage across from the door. Then he gripped the bars tightly with his hands and focused his eyes on the object that could bring him his freedom. His strong will was his greatest gift, thanks to his mother and grandmother, who had taught him to use the most peculiar and inexplicable of all his family's unusual mental capacities.

Concentrating all his energy and will on the object of his desire, he let the force build inside his brain, let the power surge and fall, higher and lower, expanding like ocean waves in his head until the thought of making the key move dominated his body, igniting every muscle, fiber, and cell to do his bidding . . . *fall off the nail, fall off the nail, fall, fall, fall, fall, fall . . .*

The key quivered.

Derek redoubled his efforts, his jaw clamped, the veins standing out on his temples . . . *fall to the floor, fall to the floor, do it, do it, do it . . .* Then the familiar, mysterious essence seemed to emerge from the bottom of his mind, a ripple that undulated up from the depths of his subconscious to burst out like a bubble breaking at the top of a boiling broth.

The key lurched and fell with a metallic clink upon the stone floor.

His head already tight and fuzzy with the beginning of a headache, Derek knelt to try to reach the key, but before he could pull it into his grasp, the outer door opened. Derek cursed his bad luck as Gus Whalen appeared.

"Now how in the dickens did that blamed key get off the hook?" Gus demanded in bewilderment, then cast a suspicious eye upon Derek.

Derek shrugged, more interested in the funny little man who accompanied the disgruntled jailor. Putting a hand to his aching temples, Derek watched the fat jailor bend with difficulty to retrieve the key.

"This here's the coffin maker who's gonna make you up an eternal home, Johnny Reb," Gus taunted with a snaggletooth smile as he rattled the key in the cell door. "Casket's gonna cost the Federal army a pretty penny with them long legs o' your'n."

Ignoring Gus's entertaining remarks, Derek leaned against the bars and the door was relocked behind the short funeral director, who was dressed in a baggy black coat and trousers. The man seemed more than strange, with his heavy black beard and a low-slung slouch hat pulled down on his forehead. Derek watched the fellow take a measuring tape out of his pocket. Wordlessly he gestured for Derek to turn around. Derek obeyed, but when his visitor raised up on his tiptoes to gauge the width of Derek's shoulders, Derek sensed strongly that the undertaker was carrying a pistol on his person.

"Dadgummit, what in tarnation's goin' on out there now?" Gus grumbled as a noisy commotion erupted in the hall. He shuffled outside of the cellblock to quell the loud argument which now filtered in through the door.

Not one to ignore opportunity, Derek realized that this was a perfect chance to take a hostage. Turning quickly, he grabbed the man and jerked him violently back against his chest. He flexed his muscular forearm around the man's neck and cut off his air.

"Hold still, mate, or you've drawn your last bloody breath," he growled threateningly while he patted his hand down over the man's chest pockets in search of the gun. His jaw went slack when his palm settled instead on a particularly full, well-formed, unmistakably female breast.

"Quit that, you idiot!" a woman's voice said furiously, muffled by his hold on her throat. "I'm here to help you."

Seized with astonishment, Derek relaxed his hold slightly, and she jerked away and whirled on him. He stared down at her and found a pair of raging light-blue eyes glaring up at him. The mustache and beard had been applied with great skill, covering nearly all of her face, but she didn't give him time to utter a word.

"I've come to tell you how you can escape," she whispered, glancing cautiously at the barred grate on the cell door, through which they could hear the rowdy altercation continuing in the corridor.

"Who the hell are you?" Derek demanded in a low voice.

"I'm Cassandra Delaney, Harte's sister. My friends and I are going to break you out of here."

"What?" Derek scowled disbelievingly. "Are you out of your mind coming in here in this ridiculous disguise? If they catch you, you'll hang for treason alongside me."

"I got in, didn't I? My contacts here in the prison made sure no one saw me but Private Whalen, and he's too stupid to know I'm not a man."

Derek pulled the young woman back away from the door and held her elbow tightly. "How do I know I can trust you?"

"You don't. But you have to believe me. I'm a friend of Lily's and I'm here to help you—"

"Is Lily involved in this too?" Derek interrupted with some dismay.

"Of course. She's terrified they're going to execute you, no matter what Harte's been telling her. Now shut up and listen to me before Whalen gets back. The escape's planned for tomorrow night. We've bribed the night guard to unlock your cell just after midnight. All you have to do is follow him outside. Everything else will be taken care of. Here, take this"—she thrust a loaded derringer into his hands—"don't use it inside the prison unless you have to. Lily and the Kapirigis will be waiting for you one block over, on O Street—you'll know the wagon by a sign painted on the side that says 'Bowden Mercantile.' They'll be hiding behind the seat under a length of canvas. Lily knows where to meet me once you cross the bridge into Virginia. She'll fill you in on the details once you're out of here."

"I don't want my sister mixed up in this. She might get hurt."

Clear silver-blue eyes met his worried frown. "It's too late for such gallantry, Captain Courtland. She's already committed to this plan and ready to do what it takes to free you. So am I."

"Yeah? Why?"

"Because I'm a Southern patriot, and you've done the South a great service by running the blockade with the *Mamu.* Now hide the gun and don't do anything stupid between now and tomorrow night."

"Gawdurned men fightin' over some woman actress they seen up on the stage, like couple of lovestruck roosters," Gus grumbled as he reentered the room and stuck the key in the lock. "Got your measurements good enough?" he asked Cassandra Delaney.

"Yep," she said in a guttural tone and was ushered out by the unsuspecting soldier, leaving Derek to stare after her incredulously. My God, the woman was either unbelievably stupid or as gutsy as hell. He didn't need his sixth sense to tell him it was the latter.

All during the day before Derek's escape, Lily felt nervous and ill at ease with the lies she was being forced to tell Harte. She was not naturally a deceitful person; the concept was as alien to her nature as it was distressing. Harte had already noticed her tension. She could tell by the way he frowned and watched her every movement.

Immediately after the evening meal, she tried to flee upstairs, reluctant to talk to him for fear that he would force the truth from her. But her hand had barely touched the newel post in the downstairs foyer when he came out of the dining parlor behind her. His deep voice stopped her on the first step.

"Lily? What's wrong with you tonight?"

Nervously moistening her lips, Lily tried to smile. "Nothing. I'm just really tired. I'm going to bed. Goodnight."

As she mounted the steps, he stood and watched her from the base of the stair. Lily wasted no time in getting to her room. Once behind the closed door, she sank down onto the bed, not sure she could keep up the charade. Harte was too smart, too used to dealing with secrets and deceptions. He would know. Suddenly she had no doubt of it.

Lily twisted her hands together. Cassandra should never have entrusted her with the plan. If she gave anything away to Harte, Derek could hang! It was imperative for him to escape before they could execute him, but she was too close to Harte to deceive him for long! He already knew something was amiss.

When the bedroom door opened, her heart stopped and filled with dread. Guilt-ridden, she stared helplessly at Harte as he stepped inside, closed the door, and leaned against the door jamb.

"Tell me what's wrong," he said without preamble.

"I . . . I don't know what you mean," she

muttered shakily. "Like I told you, I'm very tired. I guess I don't feel just right."

His brows drew together in a frown, and he crossed the room. Gripping the bedpost, he examined her with such penetrating scrutiny that Lily had to fight the irrational urge to blurt out every detail of Cassandra's clandestine activities.

"Is it because I haven't been able to get you in to see Derek yet? I'm trying my best, I swear it, Lily. And I'm on the verge of getting a stay of execution—you have to believe me."

"I do believe you," she lied, rising nervously and making her way to a chair beside the window. She sat down and took a deep breath to compose herself.

Harte sat on the bed and stared at her across the room. He glanced around distractedly for a moment or two, then took several agitated steps toward the hearth. He braced both hands against the mantelpiece and fixed his gaze on the grate.

"I don't want to lose you, Lily," he said, so low she could barely hear him. "I'm afraid you're going to leave me."

Lily's lips parted in shock. The admission had been torn from him haltingly and with a thread of vulnerability that Lily had never expected to hear from him. She sat silently as he turned to look at her.

"I'm not very good at apologizing, but I will if that's what will keep you here with me. I shouldn't have used you to get to Derek. It was wrong, and I'm sorry for hurting you." He hesitated again. "I haven't had much luck with trusting women in my life. Every one I ever cared about took off and left me in one way or another, but I've found that you're not like my mother or my grandmother or Camillia. I'm trying to be different, more open with you, but it's difficult for me. I'm not used to telling anyone how I feel."

Lily's heart melted. She had longed to hear him speak openly, to admit that he could do wrong. Never before had he revealed anything about himself, other than Camillia's death. He was finally beginning to trust her, and now she was the one who had to betray him. She bit her lip, not wanting to hurt him but knowing she no longer had any choice.

"Oh, Harte, why can't things go smoothly for us? Why can't we just be happy?"

At the distress in her voice, Harte came quickly to her and pulled her into his arms. "We can be, I promise you, sweetheart. Be patient with me. I want you. I want us to be together. No more lies. I swear it. No more."

His mouth found hers, warm, insistent, molding her lips, conquering her mind and her fears, but even as he carried her to the bed, even as he made love to her with passion so tender it brought tears of unbearable joy to her eyes, she knew she had to leave him. Now that she had finally broken through his shell, persuaded him to trust her and love her, she was going to wound him just like every other woman in his life had done. She could hardly bear to think of it. When their passion was spent, Harte held her and whispered sweet words that she knew she would never hear him say again after she and Cassandra helped Derek escape.

# 18

Twenty minutes after midnight. Lily sat shivering in the Bowden Mercantile wagon hidden in the darkness where O Street joined the eastern shore of the Potomac River. The Kapirigis were huddled close on each side of her, and she hugged them tightly, terrified that something would go wrong with Cassandra's plan.

She strained to see the time on the watch pinned to the lapel of her coat, but it was too dark to read the dial. Where was Derek? Cassandra had said he would be freed at twelve o'clock. Then all they had to do was drive the wagon across Long Bridge at the end of Maryland Avenue and out of the city to safety.

"What we do when Derek come?" Kapi whispered in a low, frightened voice.

"We go home?" As Rigi asked his tentative question, he clung tightly to Lily's hand.

"I don't know. Derek will tell us what he wants to do. We have to trust him to take care of us," Lily told them, but she didn't believe it herself.

"What 'bout the green-eyed one? Where he be?"

"Cassie said her friends were creating some kind of diversion to keep him busy. That's why he was called away earlier tonight. I don't know where he went."

"Why you go off without him? 'Member, Lily, back home you say you would not leave the green-eyed man when you find him. You say you love him, even way back then when you was little as us is now."

"Oh, quit asking me so many questions!" Lily muttered curtly, but her voice caught and she was instantly regretful. "I'm sorry. I'm just scared that something's going to go wrong and somebody's going to get hurt."

"Did you see bad dreaming 'bout us comin' here?" Kapi inquired with trembling voice.

"No, nothing. I'll just be glad when Derek gets here."

Ten minutes later, they all tensed with apprehension as the silence of the night was disrupted by the staccato sound of running footsteps. What if it was the night watch? she worried. Or the prison guards looking for them?

"Lily? Are you in there?"

"Yes," Lily whispered, melting with relief when she recognized Derek's low voice.

"Thank God, you're all right," he murmured softly as he climbed aboard. He gave her a quick embrace, then grinned at the twins as they scrambled up for their own hug. "Now you two need to lay low until we get out of the city. Lily, you'll have to ride up here with me. We'll pretend to be a married couple."

"Cassie assured me that no one would stop us if we used the right password at the bridge," Lily said. The Kapirigis quickly disappeared beneath the canvas cover, and she climbed over the seat and sank down very close to her brother. "Do you think we're going to make it, Derek?"

Her brother patted her arm reassuringly, then surprised her by chuckling softly. "Yeah, I do. That little daredevil Cassie's got everything planned out like clockwork. I'm looking forward to seeing what she looks like without her beard on."

"Beard? Whatever do you mean?"

"Never mind. Just stay quiet when we reach the bridge. It's not far from here. She said to follow the riverbank. Give me the password and let me do all the talking."

Lily told him quickly, glad to let him take charge, but she sat in tense dread as he drove the horse down the quiet, deserted streets until they reached the point at which E Street intersected with Maryland Avenue. Every clop of the horse's hooves took her farther away from Harte, and her heart grew heavier and heavier until it felt like a stone slab inside her chest.

She pressed her palm to her mouth, thinking how deceived Harte would feel when he found her gone. After she had finally persuaded him to share his feelings with her, she had left him without a word. Not only would he be hurt and disillusioned by his sister's disloyalty, but now he would think that Lily too was his enemy. He would never forgive her—never.

"All right, Lily, here goes. Act like you're asleep," Derek told her, pulling up on the reins and slowing the horse to a walk as they came to the soldier's post that guarded the south end of the well-fortified bridge.

"Hold up!" cried a gruff voice from the shadows. "What's your business here?"

"I'm taking my wife to visit her family in Alexandria. Her mother's dying of consumption, man. Let us pass."

"Nobody goes through without the password, mister. Them's my orders."

"Crosswinds West."

"Okay, drive on. What're you carrying in the back?"

"A couple of nigra boys is all. Take a look if you want."

The soldier did look, but the Kapirigis feigned sleep. The guard motioned them on, and Lily's breath came easier when they rumbled loudly across the planks toward freedom.

Derek laughed softly as they drove off the south end of the bridge and onto Virginia soil. "Cassandra Delaney must be one hell of a lady to pull off something like this without a hitch."

"Cassandra's very smart," Lily answered quickly, "and she believes in what she's doing."

"I'm eager to thank her in person," Derek replied, slapping the leather reins. The wagon lurched forward into a faster pace, and Lily looked worriedly back at the sleeping city, wondering if Harte would hate her when he found that she was gone.

Harte was dead tired. He had ridden all night to get back from Surrattsville. As he led his lathered horse across the Navy Yard Bridge into the southwestern section of the city, he admitted to himself his relief that the tip he had received three days before from a Southern informer had come to naught. No courier had dashed past the road where he had lain in wait for two days and nights to intercept Confederate orders purported to be coming out of Lee's camp.

Harte shook his head in self-mockery. In the past he had gathered data before enemy lines for days, even weeks at a time, but now that he had Lily waiting for him at home, he wasn't as eager to stay away so long. All he had thought about was the way she felt in his arms, the sweet fragrance of her hair and her soft skin, the moans of pleasure he could draw from her with the barest touch of his lips to her naked flesh.

Shifting uncomfortably in the saddle, he coaxed his mount onward. He was eager to see her again. Maybe there would be good news about her brother as well. Pinkerton had been working diligently on procuring a presidential pardon, but it wouldn't come easy or without criticism from Grant's staff. Only Harte's own services would convince the government to overturn the verdict—that and the fact that Derek was an Australian citizen. God, if the sentence had to be carried out, he couldn't bear the thought of the pain Lily would bear. She worshiped her brother.

Frowning, he saluted the soldier on duty, an old friend from Baltimore who had once worked undercover for him. He pressed on toward Georgia Avenue, then northwest on Pennsylvania toward the War Department building just past the White House in President's Park. He wanted to be done with the debriefing in time to join Lily and the boys for breakfast. Then he would bathe and go to bed, and Lily might just be persuaded to accompany him.

There was more activity than usual around the immense three-story building, and he wondered what had caused the commotion as he strode down the corridor toward Pinkerton's office. When Harte entered, Pinkerton looked up from his desk in front of double undraped windows.

"You're back earlier than expected," Pinkerton said, standing up quickly.

Harte thought he looked worried as hell. "Yeah. I decided I'd gotten a bad lead, so I came on home."

Pinkerton hesitated. "You haven't heard yet, have you?"

"Heard what?"

Pinkerton looked uneasy, and Pinkerton wasn't the sort of man to look that way.

"What happened?" Harte said, a terrible premonition twisting his gut. His first thought was that Lincoln had been attacked. "Did they get to the president?"

"No," Pinkerton paused again, glancing around as if unsure how to proceed. "Sit down, Harte, and I'll tell you."

"What the hell's going on?"

"Courtland escaped two nights ago."

Shocked, Harte could only stare at him. He couldn't believe it. "That's impossible! He's under guard night and day. Dammit, how the hell did he do it?"

Pinkerton studied him silently for a few moments. "I don't know how to tell you this, Harte, but they think your sister and Lily Courtland were instrumental in planning his escape."

Harte's face dissolved into a look of pure stupefaction, then he barked out a humorless laugh. "That's ridiculous. Cassie and Lily? Cassie's never even laid eyes on Courtland, and Lily wouldn't know how to get across the city to the prison by herself."

Pinkerton shrugged. "Everything points to them."

"You're really serious, aren't you?"

"We aren't a hundred percent sure about Cassandra's involvement yet, but word has just reached us that a cavalry unit on the road to Alexandria captured a farm wagon with four people aboard. The man and woman answer to descriptions of Derek and Lily Courtland. There were two negro boys with them as well. They all made a run for it, but the woman was captured this morning."

"It can't be Lily. Lily's at my house, I tell you. She would never do anything like this."

"She's not there, and she hasn't been seen since the night her brother escaped. I checked. And neither have the two young aborigines she brought here with her."

Their eyes locked, and in that awful moment Harte knew it was true. His heart seemed to slowly freeze over until each beat was dull and hollow. Oh, God, he didn't want to believe it. He could understand if Cassandra was working for the Confederacy. Sister or not, he had never trusted her, knowing the way she felt about the South.

But not Lily. Sweet, innocent little Lily, who had spouted the importance of truth and honesty and love until he had shared everything with her and begged her to stay with him like some goddamned two-year-old. Something snapped inside him, something deep in his soul. He wanted to fall down on his knees and groan out his grief. Oh, God, when would he learn? When would he ever learn that he couldn't trust a woman?

Harte struggled for a long moment to get hold of his emotions. Pinkerton waited patiently, gazing out the windows toward the capitol.

"Where is she now?" Harte's voice was not his own; it was hoarse and grating and full of pain that even he could hear. He swallowed hard to make it sound normal, furious at himself for being such a fool.

"They're on their way back with her now. They'll probably arrive later today. They've been ordered to take her to the Washington Arsenal for interrogation."

"I'd like to be present, if I'm allowed."

For the first time, Pinkerton showed his compassion for his good friend. "Of course. I'm sorry, Harte. I hope there's been some kind of mistake."

"My only mistake was bringing her here," Harte said coldly. Then he turned and walked out without another word.

Lily was so frightened that she could barely control the shaking of her limbs. When the soldiers had accosted them, Derek had told her to flee into the woods with the Kapirigis. In the darkness they had gotten separated, but it wasn't until dawn that the soldiers had found her in the thicket of cedars where she had hidden through the long, drizzly night. Thank God, Derek and the Kapirigis had managed to escape. In truth, she had been almost relieved to have a reason to return to Washington, even if it meant facing Harte's wrath.

Since she had been brought to the big prison and locked up in a solitary cell, another thought had plagued her, filling her with uncontrollable fear. The soldiers escorting her had been courteous and treated her well, especially when they realized she was half sick after the cold night she'd spent exposed to the elements. But she had seen their expressions and heard their whispers of concern when they learned of her involvement with Harte Delaney.

What if they thought he was part of Cassie's plot? What if they accused him of treason? Such a thing could happen in this terrible American war—families became enemies and sisters thought nothing of betraying their brothers. She forced a hard swallow down her burning throat, just thinking of the humiliation that Harte was going to endure once the whole story came out.

Wrapping the gray wool blanket tighter around her shoulders, she shivered with the chills she had been having all day and stared disconsolately through the bars. She felt so alone and empty, as if she were already dead. What would they do to her? Would she be hanged? She remembered the dreaming she had experienced the first time she had held Harte's medallion in her hand and known the terror of his hanging—the horror of the scratchy hemp rope around her neck, the feel of the horse beneath her, the jerk, the tightening of the noose—

Trembling, she came to her feet when the outer door swung inward. A slightly built man walked into the room. He was dressed in a dark frock coat and a flat-brimmed black hat, but her eyes saw only Harte, who entered after him but stopped in the doorway the moment he saw her. Her pulse quickened hopefully then almost stopped completely when he said nothing. He merely gazed at her out of eyes no longer warm and green but cold as frozen jade.

"Harte?" she muttered thickly, her heart in her throat. "I'm so sorry."

Harte looked away and moved to a grated window that overlooked the courtyard.

"My name is Allan Pinkerton, Miss Courtland. I'm afraid I'm going to have to ask you some questions. You'll be wise to tell me the truth. If you do, things'll go easier for you."

Lily tore her eyes away from Harte and looked at the man named Pinkerton. "I'll tell the truth. I swear it."

"Please sit down."

Lily looked at Harte again, but he still stared outside, his back to her. Swallowing hard, she fought back the tears, trying desperately to retain enough dignity at least to last through the interview to come. She felt so bad anyway. Her head ached, her muscles were stiff and sore, and now her heart felt broken and cold with despair. If only Harte would say something, anything.

"Are you a Confederate agent, Miss Courtland?"

"Oh, no. I'm not even an American. I have taken no part in your war except that when I first came to Washington Harte asked me to identify some Southern sympathizers."

"And did you falsify the information you gave to him in order to confuse our government?"

Lily shook her head. "No, I swear I didn't. Harte, you know I told you the truth about Mr. Minner and the others. Please, tell him."

Harte's shoulders tensed visibly, but he didn't turn around or speak in her behalf. Lily realized that he wasn't going to help her. He could be very ruthless and brutal when he wanted to be, and at the moment he felt angry and betrayed. A different kind of alarm swept over her, raising goose bumps on her arms and legs. She stared, wide-eyed with fear, at Allan Pinkerton.

"Please, madam, don't be afraid. You'll be given a fair hearing. Tell me how you managed to get Derek Courtland out of his cell."

"Cassie bribed a guard," she whispered hoarsely, wringing her hands nervously. "But I don't know who the man was. You must believe me."

"We know who he was, because he disappeared the same night you did," Pinkerton answered brusquely. "The sentries at the bridge that night said you knew the password. Where did you get it?"

"Cassie."

"Has Cassandra Delaney been working for the South ever since she came to Washington?"

"I don't know. I've only been here a short

time. I didn't find out about her spying until a few weeks ago."

"How did you find out?"

Lily hesitated. When she looked at Harte again, she found that he had turned and was watching her. She couldn't bring herself to meet his eyes. "Harte brought me a document that he wanted me to hold so I could identify the person who wrote it. When I sensed a white rose, I knew it was Cassie because I had associated the same thing with her before."

"Why the hell didn't you tell me, damn you?" Harte ground out in the harshest, coldest voice Lily had ever heard leave his mouth. Pinkerton averted his eyes.

"Because I didn't want to hurt you," she choked out. "I wanted to make her stop before you found out."

Angrily, Harte approached her and braced both hands on the table. He leaned down close to her face. "But instead, you decided to join forces with her so both of you could betray me, isn't that right, Lily? You pressed yourself up invitingly against me and told me how I had forgotten how to trust, how you wanted to show me about the good in life until I finally got careless and actually thought you were something more than the lying little bitch you are."

His accusations were delivered with such quiet, brutal cruelty that Lily felt as if she had been assaulted with fists instead of words. Her face ashen, she felt the hurt begin to expand her chest. It was the most awful, constricting pain that she could ever remember. Tears burned, welled up, and fell over her lashes to roll unrestricted down her cheeks.

"Would you like a few words alone with Miss Courtland?" Pinkerton said aside to Harte.

"Hell, no," Harte answered, his face tight with controlled rage. "She's all yours now. Do whatever you like with her. I don't give a damn what becomes of her."

Lily put her hand over her mouth and wept softly as he stomped angrily from the room. Pinkerton reached into his pocket and brought out a clean white handkerchief. Silently, he handed it to Lily.

"I'm very sorry, Miss Courtland. I can see you're distraught now. We'll talk again later."

After he was gone, Lily lay on the narrow prison cot and shook with hard, wracking sobs. Now she knew that Harte would never be rid of the demons that controlled his life and made him so cold and unhappy. And now all his pain and disillusionment had come about because of her.

# 19

Fists stuck into her ample hips, Hannah Jones stood with feet planted apart on the front stoop, peering down the tree-lined avenue in front of Harte Delaney's red-brick home. Worry lines dug furrows into her wide brown brow, and she chewed on her bottom lip in a fashion completely alien to her usually taciturn nature. At the moment, the state of affairs in her household seemed particularly distressing and topsy-turvy, even more so than was common in the reckless, danger-ridden lifestyle of the man she had cared for since he was a tiny baby.

"Oh, lawsy, why does he have to have such grief?" she mumbled, sighing heavily and fixing her gaze eastward toward the capital. Poor little Miss Lily, the sweetest lady she had encountered in many a day, having to spend time in jail. A shudder of dismay coursed through her whenever her thoughts lit on an image of that pretty child locked up in a prison cage like some kind of wild beast!

Thank the Lord that Mr. Harte had arranged to have her brought home, even if he did take himself off to Virginia right away on one of his secret missions. What broke Hannah's heart nearly in two was that all the happiness she had seen on his face since he had returned from Bermuda had disappeared, and he had become as cold as a subzero freeze once more, hiding behind the icy facade he had first built the day his mama had left him behind so many years ago.

When a flag-flying black military coach finally rolled into sight at the distant intersection, Hannah hastily made her way to the curb, glaring across that street at old Mrs. Hoople, whom she could see peeping out from behind her lace curtains like a nosy crow. Such attentions from the neighbors would only cause Miss Lily to feel even more guilty and self-conscious about her arrest. The poor girl had just been trying to help her only blood kin in the best way she knew how. *Oh, my,* Hannah thought, dismay overwhelming her again. *Miss Cassie done got herself and Miss Lily into a heap of trouble!*

When the two uniformed soldiers driving the conveyance jumped down from the high driver's seat and swung open the passenger door, Hannah leaned forward to look inside and was stunned by Lily's appearance. She looked plumb awful, her face drawn and white, but she did force a wan smile for Hannah. Even though Hannah had been informed that Lily had not felt well during the week she had spent at the prison, the housekeeper had not prepared herself for just how poorly she would look. It was plain to see that no one had been taking care of her, and Hannah bristled with outrage that a woman should be treated so vilely.

"Oh, Miss Lily, please take my hand and let me help you down here. What it be that's causin' you to ail, chile?" she clucked in concern, taking a firm grasp on the white girl's slender arm as the silent guards helped Lily to the curb.

"I don't know, Hannah," Lily answered softly, but her eyes searched the draped windows of the house. "Is Harte here? He did send for me, didn't he?"

Hannah's heart clutched with compassion, and she lied, telling herself she would ask forgiveness when she got down on her knees beside her bed that night, but she could not bring herself to wound Lily Courtland any more, not when the girl already looked as though she might collapse at any moment. "He sure wanted to be here, he did for a fact, but I declare if'n he din't have to take hisself off'n one of his important jobs. You know how they's always callin' him out at all hours of the day and night. Well, that's where he be, child."

"I understand," Lily murmured, but her sweet face looked so sad and disappointed that Hannah felt her heart bat this way and that like a rope twisting in the wind. She put a comforting arm around the girl's shoulders and guided her up the sidewalk, determined to take care of her every need now that she was back at home where she belonged.

"What exactly is it makin' you sickly, Miss Lily? Is it a stomach ailment or a touch of the influenza? I've got a whole bevy of goodly remedies that be sure to havin' you feelin' good as new in no time a'tall, mark my words on't."

"I've been nauseated a good bit, and I just feel so tired and feverish all the time, Hannah. I don't know why. I think it's because I miss Harte and the Kapirigis so much."

"Now don't you worry about any of them things 'cuz everything's gonna be just fine. You'll see, just as soon as you gets you some rest and Mr. Harte gets back home with you," Hannah murmured in a soothing voice, at the same time presenting the young armed soldier with an angry glare as he took up a sentry post at the front door. As the driver shook the reins and the coach pulled away, the second guard took the bricked path around to watch the back door.

Inside the house, however, Hannah wasn't at all sure that the situation would improve with the arrival of her young master. If he wore the same cold, angry mask as he had when he rode away, poor Lily would probably feel even worse than she did now.

A fortnight after Harte had left Lily to her fate, he walked his mount down the west end of M Street, where it entered the outskirts of Georgetown. Rubbing his heavily whiskered jaw, he tried to erase her image from his mind, an effort he had been occupied with every minute of every day since he had ridden south into enemy territory. But he had not been successful, and her face haunted him like a vengeful apparition, especially the hurt and fear in her topaz eyes when he had turned on his heel and left her to Pinkerton's mercy.

Grimacing, he ground his teeth until they ached. Why should he feel bad about anything? Damn them all to hell! Lily was the one who had committed the crime against him. She was a woman, wasn't she? He should have known better than to believe anything she said. Women used themselves, their silken bodies and their soft looks, to make a man drop his guard; then they destroyed him—consumed him with the abandon of hungry black widow spiders.

The anger hit him again, so hard and lethal that it formed a thick knot inside his chest cavity, so tight it felt as though his heart would explode. Even then, as he struggled with the turmoil of emotions that Lily had dredged up to torment him, he missed her. Damn her! And damn himself for being so stupid!

As he cantered down the street toward his home, he realized with disgust that a visitor was there. He didn't recognize the compact, single-horse trap that stood out front as belonging to any of his colleagues in the military. He cursed under his breath; he hated it when people dropped in at his house.

In truth, only a privileged few even knew where he lived, and that's the way he liked it. He had always managed to keep pretty much to himself until he had been fool enough to bring Lily and the aboriginal twins home with him, and that sure as hell had been the worst mistake of his life.

His frown black and unwelcoming, he thrust open the front door and entered the empty foyer, determined to get rid of whoever it was without delay—and he was in exactly the right frame of mind to do the job well. He glanced into the formal parlor and adjoining dining room, then up the stairs and saw Hannah leaning over the second-floor banister.

"Mr. Harte, thank goodness you've come back. Miss Lily's been real sick."

Harte's insides went cold. He took a step toward the staircase, completely involuntary and instinctive. Fear, stark and awful, riveted him. For a moment, he couldn't speak.

"What's wrong with her?" he asked, his voice thick and strained.

"I don't know yet, the doctor still be with her. She wouldn't let me call him over to tend to her 'til this very mornin', but she's been havin' a terrible bout with her stomach since you had 'em bring her back home."

Harte hadn't told anyone to bring her to his house. He didn't know a thing about her arrival, and he wondered who had taken it upon himself to make that decision for him. Probably Pinkerton, he thought, but deep inside where it was hard to admit his own relief, he felt grateful to the man. Over and over in his mind's eye throughout the days he had been away, he had seen Lily sitting on that damned prison cot, looking so small and afraid. He had hated himself for leaving her there alone, almost as much as he hated her for conspiring with the enemy.

"How long has she been here?"

"She came a day or two after you rode off, and there be guards here awatchin' her 'round the clock ever since she set foot in the house."

His old retainer's subtle rebuke came through to Harte loud and clear in a tone Hannah had not used with him since he was a boy up to mischief in his Grandmother Delaney's mansion. "Perhaps, Hannah, that's because she committed an act of high treason against our government."

Hannah only looked disgusted with him, and Harte quickly turned to the doctor, who had slipped out of the guest room and was putting on his brown frockcoat as he moved past Hannah and descended the steps toward Harte.

"How do you do, sir? I'm Doctor Havery," the diminutive, neatly attired man said. He adjusted his wire-rimmed spectacles as he gave Harte's travel-stained clothes and mud-crusted knee boots a disapproving once-over.

"The young lady upstairs is your wife, I imagine?"

"No."

"Then I'd be obliged if you'd send for her husband, whoever he might be. I have need to speak with him about her condition."

"She doesn't have a husband."

The doctor's alert blue eyes darted to him in obvious shock; then the little man frowned with a different kind of condemnation. *Who the hell does he think he is to judge Lily?* Harte thought in irritation.

"May I speak freely, sir?" the doctor said briskly. "I trust you take responsibility for her since she's staying here in your home."

Harte clamped his jaw shut as Hannah made a reproachful sound, then loudly cleared her throat in a display of her displeasure with him. "Please do."

The doctor lowered his voice. "The young lady is expecting a baby. She's not far along, just a month or two, I suspect, but she's rather frail and apparently isn't taking very good care of herself. She's not eating well, is she?"

Harte was so stunned by the physician's revelation that he couldn't answer for a few seconds. He shook his head, but even as the doctor prescribed bedrest and a healthy diet of milk and vegetables, his mind reverberated with the knowledge that Lily was carrying his child. There was no doubt that he was the father. Lily had been with no other man. He knew that without question, but he just hadn't expected her to conceive so quickly. Despite his anger with her, despite her betrayal and everything else that had come between them, he felt a warm wave of pleasure begin to spread through his body.

"I'll check back again in a few days, but I do believe she'll be fine if she can get the rest she needs. She seems quite melancholy and sad. Has she borne a loss of late? A family member, perhaps?"

"She's been separated from friends," Harte told him brusquely, wanting to get rid of the man. "Please don't concern yourself, Doctor. We'll see the she follows your orders."

After escorting the doctor to the door, Harte hurriedly climbed the steps. Hannah was waiting on the top landing, fixing him with a dire stare. "She don't have nobody but you," she said with pointed effect. "And you be turnin' your back on her when she needs you the most."

Harte ignored the barb. "I'm going in to see her now. Please don't disturb us."

He walked to Lily's bedchamer and opened the door. Lily was propped up against the pillows, and she did look so pale and unlike herself that he was a bit startled. She was so fragile of frame, so delicate, so much like a child herself that the thought of her delivering a baby suddenly loomed as a dangerous event. He wanted to take her in his arms, hold her, close his eyes and take comfort in the feel of her body pressed up against him, but he couldn't bring himself to do it. Not yet.

"Harte?" she said, looking and sounding wary. "I didn't know you were home."

"I just got here," he answered, striding over to her side. His eyes swept downward over her abdomen under the coverlet, but as far as he could see she looked as slim as ever. There was no sign of her pregnancy.

"Did you speak with the doctor?" she asked softly, her eyes searching his face.

"Yes."

A wave of color rose into her cheeks, and obviously embarrassed, she kept her eyes downcast when she spoke. "Are you angry about the baby?"

Harte hated the question, hated what it implied of him, but he had given her every reason to think he wouldn't want a child from her. Still, something inside him kept him from telling her otherwise. He didn't trust her anymore. He was afraid to touch her, for fear that his willpower would crumble at her feet, and he would cling to her like a weak, besotted fool.

"Being angry wouldn't solve anything."

Lily looked up then, and Harte saw the hope that had dawned in her eyes. He forced a matter-of-fact tone into his voice. "I guess I'll have to marry you. I know the baby's mine."

The nonchalance of his remark at first shocked her, then hurt her feelings. Lily always showed her emotions so openly. She hadn't learned how to hide them in order to protect herself, the way he had. She bit her lip and dabbed away a tear with the white lace handkerchief she held in her hand.

"Don't cry," he ordered impatiently.

"I'm sorry. I just can't seem to help it lately. My emotions are all so mixed up. I guess it's because of the baby." She sobbed again and tried to stifle it.

Harte couldn't bear to see her weep. But neither could he bear to touch her. He turned away and stood looking out the window beside the bed until she got control of herself. He ought to try to comfort her. She was sick, the baby was his, and Hannah was right. Lily didn't have anyone but him. Every fiber in his body urged him to turn around and take her into his arms.

"Have you heard any word about Derek and Cassie?" she asked a moment later in a low, worried voice.

At the question his anger returned full force. He hid the rage burning his chest as he had learned to do when he was eight years old. "Apparently they got away. But they'll be captured eventually. Grant's about ready to seize Richmond. It's only a matter of time before the Confederacy crumbles."

"Good. I want it to be over," she whispered, moistening her dry lips. "I only want to be with you again, the way we were at Moon Cove."

God help him, that's what he wanted too.

Why couldn't he just tell her so? Why couldn't he just sit down beside her and put his hand upon her belly where their child now grew? Could he ever do it again?

"Do you really intend to marry me?" she asked him quietly.

"Yes. The child should have a name. I'll arrange all the details, so try not to worry. The doctor says it's bad for the baby."

"Please, Harte, put your arms around me and tell me you want me too," Lily said, her words catching pitiably in her throat.

Harte hesitated for so long that another tear escaped. When it rolled down her cheek, he sat down and put his arm around her. He shut his eyes and lay his cheek against the top of her head.

Lily clutched the front of his shirt and wept, but Harte knew that everything was different now. Perhaps time would put things right between them—time and the baby inside Lily's body—or perhaps it wouldn't. Regardless of how that turned out, his child would have his name and Lily would be his wife.

# 20

"In the name of the Father, and of the Son, and of the Holy Ghost. Amen. Dearly Beloved. Forasmuch as Marriage is a holy estate, ordained of God . . ."

Lily lay silently against her soft, lace-crocheted pillows as Reverend Derrick began the marriage ceremony in his solemn, sonorous voice. Tall and dignified, with pure-white hair and kind brown eyes, the black-robed Lutheran minister stood with great presence at the foot of Harte's gray-and-black-draped four-poster bed.

Harte had assumed a stance close beside her, appearing erect and imposing in his formal black frockcoat and white satin vest. He looked handsome and totally at ease as he listened calmly to the words being spoken, and Lily wished she was strong enough to rise and take her place beside him the way a bride should.

Although she had foreseen months ago that their wedding would take place in his bedchamber, she could never have guessed that she would be married in bed, dressed in a white satin nightgown and a Venetian lace bedjacket instead of the wedding gown she had always wanted to wear. The brief dreaming she had envisioned just after she came to Washington had in no way prepared her for the terrible circumstances surrounding her union with Harte.

". . . and to be held in honor by all, it becometh those who enter therein to weigh, with reverent minds, what the Word of God teacheth concerning it . . ."

*Has Harte weighed his decision reverently?* she wondered, her teeth catching at her lower lip. Harte had told her he would never be married again, not to her or to anyone else. Had he changed his mind because of the baby she carried inside her? Was he wedding her out of a sense of duty, without a shred of love left toward her? Familiar fingers of nausea gripped the pit of her stomach. Lily put her gloved hand to her mouth, trying to fight back the awful sick feeling.

Hannah, who stood on the other side of the bed as the sole witness, leaned forward and looked down at Lily with concern, but she said nothing as the preacher turned his gaze upon the silent bridegroom.

"Harte, wilt thou have this Woman to be thy wedded wife, to live together after God's ordinance in the holy estate of Matrimony? Wilt thou love her, comfort her, honor and keep her in sickness and in health, and, forsaking all others, keep thee only unto her, so long as ye both shall live?"

Lily waited with bated breath, half expecting Harte to change his mind now that the moment was truly at hand.

"I will," he said firmly in his deeply resonant voice with all the self-assurance that characterized everything he did.

The cleric repeated the vow to Lily, and with her heart overflowing with love and emotion, she murmured her own acceptance of Harte as her husband.

"I will."

The kindly minister smiled and squeezed her hand as he placed it in Harte's larger one. "Now we will exchange the vows," he told them, turning first to Harte. "Please repeat after me: I, Harte, take thee, Lily, to my wedded Wife, and plight thee my troth, till death us do part."

Lily smiled tremulously as Harte finished his vows and the clergyman turned to her. She reiterated his words, low and soft and so full of love that no one could doubt how she felt about the man at her side. "I, Lily, take thee, Harte, to my wedded Husband, and plight thee my troth, till death us do part."

Lily trembled, overcome with emotion, as Harte slid a slim wedding band of unadorned gold upon the fourth finger of her left hand. Tears of bittersweet joy welled up in her eyes as the Reverend Derrick blessed them as man and wife. When the time came for the groom to kiss the bride, Harte leaned down and kissed her forehead. A faint brush of lips to consecrate an agreement meant to last throughout the rest of their lives. But would it?

Afterward, Hannah set about fluffing up her pillows with a great show of vigor, and Lily watched forlornly as Harte courteously led the black-robed preacher out of the room. The wedding was over, and Lily felt even emptier inside now that she had become Harte Delaney's wife.

"Now you try to get some sleep, sweetie-pie," Hannah was telling her briskly. "I know you is plumb tired, as weak as you be. Mr. Harte's gonna go off on duty again, so there's no need for you to worry 'bout waitin' up for him. You can just rest 'til later when he gets home." She looked down and smiled fondly at Lily. "Do you need anything? Would a cup of chamomile tea help you to drowse off?"

"No, thank you, Hannah."

"Well, if you do wants anything a'tall, or if you starts gettin' sick again and needs me, just ring this here bell"—she set a long-handled gold bell on the bedside table within Lily's reach—"and I'll come runnin', you hear?"

Lily nodded. Hannah bustled busily from the room to prepare a wedding supper, which probably no one would eat. She left the outer door ajar, and the usual undisturbed quiet of Harte Delaney's lonely house resumed. No sound came from downstairs or through her open window. It seemed as if nothing momentous had happened, as if this day were not the one Lily had waited and longed for since she was six years old.

Rolling over onto her side, she stared at the tiny gray scallops on the border of the wallpaper. In truth, nothing had really changed at all. Despite the fact that she and Harte were now man and wife, they were as much estranged as ever.

After the wedding day, time seemed to take on the crawling pace of a snail. Lily obeyed the doctor's directives to the letter, and as a result her health began to improve. As the bouts with morning sickness subsided, she began to feel like herself again. Harte was gone more often than not, and when he was home, he remained closemouthed about his absences.

Lily had learned from Hannah, however, that he spent many of his nights at the White House, on duty as a special bodyguard to President Abraham Lincoln. She had begun to believe that her husband used his orders to guard the door of the presidential bedchamber as a good excuse to stay away from his own bed.

Not that Harte wasn't kind to her. On the contrary, he was attentive in an absentminded sort of way and always concerned about the state of her health. But he rarely touched her, and she missed the physical contact between them more than anything else. She lay in her lonely bed at night, wanting him, wishing he would come and make love to her as eagerly and passionately as he had done at Moon Cove. But he never came, and he probably wouldn't as long as he believed that she couldn't be trusted.

One evening in early April she strolled listlessly through the empty rooms of the house, longing for Harte to return home. He had gotten back to Washington again just that day, after a weeklong stint at City Point, Virginia, where Lily had overheard him remark to a courier that Grant was preparing to launch a full-scale attack on the Confederate capitol of Richmond.

She peered out the tall, narrow sidelight window beside the front portal and sighed morosely, then stood for a few moments in the cool evening breeze that swirled inside through the open fan-shaped transom above the door. She was glad that the cold, gray days of winter were almost over.

Springtime in Washington was proving to be beautiful, with warm, sunny days that coaxed into bloom the circular beds of huge trumpet-shaped yellow jonquils in the front yard and the tall purple irises that lined the garden wall. Even with so much awakening life and beauty surrounding her, Lily's heart still felt encased in icy winter.

On the oval marble-topped table in the center of the foyer, Hannah had placed a large vase of fresh flowers. Lily wandered toward them, admiring the pink peonies and bright daffodils, but the hothouse white rosebuds were a painful reminder of Cassandra. Her mood became even blacker as she reached out to stroke one of the soft white petals.

At once she froze, with her hand still on the flower, as dark winds began to howl all around her, strong and icy cold, thrusting away the present and the peaceful house, and she was in some strange tent-like structure hung with shimmering gold silk, and Derek was there, she realized with excitement, striding toward her wearing high-topped leather boots and the loose, flowing black robes of a desert sheik . . . *and she was Cassie, and she was furious with Derek, outraged with his arrogance. He had done something awful to her . . . he was laughing when he reached her and as he swept her up in his arms against her will, she wanted to kill him but even more she wanted him to kiss her, hard and eagerly, with both his fists tangled in her hair . . .*

"Lily? Are you all right?"

Harte's voice brought Lily out of the unsettling trance, but she was shaken and pale from the scene she had just witnessed. She turned to see Harte shrugging out of his military cape in front of the mirrored coatrack.

"Cassie's with Derek, and she's angry and upset, but she wants him to kiss her. He was laughing, and I think they're in the desert somewhere."

Her remark claimed Harte's attention from his examination of the mail in the silver tray on the polished hall table. For a moment she thought she saw a hint of interest flit across his face, but then the implacable mask dropped back into place—the one he had worn in her presence since the day he had come to her prison cell.

"Cassie's going to be all right," he told her, with his usual detachment. "Derek's taking her to Australia with him."

"To Australia? How do you know that?"

"I have my ways," he said dismissively, moving past her down the hall and through the open door of his private office at the back of the house.

Lily followed him to the threshold, hoping he was right about Cassandra and Derek. If either of them were caught by Federal forces, they could be hanged. They would be much safer far away from the America war. She watched Harte pour himself a shot of bourbon from one of the crystal decanters in the liquor cabinet set between tall built-in bookcases. She wanted to tell him about the other dreaming she'd had just the night before, the one that had brought her bolt upright in bed. She hesitated, not sure he would want to discuss the baby. He had said nothing about it since the wedding.

A sudden loud booming in the distance startled her, and she darted a fearful look toward the windows. Cannonfire, she realized, turning questioning eyes to Harte. He didn't seem alarmed in the least by the sound of artillery so close by.

"Harte? Did you hear that? What is it? The city's not under attack, is it?"

Harte glanced up. "No. Richmond fell today. Union forces entered the city this morning."

Lily smiled slightly, not understanding his lack of emotion. "Why, that's wonderful, isn't it?"

Their gazes caught and held. "It is for our side," Harte said coldly. "I have no idea how you feel about it."

Lily didn't respond in kind, by now well accustomed to his thinly veiled barbs concerning her disloyalty to him. "Well, I'm pleased, if for no other reason than that you'll probably be home with me more often once the war is over."

Her words surprised him. She could see it clearly in the green of his eyes before he turned away and tossed down the remainder of his drink. Suddenly she had the most aching need to weep again, for him, for them—but she wouldn't let herself. She set her chin obstinately, deciding she was tired of standing back and letting him shut her out of his life. She would make the first attempt to reconcile things, even if he would not.

"I had a dreaming last night."

"Oh?" he murmured, loosening his gray silk cravat and seating himself behind his desk.

Lily hesitated, half afraid to mention the baby for fear of his reaction. He was in a funny, uncommunicative mood, even more so than usual, and she wasn't sure what had caused it. If only he would stop being so guarded and distrustful all the time, they could be happy again. But he made everything so hard for her!

"I don't know if you'll want to hear about it," she began, forcing a hopeful smile, "but our baby's going to be a boy."

Harte's head jerked up, and as he stared silently at her, she went on quickly, eager to share the exciting revelations. "We're going to name him Courtland, and he's going to be a senator here in your country someday. And, Harte, he's going to look exactly like you. I saw him after he had already grown to manhood, and he's going to be strong and good . . ."

When her voice cracked with emotion, Harte pushed back from the desk and swiveled his chair around to face the windows. He had turned his back on her eager excitement, and the effect on her happiness was so cold and dismissing that Lily felt as if he had taken her by the shoulders and given her a violent shake. Fighting hurt and disappointment, she took in a deep breath.

"I'm sorry, Harte, I shouldn't have said anything. I thought you might be interested in the baby, but now I know you're not."

Lily turned to leave. Now she wanted to be alone. But before she had time to quit the room, Harte's voice stopped her.

"Lily, wait."

Wary now, she turned back and watched him cross the room to her. He came so close that she had to tilt her head back to look up at him. He reached out suddenly and brought her in against him, and Lily shut her eyes, going physically limp with relief and pleasure.

"I am interested," he muttered gruffly, his mouth muffled against the top of her head. "I do care about the baby. I want you to know that."

"Oh, Harte, I love you. Can't you see that? Can't you see how much I'm suffering without you?" Lily cried, her fingers clutching the front of his starched linen shirt. "I want us to be happy again. I want it to be the way it was. Tell me what to do to make it that way again."

Harte held her close, stroking her hair, and the thud of his heart was slow and steady beneath her ear.

"I don't know," he said at length. "But no matter what you think, I'm not trying to hurt you. Be patient with me, Lily. I'm trying, but it's hard for me. I quit letting people get close a long time ago, when my mother walked out, and it's hard to change that."

Lily pressed closer, thrilled to hear his low words.

"I'll never leave you again, Harte. Please believe that," she whispered urgently.

To her disappointment, Harte suddenly released her and stepped away. Only a brief instant of intimacy had passed between them, but that momentary thaw of his icy indifference renewed her hope. Perhaps the baby would make a difference between them. Perhaps after Courtland was born, they would come together as a family and everything would be as good as it had been before things had gone so terribly wrong. She had to believe that the rift between them would heal. If she didn't have that hope to hold on to, she wouldn't be able to bear another moment of having Harte so close but held apart from her by his own cold indifference.

# 21

As Hannah brushed a long blond strand around her finger then draped the curl over Lily's bare shoulder, Lily examined her reflection in the tall gold mirror above the silk-draped dressing table. Though pleased that Harte had asked her to attend a play with him, she was extremely nervous about her first public appearance as his wife among the social elite of Washington.

Lowering her eyes to the plunging neckline of her gown, she was a bit astounded by the provocative way her breasts swelled over the tight white-satin bodice. She had never before worn an evening gown or even had the opportunity to enjoy an evening out with a gentleman, but since Harte had chosen the garment himself, the style was no doubt appropriate for the occasion. She would certainly wear it to please him. In truth, since their wedding she had been willing to do just about anything her husband had asked in order to make things right between them.

Since General Robert E. Lee had surrendered five days earlier, on April 9, thus ensuring victory for the Union, Harte had been a noticeably different man. Not only had he invited her to accompany him out for a social engagement for the first time, but the habitually worried ridges in his brow had nearly disappeared. She hadn't seen him so relaxed since the carefree days they had spent together at Moon Cove.

To Lily's disappointment, however, their marital relationship had not improved. Harte still had not come to her bed or treated her with the easy, affectionate regard that he had before she became part of Cassandra's plot.

Tonight, she hoped, would be the turning point. They were to attend a play at which she might be fortunate enough to be introduced to the president and his wife. Afterward they would dine at the National Hotel, and Lily meant to do everything in her power to make sure Harte could be proud of her.

She wanted to look her best, and therefore she had sat patiently through an hour of Hannah's endless fussing with her thick wayward tresses. With unstinting patience, the woman coaxed and patted the soft curls until they lay in intricate coils on top of Lily's head. While Lily watched, she tucked several miniature white lilies into the stunning coiffure, then as a finishing touch curled a few wisping strands in artful disarray over Lily's forehead and temples in the latest Washington fashion.

"There you be, Miss Lily, just like the society ladies fix their hair for the evenin'. You be prettier than all of dem, mark my words on't."

"Thank you, Hannah," Lily said. As the woman left the room, she leaned forward and critically examined the coral-colored lip rouge. When she turned her head, the diamond earrings that Harte had given her winked and flashed in the gaslights. She wanted so desperately to look nice tonight in case they encountered any of Harte's friends or fellow officers at the Ford's Theater. She pinched her cheeks to give color to the pale complexion she had suffered since her bouts with morning sickness.

Pausing to fetch a short black-velvet cape for the cool spring night, Lily slipped the ties of her velvet drawstring purse over her wrist. The time was at hand to make her premier appearance as Mrs. Harte Delaney, and she rose and hurriedly left the bedchamber, filled with anticipation of the evening ahead.

When she reached the top of the steps, she found Harte waiting below in the foyer. As Lily stared down at him, a great wave of pride swept over her. Tall and bronzed by the sun, he looked nothing less than magnificent in his charcoal-gray frockcoat and black brocade vest. Never in her life had she seen a man who could rival Harte's masculine appeal, not even her own handsome brother. The thought of Derek struck a chord of sorrow deep in her heart, and she murmured a silent prayer that he and Cassandra were safe, wherever they might be.

When Harte suddenly looked up and saw her, standing with one white-gloved hand on the banister, he stepped closer, his intense eyes moving down the length of her pearl-encrusted white gown.

"Good God, Lily, you're enough to take a man's breath away," he muttered, half to himself.

Lily's heart flip-flopped with pleasure, and she lifted the heavy satin skirts and slowly descended to the bottom step, where he stood waiting.

"Allow me," he said with a slight smile. He took her cape from her hands and placed it carefully around her shoulders.

Looking forward to an entire night in Harte's company, Lily took a deep, fortifying breath. She smiled up at him, and he took her elbow and led her to the coach that awaited them out front.

During the carriage ride into the busy streets of downtown Washington, Lily couldn't take her eyes off her husband, who sat opposite her, gazing out the window. He seemed even more quiet and reserved than usual, and Lily wondered what was troubling him.

"Is anything wrong, Harte?" she asked after a time.

"Not really. I was thinking about General Grant. He's returned to town and, in fact, I heard today that Mrs. Lincoln invited him and his wife to sit in the presidential box with them tonight. Perhaps you'll be able to meet them."

"I tremble to think of meeting someone as powerful and important as Mr. Lincoln."

In the dim light filtering from the lantern hanging outside the door, she saw Harte's faint smile. "You'll probably feel more comfortable around him than anyone else in the city. He considers himself just a man like any other, but he isn't. He'll be remembered throughout history as one of the greatest Americans who ever lived. I'm just glad the war's over and we don't have to worry as much about the threats against him. It's been hard for the secret service to protect him, because he hates being guarded."

Lily thought it must be terrible to be despised by so many of your own countrymen that your life was constantly in danger.

"Lincoln said once that we couldn't possibly guard him against all dangers unless we locked him up inside an iron box. He said if there was someone willing to give his life for his, there was nothing that could be done to prevent it. After Lee surrendered, he even walked through the streets of Richmond. Fortunately, no one there lifted a finger against him. He's a man of remarkable courage."

Lily smiled, pleased that he was talking with her, even sharing his thoughts and feelings again. Maybe they were on the right track at last. Somehow she knew that tonight was a new beginning.

Though the hour was half past seven in the evening, the wide, lamp-lit thoroughfare of Pennsylvania Avenue was filled with horses and pedestrians hurrying this way and that on various urgent missions. The wild, jubilant celebration over the Northern victory still continued with daily fireworks, impassioned speeches, and booming cannon fire. Everywhere uniformed troops patroled the streets in even greater numbers than before the surrender.

By the time they turned onto Tenth Street, where the Ford's Theater was located, traffic was heavy and slow-moving, with carriage drivers leaving off parties of well-dressed theater patrons.

As Lily watched the hustle and bustle outside the coach window, her own enthusiasm grew into a rush of excitement. Everyone seemed in a joyous, lighthearted mood, but she couldn't help but think of Cassandra and her countrymen of the South, who had been so soundly defeated. She feared that the roads and sidewalks of their vanquished cities would not be filled with laughter and celebration. She pitied their grief and the humiliating loss, even though she herself considered the institution of slavery completely immoral and wrong.

In front of the theater, Harte stepped down, then helped his wife to the sidewalk. Fascinated, Lily listened to the chatter of the other playgoers as he escorted her into the lushly decorated lobby with its arched doors hung with burgundy velvet draperies. Harte steered her through the buzzing crowd to the north side of the foyer, where a curving staircase led up to the mezzanine.

"I've rented a private box overlooking the stage," Harte told her, bending down close to speak near her ear as he led her down the aisle between the curving rows of cane seats. When they reached a closed white door, Harte opened it and they passed into a short, narrow vestibule with two more doorways that opened into separate boxes.

"Here we are," he murmured, checking his tickets against the brass number on the closed door. "Come, let's get settled so we'll have a good view of the president when he arrives."

While Harte stood back, Lily preceded him into the private box that overlooked the left side of the stage. Beautiful sheer draperies framed the ornate balustrade, and the box was furnished with a red-velvet camelback settee flanked by two matching overstuffed chairs. Lily moved to the rail and looked down into the cavernous interior of the Ford's Theater.

Below her vantage point, which was about twelve feet above the stage, semicircular rows of seats curved around the floor behind the orchestra pit. She was amazed at the number of people milling about and visiting with one another. After Harte helped her off with her cloak and draped it across one of the chairs, she seated herself on the couch. To her disappointment, he chose the other chair instead of joining her.

"It looks like a packed house tonight," he remarked, removing a small pair of opera glasses from his coat pocket. "Would you like to get a good look around before the lights go down? That's the presidential box just across from us, but it looks like the president's party hasn't arrived yet."

Lily focused the tiny glasses on the draped alcove directly across the stage from them. Elaborately decorated with a patriotic theme, the president's box had red, white, and blue American flags hung from poles on each side and several more draped on the railings as swags of bunting.

"What is the flag in the middle, the navy-blue one with the eagle?" Lily asked curiously, never having seen it before. "And who's the man in the portrait hanging beneath it?"

"The flag is the regimental banner of the Treasury Guards, and the engraving is a likeness of George Washington. He was the first president of the United States."

"Oh, yes, I remember that Cassie told me about him. He was the founding father, the one the city was named after, wasn't he?" Lily murmured, turning her attention to the people on the orchestra level.

"That's right," Harte told her. "Tonight's play is called *Our American Cousin*. It's a comedy about an English dowager trying to marry off her daughter, I believe. Laura Keene is the lead actress."

"I've never seen a play performed before. Malmora was so far away from Melbourne," Lily admitted, but before she could say more the lights began to dim. The heavy brocade curtains were slowly drawn apart to reveal the painted scenery decorating the stage. Breathlessly, Lily waited for the spectacle to unfold.

At once the crowd quieted around them, and Lily was instantly caught up in the story line and delighted by the rich costumes of the actors. When the play suddenly stopped around eight-thirty, she was disappointed. But then the orchestra struck up "Hail to the Chief," and all eyes turned to watch the presidential party enter.

"I believe that's Clara Harris who just sat down on the right," Harte told her, gesturing toward a young woman who had seated herself near the front of the flag-draped box. "She's the daughter of Senator Harris. That's Major Rathbone behind her. I guess the Grants couldn't make it after all."

"Is that Mrs. Lincoln?" Lily asked, indicating a small woman in a low-cut gray-silk gown who sat on the younger woman's left.

"Yes, and that's the president beside her."

Lily couldn't see him well because of the hanging banners, but she could tell he was a large man with a dark beard. He wore a long-skirted black frock coat and a matching vest, very conservative attire for such a distinguished man.

When the play resumed, an actor on stage by the name of Harry Hawk brought a burst of merriment to the audience with his adlibbed quip "This reminds me of a story, as Mr. Lincoln would say."

Harte laughed, and Lily smiled, but as the story unfolded, further introducing the avaricious dowager named Mrs. Mountchessington, Lily began to feel unsettled by a vague feeling of unease, the kind that often assailed her shortly before a violent dreaming took possession of her mind.

"How do you like the play?" Harte whispered, draping his arm around her on the back of the sofa. His lips were so intimate against her ear that the shivers raced each other down her arms and she forgot the strange sensation that had disturbed her. Once more she became absorbed in the comedy, laughing often at the absurd dialogue and ridiculous actions of the players.

". . . I am aware, Mr. Trenchard, that you are not used to the manners of polite society," Laura Keene said from the stage below, sweeping haughtily offstage, to the delight of the onlookers.

Droplets of cold sweat beaded Lily's brow, and she once again began to feel extremely uncomfortable and ill at ease.

". . . Heh, heh. Don't know the manners of good society, eh? Well, I guess I know enough to turn you inside out, old gal—you sockdologizing old man-trap," Harry Hawk pronounced enthusiastically, his suggestive tone and exaggerated facial expressions drawing a roar of laughter from the crowd.

The hairs on the back of Lily's neck stood on end, and she gasped and entered the roaring, rushing blackness . . . *he was creeping through the darkness, stealthily stealing up behind a man . . . the man sat in a tall rocker . . . a light shone behind him and he held something in his hand, a gun, he was going to murder the man, oh, God, it was the president, he was going to murder Abraham Lincoln* . . .

Lily came out of her trance and lunged to her feet, her fingernails digging into Harte's arm.

"Lily, what is it?" he cried in alarm, coming to his feet and clutching her shoulders. "Is it the baby?"

"A man's sneaking up on the president! I saw him! He's going to kill him . . ."

Her words were drowned by the loud laughter of the crowd, but she cried out again, pointing frantically at the presidential box. When Harte realized what she was telling him, he dropped his hold on her and drew the pistol he wore strapped beneath his coat.

Across the theater, a figure had climbed onto the decorated railing. As Lily watched in shock, he leapt the twelve feet down onto the stage, but his right foot caught in one of the draping flags. He landed off balance on his left foot, then jumped back up on his feet.

"*Sic semper tyrannis!*" he snarled, brandishing a knife at the audience, then limped with a kind of bullfrog hop across the stage and out of sight.

The people in the auditorium laughed again, thinking the man an unexpected part of the performance. Then they heard the terrified screams of Mrs. Lincoln and the harsh cries of Major Rathbone to "Stop that man!"

"Stay here," Harte said to Lily, and he was gone before she could answer.

"The president's been shot!" came a hysterical cry from across the theater, followed by a great moan of horror as pandemonium broke loose, with everyone rushing toward the exits.

Lily sank down and leaned weakly back upon the sofa cushions, watching with horrified eyes as several men converged on the president's box to aid the wounded leader, amid a terrible wailing and screaming from below and all around the theater. Shakily, Lily put a hand to her forehead as a rolling wave of sickness came over her. In her head she saw the black crepe bunting on the balustrades of the domed Capitol building, heard the wailing of the grief-stricken masses, saw Abraham Lincoln lying in state beneath a black-draped canopy. She knew then that President Lincoln would die before the night was over.

* * *

At half past eight the following morning, Lily still lay awake in bed, waiting uneasily for Harte to return. He had taken time the night before only to put her in the coach bound for Georgetown. Then he hurried away to pursue the escaped assassin. She hadn't heard a word from him, or from anyone else, since Hannah, weeping and distraught, had left the house just after midnight to spread the dreadful news of the death of the man who had signed the Emancipation Proclamation to free her people.

Lily was exhausted, but sleep was out of the question. She was too worried about Harte. Restless and upset, she rose and donned her soft wrapper and house slippers. Drawing back the curtains, she looked out on the deserted street, then quickly dropped the drapery when she heard the front door open and close.

She rounded the newel post of the upstairs hall just in time to see Harte coming up the steps toward her, his face so stricken that her own heart ached for him. She hurried down the steps to meet him. Halfway down they met, and Harte put his arms around her. Silently he laid his head tiredly against her, and she cradled it tenderly against her breast.

"He's dead." His voice was thick, unnatural. "He died from a bullet wound to the head, just after seven o'clock this morning."

"I'm so sorry, Harte. I know how much you

thought of him," she murmured, gently stroking his soft, dark hair.

He held her tightly for a long time, saying nothing else, and she didn't speak either, aware there were no words to comfort his sense of loss. But his grief communicated itself to her as she held him, terrible and stark.

"Let me make you some coffee, or something to eat," she whispered tenderly. "Hannah's gone to her daughter's house but it'll only take me a moment to fix something."

"No," he muttered, drawing away from her embrace. "Let's go to bed. I want to hold you."

Harte led her upstairs without speaking, his arm around her shoulders, and Lily realized he was utterly exhausted, his emotions raw and ragged from the shock of the assassination. She helped him undress and, once in bed, he drew her body close against his hard, lean frame as if craving her warmth.

"I've just got a few hours to get some sleep before I have to go. They think Booth has escaped into the Virginia countryside. I've been ordered to accompany a cavalry company headed south to find him."

"Booth? Was he the killer?"

"Yes. John Wilkes Booth." He released a heavy sigh against the top of her head. "He's an actor, believe it or not, a famous one. God, I've met the man. I actually admired him. I still can't believe this has happened. No one can. It's like a horrible nightmare."

"How did he get away?"

"He had a horse waiting in Baptist Alley—that's the street behind the theater. But we'll find him. Everyone's being questioned. Several men have already been arrested. The Secretary of State, William Seward, was attacked as well and is seriously wounded."

"Was he in the box with the president too?"

"No. The damned murderer forced himself into the Seward house and stabbed him as he lay in his sickbed. Several other men in the house were wounded too, but the doctors seem to think they'll all survive the attack, thank God. There was a conspiracy. Vice President Johnson was to be slain as well, but something must have happened to prevent it. We'll get them, every last one of the murdering bastards."

Lily pressed closer, hating the idea of his leaving but knowing he would never rest until he had caught the assassins.

"How long will you have to be gone?"

His arms tightened around her. "I don't know. It could be months if he gets away and goes into hiding down south. Pinkerton thinks he'll head for Richmond or Charleston, and if he does, we'll get no cooperation from the Southerners in apprehending him."

"Please be careful."

"I will. You'll be all right here with Hannah."

For a moment they lay silent, but Lily could feel the tension in his body.

"Dammit, we should have stopped this! We were responsible for his safety! We let down our guard when Lee surrendered, especially after Lincoln walked through the streets of Richmond without incident."

"You can't blame yourself, Harte. You did your best to protect him. No one could have expected this, not now that the war's over."

Harte didn't answer. Lily put her arms around his neck and held him close until he fell into an exhausted sleep. She felt content that she lay within his embrace once again.

# 22

In the days following the assassination of Abraham Lincoln, the city of Washington lay in deep mourning. Along the streets black crepe hung from lampposts and festooned door frames, and the Capitol dome was swagged with the same funereal adornment. On April 18, 25,000 people spoke in hushed whispers and filed sorrowfully through the White House, where the slain president lay in state.

From the White House, Lincoln's body was taken under escort to the Capitol Rotunda. Cannons boomed, church bells tolled, bands played dirges, and 40,000 mourners followed the fourteen-foot hearse drawn by six gray horses as the procession made its way up Pennsylvania Avenue.

On street corners and in smoke-filled saloons, the more vengeful Unionists preached angry rhetoric insisting that the South should pay dearly for the cold-blooded murder of their beloved leader. The euphoria of the North's long-awaited victory had been instantly transformed into the most bitter grief imaginable.

After the funeral services, held in the East Room of the White House on April 19, one lady in staid black silk climbed into her black coach and leaned back against the plush black-velvet squabs. Lifting her right arm, she rapped the gold head of her white cane against the top of the carriage in the signal to proceed. Her Negro driver obediently set the coach in motion, and she lifted her heavy black-net veil to reveal the proud, aristocratic bone structure of her face.

Though her skin exhibited the spidery lines of age around her large, dark eyes and at the corners of her thin mouth, Sarah Delaney hardly showed the sixty-seven years she had lived upon the earth. In truth, even with her advanced years, one could readily see how beautiful she had been in her youth. Her hair, now the pure white of fresh cream, was parted down the middle and pinned at the back of her head in a thick chignon. She had no use for spectacles, and indeed, her eyes were not the faded blue of those of many elderly people but keen and piercing, the color of an azure summer sky.

Sighing deeply, she allowed her lashes to drift downward and rested her head against the seat. She thought sorrowfully of her dear friend Abraham and of the peacefulness of his craggy face as he lay in his coffin beneath the four-pointed black canopy erected over his death bier. She had known the president for many years, ever since Lincoln and her dear, departed husband had been colleagues in the Senate.

Abraham Lincoln had been an extraordinary man, a good man of strength and vision. His courage and determination to do what was right had won the war for the North and preserved the Union. What a tragedy for him to be cut down at the moment of his greatest triumph—Lee's surrender near the Appomattox Courthouse.

Harte would be taking the president's murder very hard. Sarah's regal face softened at the thought of her beloved grandson. Harte had idolized Lincoln from the first day they had met at her house in Newport, and Sarah vividly remembered Harte's vow to lay down his life for Abraham. Sarah didn't doubt that he would have done so if called upon.

Her estrangement from Harte had gone on close to ten years now. Indisputably, their quarrel had been the greatest catastrophe of Sarah's life. Even with her loyal Hannah sending her weekly letters informing her of his health and activities, Sarah still missed him terribly.

After she had lost her own dear husband to diphtheria, Harte had been a cheerful young boy who had helped her survive the devastating loss. Even with Harte's mother, Charlotte, constantly interfering and filling the boy with her pro-slavery sentiments, Harte had loved Sarah more than any other member of his family. He had been her strength through the years following her husband's death and her hope for the future of her family.

Then he had brought home poor Camillia. Her face tightened at the thought of the peasant girl. Camillia had driven a wedge between Sarah and Harte that remained as rigid and unyielding as the day he had walked away empty-handed from The Oaks, wanting nothing further to do with Sarah or the family name. Sarah had mourned deeply his decision to blame her for Camillia's death, but she could never tell him the truth about what had really happened to the Mexican girl.

Now he had wed a second time, after he had sworn never to take another woman into his life. According to Hannah, this new bride had a stronger hold on his heart than Camillia ever dreamed of having. The young woman named Lily could possibly be a powerful ally to Sarah. Or perhaps, like Camillia, she would become another adversary.

When the rumbling conveyance came to a standstill in front of her grandson's house in Georgetown, she unlatched the door and stepped down by herself, haughtily waving away the driver's attempts to assist her. Bidding the hired servant to wait at the carriage, she gazed up at the facade of the large brick residence.

Sarah had never before been allowed to set foot in Harte's house, but her grandson was not at home. Hannah had reported that he had been away since the day after the assassination and was not expected back anytime soon.

Sarah was glad. He would not welcome her with open arms, but his bride would no doubt be pleased to entertain an important member of her husband's family, especially with Hannah's encouragement.

When the old black housekeeper opened the front door, Sarah hugged her dear friend warmly. Charlotte had brought Hannah north from Virginia as her chambermaid. After Harte had been born, she had made Hannah his mammy. Charlotte had treated the Negress as a piece of chattel until Sarah had coerced her daughter-in-law into giving the woman her freedom. Since that time, Hannah had been Sarah's loyal friend.

"I'm so pleased you be here," Hannah whispered, helping Sarah out of her rich black-velvet cloak. "Miss Lily's been eat up wid lonesomeness since Mr. Harte went south wid de army."

"Does she know I'm here?" Sarah asked in a quiet voice, her gaze sweeping approvingly over the fine furnishings of her grandson's house. He had always had impeccable taste, even when he was a small boy. She had taught him how to choose the best of everything.

"No, I didn't say a word 'bout it. But she's a sweet little thing, Miz Delaney. She'll welcome you warm as pie, I know. She's been havin' a bit o' trouble with the baby, so de doctor, he tell her to stay off'n her feet. So she be spendin' near all her time back there in the little parlor. Dat way, she say, she can see Mr.

Harte's horse the minute he ride into the stable yard."

"I'm very eager to meet her," Sarah told her quite honestly. "I suppose she must be quite a girl, considering Harte's determination never to remarry."

"Lily be an easy one to love and want to take care of. You kin just ask anybody who's met up wid her," Hannah said with an affectionate smile as she led Sarah toward the rear of the spacious house.

Sarah certainly hoped that Hannah's instincts about the girl could be trusted; nevertheless, she prepared herself for the possibility that Harte had already poisoned his young wife against her. She steeled her own resolve as Hannah announced her.

"Miss Lily? I do got a nice surprise—"

"Is it Harte? Has he come home?" came a hopeful feminine voice from within the room.

"No, ma'am, he ain't. But Harte's grandmama has come for a visit. It be Miz Delaney to see you."

After a fractional hesitation, Hannah was instructed to admit Sarah into the sitting room. The pleased housekeeper beckoned to Sarah, a wide white smile wreathing her dusky face. Sarah lifted her chin and proceeded into the back parlor, not sure what to expect.

Her grandson's new bride was seated in a violet-sprigged rocking chair beside the rear windows. As Sarah came forward, the young woman lay her book down on the marble-topped table beside her.

"How do you do?" she said in a faint Australian accent as she rose to her feet. "I'm Harte's wife, Lily."

"How do you do, Lily? I am Sarah Delaney, Harte's paternal grandmother."

Sarah was momentarily taken aback when Lily stretched out her palm for a handclasp as if they were two gentlemen meeting for the first time. She was even more startled when the young woman gripped her fingers very tightly for a moment while gazing deep into Sarah's blue eyes. Her new granddaughter-in-law's eyes were very beautiful—a lovely topaz that reminded Sarah of the maple trees lining the winding drive of The Oaks when the autumn sun set them ablaze with fiery color.

"Please sit down, Mrs. Delaney. I'm very pleased that you've come. I've often wondered about you."

Seating herself on a blue-and-white floral wing chair near Lily's walnut rocker, Sarah decided the girl wasted no time getting to the point. That was good. Sarah had always been a straightforward person herself. In a day when so many young women recited inane niceties drilled into them at frilly ladies' academies, she found it extremely refreshing to find a young lady who did not mince words.

"My grandson hates me," she told Lily with equal candor. "That's why I'm not welcome in this house. If he were here today, I daresay I wouldn't have been allowed to step inside the front door, much less speak with you."

Lily remained silent for a moment. "He has changed of late. He has forgiven me for something I did. Perhaps now he will soften toward you as well."

A tiny kernel of hope began to take shape inside Sarah's breast, and she was shaken by an absurd rush of gratitude. Could this slight girl, this child-bride of Harte's—could she help Sarah regain her grandson's love after so many years of bitter strife between them?

"Is Harte well?" she asked, immediately embarrassed at the way her voice faltered. She went on quickly in an attempt to hide her vulnerability. "Hannah told me he suffered a wound not long ago."

"He was shot in the arm, but his injury has long since healed. I pray every day that he won't be hurt again before he can come home to me."

Sarah had repeated countless similar prayers since the beginning of the conflict with the Confederacy, but she found herself wanting to reassure Harte's young wife. "Now that the war's over, he'll be a good deal safer, I suspect," she said, reaching for a cup of tea from the tray Hannah had brought into the room.

"True, but the surrender had already been signed when the president was killed, and Harte is serving down in the Southern states, where the people are angry and defeated.

Union soldiers such as he won't be welcome there."

Sarah watched Lily take one of the fragile white porcelain cups and saucers and rest it gingerly on her lap. The girl was very small-boned, almost frail-looking, and her slim body still showed no sign of the child she carried.

"I understand, my dear, that you are expecting a child," Sarah remarked, sipping the aromatic tea.

The most beautiful smile lit up the young woman's lovely face. "Yes. Harte and I are both very happy about it. I had quite a lot of trouble in the beginning, nausea and such, but I'm being very careful now to take good care of myself so the baby will be born healthy."

"I'm happy for you. Bearing a child is a great blessing for a woman," Sarah told her, realizing that she was indeed pleased at the prospect of having a great-grandchild from Harte at last. There had been a time when the young lady sitting across from her would not have met her approval as a suitable wife for her grandson or as a mother to Harte's sons. However, she had changed in that regard during the long years when Harte had scorned her because of her treatment of Camillia. She had been lonely and filled with guilt for so long now that she had learned the virtue of tolerance. Never again would she drive someone she loved away from her.

"Thank you, Mrs. Delaney," Lily said with a gentle smile. "I do hope you'll come again when Harte's at home. I believe that if the two of you could bring yourselves to talk together, perhaps a reconciliation might be possible."

"I've been praying for such a thing for years, but Harte has never been one to forgive and forget. He loved The Oaks, my estate in Newport, more than any place on this earth, but he has never set foot there since he walked out years ago."

Lily seemed to consider Sarah's remark with great seriousness as she sipped her tea and watched Sarah intently over the edge of the cup. She was certainly a pretty little thing, Sarah thought, beautiful in a genuine, fresh way that had no need for artificial enhancements. She was artlessly lovely. Sarah could understand how a girl so obviously innocent could mesmerize a man, even one as arrogantly masculine and aloof as Harte had always been.

"That is a very finely carved cane you have there," Lily remarked unexpectedly, with another soft, endearing smile. "May I examine it closer?"

Startled by the unusual request, Sarah looked down at the cane that she had propped against the arm of her wing chair. She passed it to Harte's wife, and Lily inspected the ivory walking stick with a great deal of interest. Then, to Sarah's bewilderment, Lily closed both hands over the solid-gold handle and shut her eyes as if she were concentrating on something far away.

*How strange she is,* Sarah thought to herself,

then Lily opened her eyes and smiled warmly, giving the cane back to Sarah.

"It is beautifully constructed," Lily murmured, then absolutely astonished Sarah with her next statement. "I think I should like to visit you at your house in Newport someday soon. Hannah speaks so often of the beautiful grounds at The Oaks and the gorgeous view from the cliffs, and I am lonely here in this big house without Harte."

"Do you mean it, child?" Sarah stuttered in complete disbelief. "Would you truly come there with me?"

"Yes," Lily said, reaching out to lay her palm on top of Sarah's gnarled, blue-veined hand. "I would enjoy the sea air, because it would remind me of Bermuda, where Harte fell in love with me. I could leave word for Harte to come there to fetch me home. Would that be all right with you?"

Scalding tears sprang into Sarah's eyes, burning her lids like moist flames. She had not wept for Harte in a very long time—because she had given up hope of ever seeing him again. Now this waif of a girl was giving her the chance for which she had hoped and prayed for so many years.

"You'd do that for me?" she whispered, forcibly restraining her brimming emotions as she withdrew a white-linen handkerchief from the tight lace wristband of her black-silk sleeve.

"And for Harte. I think his heart will be troubled as long as he does not face what has happened in his past. I want him to be free of all the demons he has locked up so tightly inside his soul. If he visits you at The Oaks, perhaps he will lose some of the anger and guilt that constantly drive him to take terrible risks and put his life in danger. More than anything else, I want him to be content to be safe at home with me and our children instead of out looking for a way to punish himself."

Sarah stared at Lily with newfound respect. The young woman whom Harte had married possessed a wisdom beyond her years. Harte was fortunate to have found her. "You must come very soon, while the peonies and forsythia are still in blossom. Harte always loved Newport the most in the springtime. I have many servants who will be happy to see to your needs and make sure you're comfortable. It'll be lovely having Hannah back with me as well." She paused, realizing that she was babbling on like a giddy young schoolgirl, something she hadn't done in decades. "Do you really think Harte will come to Rhode Island? He could just summon you back here to Georgetown instead of coming there himself, you know."

Lily smiled. "I think he'll come for me, but I also think he'll be very angry about having to do so."

"I wouldn't want to cause trouble between the two of you," Sarah said quickly and sincerely.

"You won't, because he'll understand in time why I've chosen to visit you." Lily smiled again, so sweetly that Sarah began to believe her. Indeed, it would be hard to remain angry for long with the beautiful, serene young lady sitting across from her.

# 23

Almost two weeks after the day Lily received Harte's grandmother in Georgetown, she rode with Sarah Delaney in the plush burgundy lacquered Delaney coach with the gold familial crest painted on each door. Their ship had landed in Newport earlier that morning, and now the short ride to the cliffside mansion was coming to an end.

As the luxurious conveyance passed through the tall brick wall decorated with ornamental black-iron scrolls and proceeded up the cobbled drive between ancient oaks and maple trees, Lily stared in awe at the gigantic graystone mansion looming before them at the end of a velvety expanse of emerald grass.

Even more grand than she had expected, the elegant house shone with row upon row of mullioned windows opening into more rooms than Lily could explore in a month. In truth, the elaborate facade brought to mind the feudal castles in the stories of kings and knights that her mother read to her when she was a little girl.

As they approached the great stone portal, Lily absorbed the grandeur of the veritable fortress where Harte had grown so unhappily to manhood, and she realized for the first time just how much wealth the Delaney family possessed. In the shadow of huge white pillars, Sarah Delaney's servant staff met their returning mistress with bows and curtsies as if she were a queen. Lily was pleased to see little Birdie among the uniformed maids, but the sight of the timid Negress also reminded her of the Kapirigis and how much she missed having the little boys with her.

Inside, the place was even more overwhelming, causing Lily to stop in wonder on the other side of the stained-glass doors, intimidated by the sheer opulence of the house—from the polished black-marble floors that reflected everything like a dark tranquil lake to the exquisite crystal chandeliers glittering from the gilt and plaster-medallioned ceilings in every chamber.

*No wonder poor Camillia was so ill at ease in such a palace,* Lily thought, as Sarah led her through a marble-walled corridor to a long gallery stretching across the rear of the house. High multipaned windows lined the back of the narrow rectangular hall, and more verdant, manicured lawns swept out from a terraced flagstone patio to the cliffs that overlooked the dark-blue waters of the Atlantic Ocean. The view of the sea reminded her of the sunwashed bedchamber at Moon Cove, and again her heart was wrenched by the desire to be with Harte. She missed him so much!

"Your home is beautiful," she murmured to Sarah. "I know Harte surely must have missed coming here all these years."

Sarah nodded, her face etched with sorrowful lines. Lily had found the elderly woman quite nice and accommodating on the voyage. Harte's stark description of her seemed a bit exaggerated, but then she had known Sarah for only a short time.

"He always loved the ocean and everything associated with it." Sarah smiled, her eyes faraway and misty as if she were recalling some fond memories of her grandson's boyhood. Abruptly, however, she seemed to come back to the present, obviously embarrassed that Lily had caught her in nostalgia. "I brought you here first because I thought you might enjoy seeing some of the Delaney forebears. Since it has been our family tradition to commission portraits of each family member, we have accumulated quite a gallery, as you can see."

Lily strolled along beside Sarah, slowing her pace to match her companion's painful gait. In the last few weeks, she had observed how Sarah suffered from her gouty right foot, though the older woman never complained about her disability. As she examined the lifesize portraits one after another down the long gallery, she understood how Harte came to possess his handsome, patrician features. How nice to have a complete record of your family for so many past generations, she thought. She knew so little of the Courtland heritage other than the stories her grandmother had told her about her youth in southern England.

"This is my son, Melvin. Harte's father was our only child," Sarah murmured, pausing before the picture of an extremely handsome young man portrayed in a gray uniform and military hat with a jaunty gold plume decorating the brim. "This was painted just after he turned eighteen, while he was enrolled in West Point. I can't tell you how proud my husband and I were the day he was commissioned an officer."

"Harte looks quite a lot like him," Lily remarked, noting especially the resemblance around the nose and the hooded eyes, though Melvin Delaney's eyes had been a warm cinnamon-brown, quite unlike Harte's cool green.

"I know. Sometimes when I looked at Harte as a child, it was almost as if I had Melvin with me again."

As they stopped before the next painting, Lily gazed up at a small group sitting together in front of one of the huge round columns supporting the front portal of The Oaks. Lily recognized it at once as a family gathering of Harte's mother and father and their three children.

Harte appeared to be around seven years old, and he stood leaning against his mother's fancy white skirts, looking stiff and uncomfortable in his tight-fitting trousers and coat of burgundy velvet. Cassandra sat on her mother's lap, a beautiful baby in a long, elaborately fashioned white-lace gown. Another little boy, nearly as tall as Harte, sat cross-legged in front of his father. Stuart, Lily thought, Harte's long-lost Confederate brother whom she had yet to meet. Not for the first time, she wondered how he had fared in the South's ignominious defeat.

Returning her attention to Harte's mother, Lily decided that Charlotte had been quite beautiful, as slender and bright-eyed as Cassandra was now. How could she possibly have gone away and left Harte behind? He had been such a beautiful child, and even in the portrait, he leaned close to his mother in a possessive way. She placed one hand on the slight mound of her abdomen. She could never go off and leave her baby. Poor Harte. He had suffered so much at the hands of his family.

Next she discovered a portrait of a young Harte sitting astride a magnificent black stallion, looking proud and handsome. A lock of his soft dark hair fell over his forehead in a way it still did at times, and Lily's heart clutched with loneliness for him.

"Harte was seventeen when he sat for his portrait," Sarah told her. "A year or so before he got involved with that man Pinkerton."

"You disapprove of Mr. Pinkerton?" Lily asked.

"Harte was an obedient boy until he joined

Pinkerton's detectives and became obsessed with danger and recklessness," Sarah said bitterly. Then she moved on to the next painting. "This is Stuart, my other grandson. He's just a year younger than Harte."

Eager to see Harte's brother, Lily moved closer and stared at the young man in the portrait. He looked very much like Harte, except that his eyes were more almond-shaped and a very clear blue, almost the same color as Sarah Delaney's.

"I've never met him," Lily remarked, "but I can remember now that Cassie told me you invited him here once to have his portrait painted. He's very handsome too; all of your grandchildren are. He was here at the same time Camillia was, wasn't he?"

Sarah looked uncomfortable and hesitated a beat too long before answering. "Yes, I believe so."

"Is there a portrait of Camillia?" Lily asked, studying Sarah's expression to see if she really detested the girl, as Harte seemed to think.

Sarah stiffened, but otherwise showed no emotion. "I had her portrait stored away in her rooms in the east wing. I found it painful to look at it after Harte left here for good."

"Will you tell me about her?" Lily asked eagerly. "Harte told me how they met and how she died, but there's so much I don't know about her."

"I would prefer not. The past is best left forgotten."

"I'm afraid Harte hasn't forgotten it at all, Mrs. Delaney. In fact, I think he's very troubled in his mind about what went on here eight years ago. I think he might blame himself as well as you, and I don't think he'll ever be happy until he comes to terms with what happened." She hesitated briefly, her eyes searching Sarah's face. "You can help me a great deal, if you would. That's one reason I wanted to come here with you."

When Sarah did not reply, Lily tried to make her understand. "I don't know if Hannah has mentioned this to you, Mrs. Delaney, but I was born with a special gift that allows me to sense things that others cannot. When I held your cane in my hands the first day I met you, I knew you loved Harte and were trying to protect him from something, but I couldn't quite see what it was. If you tell me the truth, perhaps I can help you both come to terms with Camillia's death."

"Dear God," Sarah whispered hoarsely, her face slowly draining of color. "You must not pry into the past, Lily. I beg you. Camillia is long dead. She died in a terrible accident. Let her rest in peace, or you'll only make things worse."

Sarah limped quickly down the gallery, her cane clicking on the marble tiles. Lily sighed, realizing that she would get no help from Harte's grandmother. Turning away from the long line of portraits, she looked out into the distance, where she could see the ocean glittering deep blue beneath mounds of white cumulus clouds. Perhaps Sarah was right. If delving into Camillia's death would cause Harte more pain, Lily shouldn't have come to The Oaks at all.

Even as she strove to push thoughts of the Mexican girl from her mind, the sunshine-bright room suddenly grew darker from the onrush of a dreaming, and she shivered. The air around her seemed cold and dank and then *she was walking down a corridor, it was the one on the third floor of The Oaks, where the staircase ended. She could feel the crimson-and-gold carpet beneath her feet, but she was barefoot and cold and sad, so terribly, horribly frightened, deep inside her heart. She felt so alone as she entered a small room at the back of the house—felt the tears running down her face as she approached a small kneeling bench set before a picture of Jesus and the holy mother—she knelt there praying for peace of mind, praying that Harte would not stop loving her—lifting her gold crucifix and pressing it against her lips—*Dio por favor, *have pity on me—*

Lily opened her eyes, and, gripped by a sudden, unreasoning sense of doom, she rushed out the nearest set of French doors, anxious to be free of the ghosts in the long gallery where Harte's ancestors stared at her from their portraits. Out on the lawn, she came to a stop against the stone balustrade and lifted her face to the warmth of the sun, trying to dispel the cold foreboding that had taken hold of her.

* * *

Later that night in Harte's childhood bedchamber on the second floor of the east wing facing the ocean, she sat before a pink-marble fireplace, her thoughts relentlessly returning to Harte's first wife. She knew so little about her, only that her memory was still with him, preventing him from being a part of his own family.

What devils could have driven Camillia to take her own life? Or had it been an accident, as Sarah professed? What had really happened that long-ago day? Lily sighed, praying that Harte would come and face his past so he could rid himself of the guilt buried so deep in his soul.

Distant thunder rumbled, echoing in a hollow drumroll over the roof of the mansion. Earlier that afternoon Lily had watched a strange, low bank of fog roll in off the horizon, like a misty carpet being spread over the land. The wind stirring the curtains hung heavy with the damp smell of impending rain.

"It's gonna storm awful bad tonight, Miss Lily," Birdie chirped in her high-pitched voice. Glancing timidly at the windows as lightning flared, she nervously twisted her fingers together. "Can I's sleep here in de sittin' room instead of goin' all de way up to de servants' attic? It be a long way through all sorts of dark halls, and Mr. Beeker, de butler, done turned down all the lights. I's scairt of storms and lightning. Dat's when de ghosts roam."

"Of course, if you like," Lily agreed, pleased

that Sarah Delaney had assigned Birdie as Lily's chambermaid.

While Birdie fetched crisp white sheets and a soft patchwork quilt from a chifforobe in the dressing closet, Lily changed quickly into a warm nightgown and used the stepstool to climb onto the high tester bed. While Birdie hurried around the room, yawning as she extinguished one gaslight after another, Lily relaxed against the pillows and stared at the golden threads of the burgundy-brocade cover gleaming in the light of the candle she had left burning beside the bed.

"Have you ever heard anyone talk about Mr. Harte's first wife, Birdie? The one named Camillia?" she asked, glancing at the window as the first drops began to hit the panes with a loud patter.

"Yes'm," Birdie whispered, drawing up close and looking around in fright. "Dey say she walks and weeps when de rain and wind is howlin' and it be stormin' like it be tonight."

Birdie's eyes looked very round and white in her dark face. She crept to the foot of the bed and shivered so violently that the tightly woven braids all over her head shook. "My cousin Jed done saw her once out in de graveyard at de top of de cliffs. She showed up when de lightning flashed, and she want him to come and jump off and kill hisself like she done, but he din't. Instead, he ran as fast as de wind, and he neber came back here no mo'."

Had Camillia really appeared as a ghost

here? Lily wondered. Had she come back to haunt the halls of the house where she had been so unhappy? Perhaps she would roam tonight because of the storm. Lily had seen apparitions before, sometimes in her dreams and sometimes when she was fully awake. The ability was yet another facet of her sixth sense, and it had terrified her when she was a child. As she grew older, however, she learned that the ghostly visions never harmed her, so she was no longer afraid of them. But what an awful fate for the girl named Camillia, she thought, to be forced to spend eternity in the very place that she had committed suicide to escape.

For a long time after Birdie was snoring contentedly under her quilts on the windowseat cushions, Lily lay wide-eyed, listening to the rain sluicing in windblown waves against the windowpanes and wishing that Harte were there to hold her in his arms and take away the chill in her heart.

# 24

Harte walked his mount up the brick-paved driveway of his ancestral estate, pulled back on the reins, and gazed up at the house he had not seen for nearly a decade. With some dismay, he realized that he had missed The Oaks more than he had ever imagined. Stricken by bittersweet memories of more innocent days, he scrutinized every inch of the great facade.

Above the front door on the balustraded balcony that led off the second-floor landing, three gigantic copper urns were filled with yellow tulips and white alyssum—his grandmother's favorite flowers. James, the gardener, who had been with the Delaneys since before Harte was born, would have brought the bulbs out of the hothouse on the first day of April, just as he had done every year since Harte could remember.

Absently winding the leather reins around a brass hitching ring shaped like a ram's head, Harte inhaled a deep, steadying breath. He hadn't wanted to come home—still didn't want to—but he didn't have a hell of a lot of choice. Not if he wanted Lily back with him. And he did want that, more than anything.

When he had arrived in Georgetown and found his house closed up and deserted, he had been shocked, then angry and disappointed. He had missed his wife's departure by a week, and when he found Lily's letter, begging him to come fetch her from Newport, there was never any doubt that he would do so. Now that the war was over and the conspirators involved in the Lincoln assassination caught and ready for trial, all he wanted was to start over again. He wanted a fresh beginning for a new, peaceful life with Lily and their child.

Over the years he had been alone, always moving from one dangerous assignment to another, his emotions had atrophied into a hard knot of dispassion. Lily had softened those long dead feelings with her love and sweetness. She had opened his eyes to a great many things, but still there was an acid burning inside his soul.

His guilt over Camillia's death was always with him. His resentment toward his grandmother was always with him. Lily was right. The time had come to exorcise the demons driving him, but now that he stood upon the portal of his past, he wasn't sure he could bring himself to face it.

A red-breasted robin flitted from the limb of a budding oak tree and lit on the marble balustrade beside him. Preening and ruffling her soft brown feathers, the bird erupted in a joyous trill as Harte slowly climbed the massive stairs to the columned portico. Ignoring the heavy gold knocker, he stared at the crimson stained-glass panels set with a giant capital D. He turned the doorknob and stepped back into his youth.

Images, memories, overpowering emotions slammed like a piston into his mind, bringing him to a standstill on the dais just inside the door. Everything looked exactly as it had the last time he had walked out the door, but that didn't surprise him. Nothing ever changed at The Oaks.

Sarah Delaney was, and always had been, a traditionalist. The plush furnishings and ornate decor that had been established and added to by countless generations of Delaneys had remained constant under Sarah's firm reign. Although religiously cleaned and refurbished every spring on the first day of June, the old-fashioned rooms with their antique furniture would never be updated or redecorated, at least not during his grandmother's lifetime.

The mingling scents of lemon oil and fragrant red roses artfully arranged in the silver urn beside the door filled his senses and sent his mind into a plunge down the slippery slopes of the past. He and Stuart had used the wide black-marble banisters of the grand staircase as a hair-raisingly steep slide on rainy days, much to the delight of giggling housemaids who had never reported their naughty behavior to Grandmother Sarah.

In a vivid burst of recollection, he saw Cassandra when she was three years old, standing at the bottom of the stairs, her angelic face set in a scowl of childish dismay. She had stomped her foot and cried because she wasn't tall enough to climb on the balustrade with her older brothers. That was before his father had died and his mother had seen fit to go off and leave him behind like some unwanted dog.

Harte gritted his teeth as the pain made his chest ache. He would never forget the way he had felt as he had run from room to room looking for his mother. But he had found neither her nor his brother and sister. They had left—lock, stock, and barrel, without even a forgotten handkerchief scented with his mother's perfume or one of Stuart's socks to remind Harte that he had truly had a family.

Wind currents from the open fanlight above his head tinkled through the hanging chandelier and made him think of Camillia. The first time she had entered The Oaks, she had stood where Harte did now, her hair covered with a black-lace mantilla, the trappings of wealth around her totally alien to her upbringing within a simple adobe dwelling in the Mexican countryside. First astonishment had filled her large, dark eyes, then tears—the beginning of many that she would shed in his grandmother's mansion by the sea. She had left him too, like his mother, but in a different way.

That had been his own fault. His and Sarah Delaney's.

Harte's rage sparked and rekindled deep within his soul. He fought against allowing it to take over his mind, then let it go as Lily came rushing into sight from a side hall.

"Harte!" she cried, running across the tiles toward him and flinging herself into his arms. He caught her up against him, his throat closing with joy. He shut his eyes and savored the pleasure of touching her again.

"Oh, Harte, I've missed you so much I could barely stand it," she murmured breathlessly against his chest. "I was beginning to fear you weren't coming." She pulled back from his embrace, anxiety shadowing her beautiful golden eyes. "Are you angry with me? Do you understand why I came here?"

"Only because it took me three extra damn days to get to you." He smiled down at her, thinking she was even more beautiful than he remembered. "Do you feel all right now? Have you been seeing the doctor?"

"Yes, and he says I'm just fine. He thinks the baby's all right, too. Isn't that wonderful?"

Harte hugged her closer and laid his cheek on her soft golden hair. He had been worried about her. He was still concerned. Lily was so small and slight. He couldn't imagine her being able to bear him a child. Suddenly every muscle in his body tensed and held. He saw his grandmother descending the stairs. Deep-rooted, bitter resentment surfaced in his heart and surged through his blood.

"Hello, Harte," she said in her well-remembered, cultured accent; it was a voice he had never expected to hear again.

Lily drew back slightly, then looked up at him beseechingly. "Sarah's been so kind to me, Harte," she whispered softly. "She's made me feel very much at home here. Truly she has."

Harte nodded, but his eyes remained riveted on the woman on the steps. She looked different, much older than the day he had left. Now her hair was completely white; before it had only been peppered with gray. The old-fashioned coiffure was the same, though—parted down the middle into two elegant wings that swept back into that tight bun. She looked as gracious and genteel as ever, nothing like a woman cruel enough to drive an innocent young girl to suicide.

"Come, darling, let's go into the sitting room," Lily was saying brightly. "Your grandmother and I were just getting ready to have afternoon tea. I know you must be tired. Did you ride all the way here?"

"I took a train to Newport, then hired a mount from a livery," he answered, allowing her to lead him through the sliding doors into the small sun porch. The sight of the yellow-and-pink floral fabric covering the overstuffed couch and rockers affected him more than anything he had seen thus far at The Oaks.

The cozy, sun-bright room had been his

mother's favorite retreat in his grandmother's mansion. She had held him on her lap by the windows and told him stories about the beauty of Twin Pines while she rocked him. She had loved her Virginia plantation much more than she had ever loved him, and she had returned there as soon as she could. He had never seen her again.

Ancient hurt tried to escape the tight bands of anger he had wrapped around his emotions the day he had found that she was gone. He had hidden under the round table in the corner and wept silent tears while his grandmother and her army of servants had searched the house for him.

"Have you been well? Has your wounded arm given you any more trouble?" Lily asked, drawing him down beside her on a soft, deeply cushioned settee.

"I'm well enough."

Harte watched his grandmother take a seat on her favorite straight-backed velvet chair, the one he had always thought of as her throne. Agitated in her presence, he stood and propped his elbow on the carved mantel. The tension in the room was so thick he could almost reach out and touch it.

"The newspapers have reported that the army has caught all the conspirators now," his grandmother said to him. "Is that true?"

"Yes. John Wilkes Booth was shot and killed inside the barn at the Garrett farm on April

26. His fellow conspirators are incarcerated in the Old Penitentiary and awaiting trial."

"Cassie and Derek weren't involved, were they?" Lily asked warily.

"No, thank God. I suspect they've reached Melbourne by now. According to my sources, the Kapirigis are with them."

"Cassandra always was a headstrong child," his grandmother remarked. "I wasn't the least bit surprised to find her working for the Confederates."

"She was doing what she believed in, be it right or wrong," Harte said sharply in his sister's defense.

His grandmother did not reply, but lapsed into silence, something she never would have done eight years ago. Lily looked upset at the way the conversation was going, and all Harte wanted was to be alone with his wife.

"I'm too tired for tea," he said tersely. "I'd like to rest for a while and be alone with Lily."

"Of course," his grandmother said, with a gracious nod. "I do hope you'll feel up to dining with me this evening. Cook is preparing all your favorite foods. How long do you plan to stay?"

"Not long. The conspirators' trial started on May 9. I'd like to be back to hear the verdict."

"I see." His grandmother's expression didn't waver. "I am very pleased that you've come home at last, Harte," she murmured quietly. "We've all missed you terribly."

Her verbal display of affection shocked him.

It was rare indeed for his controlled, self-contained grandmother to reveal any kind of personal feelings. Perhaps she had changed—but he really didn't give a damn. He had come to The Oaks to get Lily. That was the only reason.

"I've been staying in your old room," Lily said, as she walked down the upstairs hallway hand in hand with her husband. She was so happy to have him back that she couldn't stop smiling. And he had been relatively civil to Sarah. Coming to The Oaks and seeing his grandmother couldn't have been easy for him, but she knew how important a step it was in ridding him of the hatred that made him so bitter. The moment they entered the bed-chamber, he shut the door, then pressed her back against it.

"God in heaven, I've missed you," he muttered gruffly, his fingers working loose the pearl buttons at the front of her bodice. "I want you so much I can't think straight."

Lily smiled, trying to help him undress her, but he was in far too much of a hurry. He swung her into his arms and carried her to the bed. He pushed her back on the pillows and dropped down on top of her, holding her face and kissing her passionately until her body grew hot and limp.

His lips were warm and firm and commanding, molding themselves to her mouth with fiery possession. His tongue sought hers, found it, and elicited breathless moans from deep within her throat as he fingered loose the tiny buttons and satin bows of her undergarments. Finally Lily lay naked and writhing, awaiting his pleasure.

"Oh, God, you don't know how many nights I've lain awake thinking about you," he breathed, rising on his knees and jerking his shirt over his head.

"Yes, I do," she whispered, breathlessly watching as he unbuckled his belt and rid himself of his trousers. Moments later, he came back into her eager arms and drew her body tight against the hard muscles of his chest.

"I don't want to hurt you or the baby," he whispered, still kissing her, his voice hoarsened with need, "but God knows I want you right now more than anything I've ever wanted."

"Don't stop," Lily murmured breathlessly. "I can't bear it if you do."

Harte laughed softly, his mouth coming down on hers again, and when she tightened her arms around his neck and arched up to meet him, his eager kisses intensified until they were clinging hungrily to each other, anxiously, desperately, as if they were drowning in each other. Lily met his desire with unchecked abandon, lolling her head back as he pulled her to her knees where he could nuzzle her naked breasts. She cried out when his lips closed over one desire-hardened nipple.

Her chest heaving with the need to have him inside her again, for them to become one, man and woman, husband and wife, Lily clutched his head against her breasts, sliding her hand through his thick dark curls, then clenching her fingers in the softness of his hair as he pushed her back against the pillows. His lips moved lower, burning a path down her quivering belly. The pleasure was so acute that she cried out, then his mouth was covering her lips once more, the gentle caress of his fingers bringing every inch of her body to a raw, raging fever.

Harte suddenly rolled onto his back, bringing Lily astride him, and she braced her palms on the swirls of hair covering his muscular chest. She wet her dry lips as he raised her and brought her down on him, the mere act of their joining after so long sending exquisite, rippling chills over her flesh in endless, tingling waves of sensation.

"Oh, my God, Harte," she managed, biting her lower lip as his hands encircled her waist and helped her to move in rhythm with each slow thrust. She had missed him so much. Her head arched back, her eyes closed in ecstasy. She had missed his touch, the feel of his hands on her body, the strength of his muscles, the clean, masculine scent of his skin and hair, everything about him.

"I love you, Lily," he breathed hoarsely. At last. The words she had never before heard him utter. She wept with joy because he had finally said them. Slowly, with gentle, tender passion, he moved within her, his words of love sweet in her ear as they climbed together to the very brink of the stars, to a paradise where they were forged into one with the heat of a thousand suns, their love consummated, as cherished as the babe forming inside her womb.

# 25

The sharp report of a gunshot woke Harte with a start. Sensing danger, he slapped at his right thigh in a frantic search for his revolver, but almost at once he realized that the noise had been a shutter banging against the house. His pulse was still racing with adrenaline, and he reached out for Lily's soft warmth to relax his tight muscles. When he found that he was alone in the bed, he frowned and sat up.

The large bedchamber was shrouded with the smoky-pearl shadows of dawn, but Lily was nowhere to be seen. Across from him, the velvet draperies billowed wildly into the room. The louvered shutter slammed again, and Harte tossed back the covers and strode naked to the windows.

The ocean breeze felt cold and damp against his bare skin, and he inhaled deeply in the crisp air as he leaned forward to grasp the handle of the shutter. A movement on the lawn below caught his eye, and he peered down at the figure moving slowly through swirling patches of low-hanging, early-morning mist.

Oh, God, it was Lily. Fingers of fear closed tightly around his heart. She was heading straight toward the walkway that ran parallel to the edge of the cliffs. What the devil was she doing outside? Didn't she realize how dangerous the cliffs were in the fog?

Bracing his palms on the windowsill, he yelled her name, but the gusts hurled his words up and away from him. He jerked on his trousers and boots, flung open the door, and sprinted down the hallway. He took the stairs three at a time, and by the time he burst out of the doors of the portrait gallery, he knew intuitively that something horrible was going to happen.

If Lily went too far out on the crumbling ledges or if she lost her way and took a step in the wrong direction, she could plummet to her death—just like Camillia had! He had to get to her first! Fear took total possession of his mind as he raced down the gravel path. He could hear the roar of the ocean now. The gigantic waves boiled and crashed against jagged rocks hidden in the dense fog far below. Then he saw her—standing at the very brink of the precipice.

"Lily, stop! Wait for me!"

To his relief, Lily heard his cries. She turned and smiled, the sea breeze molding her diaphanous silk nightgown to the slender curves of her body. Harte breathed easier as she took a step toward him, but then another person materialized out of the clinging gray mist—

Who was it? Oh, God, it was his grandmother, and she was trying to push Lily over the edge! Harte tried to move, tried to get to her, but his feet seemed mired in frozen mud, and then Lily went over backward, falling, falling down through the murky grayness, and Harte screamed her name in pure, mindless horror.

"Harte! Harte, what's wrong?"

His chest heaving with his labored breathing, Harte opened terrified eyes and found Lily's concerned face just above him. Slowly he became aware of the mattress under his back and the cool kiss of the breeze as it gently stirred the crimson-velvet bedhangings.

He lurched upright and dragged both trembling palms down over his face. He tried desperately to get a hold on his shattered emotions, but when Lily laid a consoling hand upon his bare back, he grabbed her close against him, clutching her tightly, never wanting to let her go.

"Oh, Lily, I had the most god-awful dream about you. I saw you go over the cliffs, and it was just so damn real—" His voice caught and failed him, and he forced down the ragged feelings that surged up in the back of his throat as he stroked her long, soft hair.

"I'm fine, darling. It was just a nightmare, that's all," she whispered, resting her cheek against his chest.

"Promise me you won't go out on the cliff walk alone," he demanded harshly, holding her out from him, his fingers biting tightly into her upper arms. "Tell me you won't, Lily."

"I won't, I promise."

Still tense, Harte released her and got shakily to his feet. He shut the open windows so he couldn't hear the distant roar of the waves crashing against the rocks. He went over to the fireplace, where they had left the dinner tray that Hannah had brought up the night before. With unsteady hands, he splashed wine into one of the goblets. The streak of fire that the liquor burned down his gullet was a welcome sensation, and he looked back at Lily, kneeling on the bed and watching him with concern.

"I'm sorry, baby," he muttered thickly. "Go on back to sleep. I'm all right now."

"Are you sure?" she asked as he jerkily poured himself another stiff drink.

"Yeah. It was just so real—" Words failed him as he relived the dreadful moment when Lily lost her footing and disappeared into the thick gray fog as he stood unable to help her. The same awful feeling of powerlessness assailed him, and he grimaced as he tipped the glass to his mouth again.

Lily climbed down from the high bed and slipped her arms into the sleeves of her dark-blue velvet robe. "Do you want to talk about it, Harte?"

When she reached his place by the fire, Harte sat down on the silk settee and pulled her close beside him. He lifted her hand and pressed her soft palm against his lips. "I thought I'd lost you."

Lily smiled and traced her fingertips down his lean jaw. "You mustn't worry about me. We'll grow old together. I've seen it in my dreamings."

Unrelieved by her assurances, Harte rested his head against the sofa cushion. His mind was still caught in a whirling turmoil; his stomach was still churning. He should never have returned to The Oaks, he thought. Coming back to his grandmother's mansion had been a mistake.

"I don't want to stay here, Lily. This place gets to me. I know you meant well, but it's not going to work. Too much has gone on between Grandmother and me for us to forgive and forget. I was willing to try, but hell, she was the one in my dream who pushed you off the cliff. I guess that shows you how much I trust her."

"Perhaps you had the nightmare because you hold her responsible for Camillia's death," Lily whispered gently. "I think you probably also still blame her for driving your mother away from here and leaving you behind. Am I right, Harte? Do you?"

"I don't want to talk about my mother or Camillia," Harte said in a terse dismissal of the subject, rising to his feet and moving a few steps away. He propped his arm on the mantel and stared into the glowing embers.

Lily remained silent for a moment. "There's some kind of mystery surrounding Camillia's death. I've sensed it strongly from the day I came here with your grandmother."

Surprised by her unexpected remark, Harte turned quickly and studied her. "What do you mean?"

"I don't know. Sarah won't discuss Camillia either, but I know she's burdened by a terrible guilt about something to do with you. I also think she's desperate to make things right between you."

"Did she tell you that?"

"No, but I've known it since the day she came to visit me in Georgetown. I held her cane in my hand—you know, the ivory one she always carries with her—and I felt her remorse so strongly that I knew I had to try to help her set things right."

Lily paused, beseeching him with a look in her beautiful amber eyes that Harte found difficult to resist. "You suffer too, Harte, just as much as she does. That's why I came here. So the two of you could realize all the terrible agony you've put each other through. You haven't been back here since Camillia's death, have you? You and Sarah have never sat down together and tried to talk about what happened. I feel certain that's what you need to do before you can put it behind you."

"There's not a chance in hell that that's ever going to happen."

"Please, Harte. Sarah's your grandmother. She's the only family you have left now other than Cassie and—"

"I said no, goddammit!"

After Harte's angry outburst, Lily lapsed into silence. Harte set his jaw. Suddenly all he wanted was to get away from Lily and her painful talk of his mother and Camillia.

"I need some air," he said, hurriedly jerking on his pants. He put on his shirt and avoided Lily's eyes as he fastened the buttons. "I'll be back in time to take you down to breakfast."

Even though Harte knew Lily would be hurt by his abrupt departure, he left. He needed to be alone, to wrestle into submission the devils that his nightmare had released from the darkest dungeons of his mind.

Later that morning, when Harte returned from his long walk along the beach, Lily saw that he had recovered his composure. He had obviously put his bad dream into perspective and had once more taken refuge behind the impassive mask of aloof indifference that he had worn so often when they had first met.

When they paused at the threshold of the dining parlor on their way to breakfast, Lily put a tentative hand on his arm. "I know you're still angry with Sarah, but please try to make an effort to be civil. Would you do that? Please, for me?"

Harte didn't look overjoyed with her request. "I suppose I can be pleasant while we're here, which won't be long. The sooner we get out of this damned house, the better."

Lily wasn't sure at all that he could bring

himself to be nice to his grandmother, even if he wanted to. The angry slant of his jaw revealed his animosity. "I think you're wrong about Sarah. I get the feeling she's trying to protect you, but I can't figure out what she could be afraid of."

"And I think that, for once, your instincts are dead wrong," he replied, as he slid open the white double doors. "When you get to know Sarah better, you'll see that she's very good at making people think the things she wants them to. The truth is that she brought you up here to Newport because she wants you as an ally against me. She hopes to use you to get me back here where I can do her bidding. But it's not going to work. I know her too well."

Lily sighed as they entered the long, spacious dining room. A gigantic fieldstone fireplace stretched across the south end; on the north side of the structure, a two-story expanse of bay windows opened upon a panoramic view of the Atlantic Ocean. A mirror-surfaced table of richly polished cherry and oak parquet was designed to accommodate fifty or more people, but at the moment it had only three settings of glittering gold-rimmed navy-blue china and long-stemmed crystal goblets arranged on fine oyster-colored lace mats. In the warmth of the sunny windows, Sarah Delaney was already seated in a special straight-backed wing chair covered in a navy-and-gold floral chintz that matched the handsome curtains.

"Good morning," Sarah said politely after Harte and Lily had walked the length of the room to join her. "Good morning," Lily murmured while Harte assisted her with her chair.

"I'm very pleased that you decided to breakfast with me," Sarah remarked with a wary glance at Harte. "I missed you at supper."

"We're sorry we didn't come down last night," Lily replied hastily, realizing that Harte wasn't about to respond to his grandmother's amenities, "but we had a lot of things to catch up on."

Lily felt heat rise in her cheeks to think exactly what those things were and how soon and how often they had caught up on them once Harte had gotten her alone in their bedchamber. She lowered her eyes as a sensual shiver crept up her spine.

Harte said nothing but merely took the chair across from Lily. A tense, oppressive silence enveloped the table like a heavy cloud of gloom.

Harte's bitterness was ruling him now, Lily thought sadly. Sarah was eager for a reconciliation, but Harte just didn't seem able to forgive her. Both of them surely ached inside from their years of estrangement. How much longer would they let it continue?

Lily looked up at her husband and felt pure love flow from her heart. He was leaning back in his chair, waiting while Birdie heaped a portion of fluffy scrambled eggs on his plate. This was yet another facet of him, she realized, deciding that he looked very much the rich aristocrat now in his fine slate-gray frock coat, with matching vest and spotless white-silk shirt. He was very comfortable indeed in the luxurious surroundings of a mansion like The Oaks. He certainly no longer resembled the tough, hard-faced man who had worn a leather vest and a strapped-down gun and had fought off Ringer's dingoes during their harrowing escape down the river.

Harte had changed so much since those first few days, and for the better, but she knew in her heart he could never truly be happy until he let go of the pain and hatred that burned like a live coal within him. Perhaps if they stayed at The Oaks for a while, and he saw how hard Sarah was trying to make amends, he might relent.

Lily was glad when Sarah made another verbal attempt to ease the strained atmosphere. "I suppose you're very happy to have Harte home with you again, Lily."

"Oh, yes, it's wonderful," Lily answered, smiling at her husband.

More unsettling quiet ensued as breakfast continued without conversation, other than occasional requests for Birdie to refill their coffee cups or replenish their plates.

"Do you have any idea how long you'll be able to stay, Harte?" his grandmother asked at length, looking directly at her grandson in an obvious effort to force a response from him.

"We'll be leaving as soon as Lily can get her things together and feels up to the trip home," he answered, reaching out to pick up an iced glass of fresh juice.

Sarah looked surprised. "But Lily's only been here a week," she pointed out quickly, "and I haven't been able to show her the estate because my gout has been so painful. Please, won't you consider staying a bit longer? Lily and I have hardly had time to become acquainted."

"I'm not sure I want the two of you to become better acquainted. I'm not sure our marriage could stand it."

"Harte!" Lily cried, dismayed at Harte's cruel taunt.

"Please don't concern yourself on my behalf, Lily. I'm well aware of my grandson's hostility toward me," Sarah replied with her usual benign graciousness. She turned her full attention back to Harte. "Since you're leaving so soon, I do hope you'll take a few minutes to meet with Mr. Criles and my other solicitors. They've readied several sets of papers which require your signature."

"What kind of papers?"

"Legal documents concerning my will and the eventual distribution of the Delaney estate and properties abroad."

"I'm not interested in the Delaney money. I

thought I made that clear to you a long time ago."

For the first time, Sarah's calm demeanor slipped a degree. "Whether you like it or not, Harte, you are my sole heir." She swept her black-silk-clad arm in a gesture that encompassed the mansion and the manicured grounds sweeping off toward the cliffs. "All this will be yours upon my death. You need to be aware of the particulars and the legal responsibilities concerning ownership. I haven't bothered you with family business for over eight years, so surely you can grant me a single hour of your time before you return to Washington."

"I don't want anything from you," Harte reiterated with slow, succinct scorn.

Sarah arched an eyebrow. "What about your wife and your unborn child? Are you so cavalier about throwing away Lily's future security and the birthright of your children?"

"Believe it or not, Grandmother, Lily didn't marry me for my money or for your empire. But I suspect her lack of greed is just a little too hard for you to comprehend, isn't it?"

"Oh, Harte, please," Lily murmured, shifting in her chair with embarrassment as their words became more heated and quarrelsome.

Harte's dark brows came together in a deep frown. "I'm going to spend the day with Lily. Perhaps later on this afternoon, I'll find a few minutes to meet with your lawyers."

"Thank you, Harte. I do appreciate your time," his grandmother said with a regal nod of her head. "I'll be in conference with them all afternoon in your grandfather's library. Please feel free to join us whenever you wish."

Harte threw down his napkin as if annoyed with the conversation. He stood and looked at Lily. "If you're finished with breakfast, I thought we'd take a walk in the gardens."

"All right," Lily said at once, eager to escape the disastrous meal.

But as Harte took her arm and led her away from his grandmother's table, she could sense the anger and resentment that his discussion with Sarah Delaney had set off within him. A reconciliation between them was going to be very hard to accomplish, if it could be managed at all.

# 26

Harte led Lily down the hedge-lined, graveled walkway of the elaborately landscaped rose garden, well aware by her silence that she was disappointed with his behavior during the morning meal. Despite his intention to be polite to Sarah for Lily's sake, once he found himself actually facing his grandmother across the breakfast table, he hadn't been able to hide his true feelings. Now Lily was upset with him, and he didn't like being at odds with her on his first day home.

When they reached the circular rose bed that formed the hub of the wheel-shaped gardens overlooking the sea, he guided Lily toward a shady arbor planted with a spectacular display of giant yellow roses.

"Why don't we sit down for a moment and enjoy the view?" he suggested, taking a seat on one of the stone benches in the shade of the fragrant, rose-adorned trellis. Instead of joining him there, Lily strolled a little way down the path to a point where she could look far out over the glittering blue ocean. The wind was caressing the long golden curls that she'd left loose and unbound to tumble down her back. Watching her where she stood facing away from him, the hem of her pale blue skirt billowing in the wind, his vivid nightmare welled up in his mind. He fought off the chill that swept through him.

"You're angry with me, aren't you?" he asked, approaching her from behind and wrapping his arms around her.

"No, I'm not angry," she replied. She sighed and relaxed into his embrace as he pulled her back against his chest. "I just don't think you're giving Sarah much of a chance to redeem herself. There, see what I mean, Harte? Your body tensed at the mere mention of her name. I could feel it."

Harte couldn't deny his reaction. "You don't understand, Lily. I've felt this way for years. I can't just switch off my emotions to please you."

Lily turned quickly in his arms. "I know you can't, but I want to understand how you feel. Tell me. Let me help you come to terms with what happened between you and Sarah."

Harte didn't want to talk about it, not to Lily or anyone else, but she continued to search his face, her beautiful eyes troubled. "The past remains constant, Lily. There's no use trying to change it."

"Of course, you can't change it, darling, but you can accept it. I think if we could find out what it is that Sarah's hiding from us, everything else would eventually fall into place. You need to ask her to tell you the truth, Harte. I know that's the answer."

With a sigh, Harte released his wife and took a step away, wishing she would just drop the subject. He looked out over the whitecaps curling and breaking on their inward rush to shore and longed for the gentle turquoise surf that washed the coral beaches of Moon Cove. He and Lily had been happy there, with no worries to plague them. The weeks they had spent in the idyllic glade had been like paradise on earth, just as she had once said. He found himself wanting that peaceful contentment again. He wanted Lily all to himself. Suddenly he decided that's where they would go, as soon as he could arrange a furlough.

"You know, Harte, when Strassman murdered Papa"—Lily's voice caught pitiably and Harte turned to look at her—"I had trouble accepting that he was really gone until I actually saw his gravestone. Somehow seeing his name carved there for all eternity made me accept that he wasn't ever coming back. That's when I decided that I had to come to America and find Derek." She paused, studying his face with imploring eyes. "Perhaps that's what you need to do. Camillia's buried here on the estate, isn't she? Maybe if you could go to her grave, it would help you put to rest some of the blame and guilt. It helped me so much, even though it was very painful too—"

Tears had welled in her eyes as she talked

about her father, and when she fumbled for her handkerchief, Harte enfolded her against him. He held her tight, unable to bear the pain in her voice.

"All right, we'll go there now, if you think it will help," he murmured in an effort to appease her, even though he knew visiting Camillia's gravesite would do nothing to lessen his resentment toward Sarah. His grandmother bore half the responsibility for Camillia's death, and nothing or no one could ever change that.

"Really, Harte?" Lily asked in surprise, her lips curving into a tentative smile.

"Yes. The family mausoleum and cemetery are not far from here, just beyond that thicket of trees over there. We'll go now if you feel up to it, but after that, I think you should return to the house and rest for a while. You've been on your feet all morning."

"But the doctor's been encouraging me to get plenty of exercise," Lily told him, and she looked so pleased and happy that Harte was glad he had agreed to the idea. Maybe she was right. Perhaps he could put Camillia's ghost to rest if he saw her tomb. Deep in his heart, however, he didn't think it would make any difference at all.

After a leisurely stroll through a shady grove of oak trees, they reached the waist-high, gray-stone wall that surrounded the family cemetery. Generations of his Delaney ancestry had been laid to rest beneath the elaborately carved tombstones set with graceful Grecian urns cascading with green ivy or under towering statues of praying angels with outspread wings.

Harte opened the spiked iron gate for Lily, and the squeak of the rusty hinges brought back the memory of the last time he had stepped onto this hallowed ground. He had been seven years old on that windy, overcast January day. His mother had taken to her bed, too distraught to walk with the other mourners behind his father's shiny black casket set with silver handles. Sarah Delaney had been the one who had taken Harte's small hand firmly in her gloved fingers, and together they had led the sorrowful procession to the cemetery.

"Do you know where Camillia would have been laid to rest?" Lily asked gently, bringing him out of his somber reverie.

"No. I never asked."

Lily gazed up at him. "Is this too painful for you, Harte? Do you want to leave? If you do, I'll understand."

Harte shook his head. Too much time had passed for him to be affected by anything other than remorse. Now, so many years later, he only felt sad for Camillia and ashamed of the way he had treated her. "We're here now. Let's go through with it. I suspect she would have been buried somewhere near my father and grandfather. Come, I'll show you the way."

Taking Lily's elbow, he guided her down the

brick path through the well-tended graves that surrounded the central mausoleum of pure white marble. Just past the pillars at the entrance of the crypt, near the spot where his grandmother had ordered a lush display of climbing red roses to be planted along the wrought-iron fence surrounding his grandfather's grave, he saw an unfamiliar headstone.

"That must be it," he said, stopping with Lily at the foot of the grave. Silently, he stared down at the simple words of the epitaph chiseled in flowing script on the graceful obelisk.

CAMILLIA GUITIERREZ DELANEY
BELOVED WIFE OF HARTE
BORN 1840
DIED 1857

Only seventeen, he thought, then was ashamed when he felt nothing other than guilt. He had liked Camillia very much. He had respected her courage and her gentleness, but he had never really loved her, not the way he loved Lily. He should never have married Camillia and left her behind to die alone and unhappy in a foreign land where she was so miserable. He would regret doing so for the rest of his life.

"Are you all right, Harte?" Lily asked softly. "What are you feeling?"

"I feel sorry that she had to die so young and for no reason."

"Would it bother you if I touched the headstone and tried to find out more about her death? If you think it would, I won't do it."

"I don't like the idea of your putting yourself through another violent dreaming, Lily. We all know what happened to Camillia. There's no need for you to have to live through her suicide. It'll only upset you."

Lily's finely arched eyebrows drew together in a vague frown. "I realize that, but I just have the strongest sensation that I must do this. I don't know why I feel it's so important, but I do."

Harte hesitated briefly, but he knew she was determined to go through with it. "All right."

Harte watched Lily walk slowly away from him until she stood behind Camillia's grave. Suddenly wary of what kind of dark, macabre scene she might envision while standing on a grave, he felt his shoulder and neck muscles begin to bunch with tension. When he realized he was clenching his fists, he consciously relaxed his fingers.

Still facing him, Lily stopped behind the four-foot monument and rested her palms on the smooth marble sides of the obelisk. She shut her eyes and seemed to concentrate very hard, in the way that had become familiar to Harte. When they had first met, he had been fascinated when he watched her being claimed by one of her bizarre dreamings, but at the moment he found the process frightening. He was worried about how she would be affected by what she saw in her vision.

For several long moments Lily held tightly to the polished stone, her beautiful face in repose, her long, curling lashes cast down to form shadowy crescents against her cheeks. She showed no emotion, and Harte waited nervously for something to happen.

Suddenly Lily jerked her hands away as if the stone had burned her fingers. She opened her eyes. When Harte saw the terrible expression twisting her face, raw, unreasoning fear mushroomed in his chest. Frozen with dread, he waited for Lily to tell him what she had seen. Nothing in his wildest imagination could have prepared him for the words that she uttered through quivering lips.

"Camillia isn't here, Harte. She's never been in this grave. No one has."

Harte reeled under the impact as if he had been physically struck. He staggered back a step, confusion storming like a whirlwind that clouded all rational thought.

"What are you talking about?" he managed somehow.

Lily shook her head. "I don't know. I just know this grave is empty. There's no one buried here. Oh, my Lord, Harte, do you think she's still alive?"

Shocked speechless, Harte could only stare at her. Camillia alive? After all these years? Oh, God, if she was alive, somehow, some way, what would he do? He was married to Lily now. They were expecting a child.

"I don't believe it," he muttered, but God

help him, he did believe it. "Grandmother's behind this!" he exploded furiously. "And by God, she's going to tell me the truth if I have to shake it out of her."

Lily ran forward and gripped his arm to stop him. "No, Harte, wait. You're too angry now to speak with Sarah, and I don't think she'd tell you the truth anyway. Don't you see? This is what she's been hiding from us. But why would she do such a terrible thing?"

"She's got to tell us the truth! Don't you realize what it means to us if Camillia's alive? Oh, God, I can't believe this is happening!"

Lily's face blanched, and Harte knew when she put her palms to her rounded belly that she had just realized the ramifications of their dilemma.

"Don't worry, Lily," Harte said quickly. "I'm going to find out what the hell's going on and then do whatever it takes to make things right."

"Harte, wait. I think I might know a better way. Sarah could tell us anything, and we wouldn't know the difference. She could deny everything. But if I could hold something of Camillia's in my hands, perhaps I could see what really happened to her. Then we'd know the truth without having to confront Sarah."

"I don't have any of her things. Grandmother probably had them packed away or destroyed. I want to make her tell me the truth, dammit."

"Please, Harte, listen to me. I had a dreaming about Camillia the first day I came here. I saw her in a bedchamber up on the third floor. She was praying on a kneeling bench. I know I'd recognize the room if I saw it. Let's go there and see what we can find. Please, Harte, let me try this before you talk to Sarah!"

Harte took Lily's arm and led her away from the cemetery and toward the mansion. He was trying very hard to restrain himself, though more than anything in his life, he wanted to search out Sarah and vent the anger burning like acid through his veins. For years he had blamed himself and resented his grandmother for the way she had treated Camillia, but this was too much. Only a devil would do something like this to a member of her own family. And why? For God's sake, why?

Though they soon reached the dim recesses of the third-floor corridor, Lily still hadn't overcome the shock she had felt at the revelation that Camillia might still be alive. The idea was terrible and overwhelming, so dreadful in fact that she couldn't believe Sarah Delaney could actually have engineered such a deception. There could be no reasonable justification for lying to her own grandson about the death of his wife.

"Are you sure you saw her up here on the third floor? We haven't used this part of the house in years. The last time I was up here was when Stuart and I used to play hide-and-seek when we were little."

Lily nodded as she preceded Harte down the

hallway toward the back of the house. "I'm positive this was where she was walking. I saw everything very clearly. She wanted to come up here where she could be alone. She was very upset and unhappy."

A few minutes later Lily stopped outside a closed door. "This is the room, Harte. She went in here to pray."

For some reason a shiver coursed up Lily's spine, and she didn't want to be the one to go inside first. She stepped back and let Harte turn the doorknob. Half afraid of what they might discover, she peered around Harte as he entered before her.

"Nobody's been in here in years, that's for damn sure," he muttered, striding through the darkness to the heavily draped windows.

When Lily followed, the musty smell of age and dust permeated her nostrils, and she blinked as Harte jerked open the curtains and flooded the room with sunlight. All the furniture was covered with canvas sheets, but Lily immediately recognized the alcove where Camillia had knelt in her dreaming.

Walking straight to that corner, she pulled off the white sheet and found the black-velvet praying bench in its place against the wall. Above it, another sheet had been draped over a picture, and she tugged it loose and discovered the painting of Jesus and the children. Her nerves rippled with apprehension.

"You're right about the prayer bench, I see," Harte said with a frown as he came up behind her. He pulled off a few more dustcovers from the furniture, revealing a cherrywood four-poster bed and a matching chest. He slid open several of the drawers. "If Camillia did stay in here, Grandmother has seen fit to get rid of her things."

"She was so full of emotions when she prayed here that I think I can get something from her if I kneel on the bench where she was when she was so distraught."

"Are you sure you want to do this?" Harte asked.

Lily nodded, but inside she felt a moment of pure panic. Now that she knew that Camillia wasn't buried where she was supposed to be, she was afraid of what she might see. Swallowing hard, she knelt upon the bench and placed her palms on the Bible that still rested undisturbed on the stand.

Instantaneously, she was shaken by a great upheaval inside her head—storm winds swirling out of the black unknown in a tempest of sound and fury and dark, rushing air. Then she saw the cliffs out past the cemetery, and it was nighttime with a full moon glowing over the ocean and *she was waiting, waiting, her heart breaking, and then a man came out of the darkness . . . and came running toward her . . . it was Harte . . . no, he looked like Harte . . . he was young and bearded . . . his hair long and tied in a queue . . . she reached out to him, appealing to him to come to her . . . he took her into his arms and kissed her . . . and she wanted him to be Harte . . .*

"There's a man with her, out on the cliffs—" Then the misty scene faded into another time, another place—no, still on the cliffs, and . . . *she was standing on the very brink of the cliff . . . looking down at the roaring waves . . . crashing and breaking against the rocks below . . . clouds scudding before a storm . . . wind blowing wildly . . . the ocean dark and angry . . . then she was no longer alone, she was struggling, fighting to free herself . . . someone was gripping her arm, holding her against her will . . . terror . . . screaming . . . her crucifix was jerked hard and she felt the chain break and the cross slide off her neck . . . then she whirled and saw the person who was fighting her . . .*

Panting hard, her chest heaving, Lily came out of her trance and shot to her feet. Harte reached out to support her as her knees crumpled beneath her.

"I saw Camillia fighting with someone on the cliffs." Their eyes locked. Lily's lips trembled. "Oh, Harte, I think Sarah was trying to kill her."

# 27

Sarah Delaney sat beneath the vaulted oak beams of her spacious library, vaguely listening to the droning discourse of the six lawyers flanking her, three on each side of the long mahogany reading table. Her thoughts, however, kept returning to her grandson and his wife. Every few minutes she glanced longingly at the door, still hoping that Harte would willingly accept his responsibility as the Delaney heir.

As the hours drifted slowly past, she began to prepare herself for the eventuality that he wasn't going to come. In truth, she had feared that possibility after witnessing his open hostility to her at the breakfast table. Lily had tried her best to unite them, bless her kind heart. She had come to The Oaks, had enticed her husband to follow her, but now Sarah felt certain that Lily's good intentions were to no avail.

Careful to keep her posture erect and to give the outward appearance of attentiveness, Sarah mentally chastised herself for her lack of interest in the accounts of her vast business concerns being presented in a rambling report by the stodgy bald man sitting on her left.

Martin Criles was the senior partner of Criles and Deaton—the oldest, most prestigious solicitors' firm in the city of Newport—and she trusted him implicitly. He was a distant cousin of her late husband and had always been a good friend and confidant to her as well. Martin never failed to have her best interests at heart, and he had given her a wealth of fortuitous advice through the years when she had been forced to run the family businesses in Harte's stead.

Sarah started visibly in her high-backed Queen Anne wing chair as the door across the room suddenly swung open and banged loudly against the wall. She jerked her surprised gaze to the open doorway, where Harte now stood. His face was dark with a stormy expression that she knew well. His fists were planted on his lean hips, his every muscle rigid with contained rage. As Lily ran up behind him, a frightened expression on her face, Sarah tensed. An awful wave of foreboding washed over her.

"Grandmother, I want to talk to you," Harte said curtly, obviously holding himself in tight rein. "Now. In private."

The collective attention of the team of legal advisers shifted back to Sarah to read her reaction to Harte's rude interruption. Though her heart had iced over with dread, Sarah endeavored to retain her dignity. "Of course, Harte, if you wish. Gentlemen, please excuse me for the time being. My grandson wishes a private audience. We'll continue this meeting in ten minutes."

Martin Criles removed his thick horn-rimmed glasses and studied Harte with overt disapproval. Then he searched Sarah's face. "I would be happy to remain here with you, my dear, if you think you should need my presence."

"That won't be necessary, Mr. Criles," Harte answered tersely. "This is a private family matter, not a business question."

Sarah's pulse pounded with renewed fear. What could have transpired to plunge Harte into such a fury? She forced a gracious smile. "Thank you, Martin, but I think it would be best if you wait outside. My grandson is obviously quite upset."

An uncomfortable hush fell over the huge library as the lawyers gathered their papers, returned them to their matching black business satchels, and filed silently out past Harte and Lily.

After the door was closed behind them, Harte came forward. When Sarah saw the cold loathing in his eyes, she felt a shiver of alarm. Extremely wary, she waited for him to speak. Oh, Lord help them, had he found out the truth? Had Lily's strange intuition uncovered Sarah's terrible secrets?

"I want the truth about Camillia, Grandmother, and I want it now. She's not dead, is she?"

Stone-cold horror flooded Sarah's mind, paralyzing her limbs, but she forced herself to remain calm. He couldn't prove his accusations. She only had to deny everything.

"Why, Harte, I don't know what you're talking about. Of course, Camillia's dead. She has been for years—"

Harte slammed his fist down on the table in front of her so hard that the accounting ledgers jumped and the antique silver inkwell overturned. No one moved as the black ink pooled on a piece of white paper, then slowly dripped onto the priceless Persian carpet beneath the desk.

"Goddammit, don't lie to me anymore! Tell me what happened here and why you've kept it from me all these years. Good God, don't you see what you've done? If Camillia's still alive, Lily and I aren't legally married and that makes our child a bastard!"

Forcing a swallow over the lump of fear clogging her throat, Sarah turned to Lily, but Harte's wife only looked back at her with sorrowful eyes.

When Sarah refused to answer, Harte gritted his teeth until his jaw locked. "If you ever want to see me again, or Lily and your great-grandchild, you had better tell me everything you know about Camillia."

Sarah met his eyes. She had to be strong. She had to continue her bluff. For him, for his own good. "Camillia is dead. She has been for a very long time. I don't understand why you've come here making these ridiculous accusations."

Harte stared at her a long moment. "All right, Grandmother. You've left me no choice. If you won't cooperate, I'll order Camillia's grave to be exhumed. We both know we won't find anyone there, don't we?"

"No!" Sarah cried in horror, unconsciously coming to her feet. "Please, Harte, you can't do such a thing."

"Oh, Sarah, please listen," Lily intervened hurriedly, obviously fearful of her husband's growing wrath. "Just tell us what really happened all those years ago. Harte deserves to know the truth. Don't you see that all these lies have to stop? We already know Camillia's body isn't in the grave. The moment I touched her headstone, I knew no one was buried there."

Sarah's lips quivered. "She's dead. Leave it be, I beg you. Your marriage is in no jeopardy, I swear it. I cannot say more."

"Oh, yes you can," Harte spit out furiously, "or I swear to God I'll raise such a stink in Newport that the Delaney name will never garner an ounce of respect around here again. This scandal will be dragged through the mud by every newspaper in New England, and you know it. And don't think I won't do it, Grandmother."

Harte's words were so lethal and determined that Sarah had no doubt he would carry out his abominable threat. She sank limply back into her chair and retrieved her handkerchief from her sleeve. Pressing it to her mouth, she stared at her enraged grandson. But how could she tell him?

"Sarah," Lily said gently, moving around the table and placing a consoling hand on her shoulder. "Please, you have to tell us. Harte deserves to know. I sensed when I first met you that you were trying to protect him. I feel certain that whatever happened wasn't really your fault. Just tell us and maybe we can end this terrible pain once and for all."

Hot tears burned behind Sarah's eyes, and she fought for control of her emotions. She had never been one to break down, even in the worst of situations. But never had she faced a task as painful as the one which now confronted her.

"All right," she said hoarsely. "I'll tell you."

Lily breathed easier, but she was still worried. Harte's eyes were narrowed and suspicious, and Lily was afraid he wouldn't believe Sarah, even if she did tell him the truth. Lily sat down in the chair beside Sarah, but her husband remained standing, seemingly unaffected by his grandmother's agitation. He frowned as Sarah stood and limped to the windows that overlooked the front drive. She leaned heavily on her cane, suddenly appearing frail and old.

"Camillia is dead—" she began softly, but

Harte exploded with anger before she could finish her sentence.

"Dammit, we know that's not true!"

"Harte, please, give her time to explain," Lily murmured gently, but Sarah turned and looked straight at her grandson.

"I will tell you the truth, but it will be difficult for you to hear."

Something in her somber tone arrested Harte's ire, and he remained silent during the short pause that followed.

"As I said, Camillia is dead," she repeated in a trembling voice, "but she didn't die the way I told you she did. She passed away in a convent in New Orleans less than one year after the date inscribed on her tomb."

For an instant both Harte and Lily could only stare at the older woman.

"What are you saying?" Harte asked in confusion. "I don't understand."

"Please, Harte, let it end here," Sarah begged. Then she quickly solicited Lily's support. "Lily, help me persuade him it's better if he doesn't know, please."

Lily's smooth brow furrowed with pity, but she shook her head. "Sarah, we can't do that. This deception has caused years of suffering for you and for Harte too. You have to tell us. You have to end it."

When Sarah hid her face in her hands, Lily began to dread the moment that the truth would be revealed. Sarah's secrets must be terrible indeed, for her to have kept them so thoroughly hidden in her heart for so long.

"When Lily knelt on Camillia's prayer bench, she had a dreaming," Harte said then. "She saw you struggling with Camillia on the cliffs. She said she could feel Camillia's fear." An awful expression flickered across his face. "Did you try to kill her, Grandmother? Did you hate her that much?"

Sarah violently shook her head. "Oh, no, no, you're so dreadfully wrong. I never harmed her. I never wanted to." She sobbed, then struggled for composure. "I was only trying to help her. That's why I kept her secrets. That's why I sent her to the convent. You have to believe me."

"Why? Why did you send her there? And why were you with her on the cliffs? Good God, Grandmother, how could you have done these things?"

Sarah's face crumbled into anguish. "It was all so awful. It would have been preventable if I had only seen what was happening. But you must believe that I had no idea it was going on. I was appalled when I found out."

"What was going on?" Harte demanded harshly, obviously impatient with his grandmother's halting confession. "Just tell me what happened!"

Her gnarled hands clutched tightly over the gold head of her cane, Sarah stared out over the lawns. She drew a deep breath. "Camillia was going to have a child."

Lily looked quickly at Harte. He looked stunned. Then his expression turned into disbelief.

"That's impossible. She wanted a baby desperately and was terribly disappointed when she hadn't conceived by the time I left for Texas—" Harte's vehemence faded when he realized exactly what Sarah was intimating. Anger twisted his mouth. "If you're accusing Camillia of being unfaithful, I don't believe it. She was a devout Catholic. She'd never have slept with another man."

Sarah didn't look at him. "It's true, Harte. That's why she tried to throw herself off the cliff. So you'd never find out."

"That's what I saw in my dreaming, isn't it?" Lily murmured, instinctively certain that the struggle she had witnessed had been Sarah's attempt to save the young Mexican girl's life. "You weren't trying to push her, were you? You were trying to save her." Lily turned to Harte, but he was still staring in shocked dismay at his grandmother.

"Oh, Harte, Camillia was so unhappy after you left her here with me. And I'm ashamed now of the way I treated her. I was cold and unkind and always expected so much because I thought she was unworthy of you. But Lord help me, I never wanted to hurt her or send her away. She was lonely and missed you terribly. That's why she turned to him, I know it."

"She's telling the truth, Harte," Lily admitted in a low voice. "In my dreaming I saw Camillia embracing a man out on the cliffs. I thought it was you at first, but it wasn't."

"Who was he then?" Harte asked, his voice nearly unrecognizable. "Tell me his name."

"Harte, stop! She's been dead for years. It doesn't matter now."

Harte ignored Sarah's pleading. "The hell it doesn't! I want to know who he was. You should have told me then instead of faking her death. For God's sake, I was a grown man. I could have handled her infidelity. If you feared a scandal, it would have been simple to tell everyone the baby was mine. Why didn't you? Why did you send her to New Orleans? None of this makes any sense."

"Yes, you could have handled it, but she couldn't. She was overcome with guilt. She wept all the time and prayed endlessly for forgiveness. And the circumstances were just so ugly—"

"What circumstances?"

Sarah shook her head. "I won't tell you any more. It will come to no good."

To Lily's alarm, Harte got up, went straight to Sarah, and pulled her around to face him. "I have to know who the man was. You're going to tell me, Grandmother."

Tears began to roll down Sarah's face, and she shook her head from side to side, but she finally blurted out the words he wanted to hear.

"Oh, Lord help us, Harte, it was your own brother. It was Stuart."

Lily gasped with shock, and Harte's face went white. A muscle twitched spasmodically in his cheek. Then he suddenly let go of Sarah's shoulders.

"No, you're lying," he muttered thickly. "Stuart was still in Virginia then."

"No, he wasn't. He came here to have his portrait painted for the gallery." Sarah's words began to flow faster, as if a dam had broken and the guilt captured inside her heart for years was rushing out in a deluge of boiling emotions. "He was exactly her age when they met, sixteen, and he looked and acted so much like you. They liked each other from the beginning. Stuart was kind to Camillia and told her all the stories about you and your childhood here at The Oaks."

Sarah's voice tightened. "He was here for a month, and they were together all the time. Heaven help me, I saw no harm in their friendship. It never occurred to me that anything else could ever develop between them. I didn't know they'd been lovers until weeks after Stuart had gone back to Twin Pines and I came upon Camillia out on the cliffs. That's when she admitted everything to me."

Lily was horrified by Sarah's revelations, and Harte couldn't seem to move. He stood very still, obviously struggling with disbelief.

"Stuart and Camillia?" he mumbled incoherently. "I can't believe it. Did they love each other?"

"Oh, don't you see? They were young, and Camillia needed someone to comfort her. Once they realized what they had done to you, he left at once, without a word of explanation to anyone. It was weeks later when Camillia realized she was carrying his child. That's when she became consumed by guilt and decided she couldn't go on. More than anything, she couldn't bear the idea of your finding out. She blamed herself for everything. She felt that adultery was the deadliest of all sins."

Sarah's tortured words stopped abruptly. She stared at Harte, then sank down on the window seat as if her legs had given way.

"Try to understand, Harte. When I found her poised on the precipice ready to jump, she wasn't in her right mind anymore. You know how religious she was, how committed she was to her faith, yet she was determined to commit suicide so she wouldn't have to face you. Think about my position. I knew she would try to kill herself again, and if she did, her unborn child would die as well. I didn't know what to do, and she begged me not to tell you or Stuart. So I arranged to have her taken to the convent where she could have the baby, and after she was among the nuns, she decided she wanted to remain there and devote her life to God." She heaved an immense sigh. "So I told everyone she died in a fall, but she didn't. She died in childbirth."

"What about the baby?" Lily asked gently.

Sarah bit her lip. "It was a little girl. I wanted to bring her back here, but how could I? How could I explain her presence to you when you already blamed me for Camillia's death? I knew you would hate me even more if you found out the truth. I made a terrible mistake deceiving you, and I've paid for it all these years that you've stayed away from me."

"Where's the child now?" Harte asked in such a terrible voice that Lily's heart twisted.

"She was adopted by some friends of mine. They took her with them to England shortly after she was born. I've made sure she's been well taken care of. I've only seen her once, when she was three years old. She was a beautiful little girl, and her family dotes on her. She'll soon be eight years old."

"And Stuart still doesn't know he has a daughter?"

Sarah shook her head. "Camillia begged me not to tell him. She was never the same after she found out she was pregnant. It was awful, all of it." When she looked at Harte, agony darkened her eyes. "I was only trying to protect you, Harte, but I wish to God I'd never done it. It was wrong. I see that now."

Sarah laid her head on the table and wept, and Lily put her arm around her heaving shoulders. "It's going to be all right now, Sarah. It's not too late to make things right. You've told the truth. Now you and Harte have to decide what must be done. Isn't that so, Harte?"

Lily looked at her husband for affirmation, then bit her lip in dismay. He had walked out without a word to either of them.

It was nearly dusk. Lily stood in the window of the second-floor mezzanine watching the gravel path that led to the cliffs. In Bermuda, Harte had always walked along the beach when he was upset or needed time alone, and she felt certain that was where he had been for so long.

Below her on the flagstone patio, Sarah Delaney sat in the shade of an awning, no doubt keeping her own vigil for his return. Even if Harte couldn't forgive Sarah and their estrangement continued, Sarah's heart would be cleansed of the lies she had told for so long. Lily was glad for that. Sarah had carried a terrible burden all those years.

Lily scanned the lawns again and saw Harte finally coming back toward the house. She sighed with relief. She wanted him to come to her and let her comfort him the way she had when he had been so bereaved by Lincoln's assassination. If he could bring himself to forgive Sarah, perhaps they could finally live together in peace.

As Harte crossed the flagstones below, Lily held her breath awaiting the moment he would become aware of his grandmother's presence at the far end of the terrace. A moment later, he did see Sarah and stopped in his tracks. He seemed to debate whether or not to approach his grandmother.

"Oh, thank God," Lily whispered to herself as she saw him turn and stride resolutely toward Sarah. When he drew near, Sarah rose, and Lily watched breathlessly as they spoke together for several moments. Her heart shivered when he stepped forward and held Sarah's frail form in a brief embrace.

Lily watched the reconciliation she had longed to see, her heart full, knowing she should not intrude on their tentative reunion, but so very glad that the nightmare of Camillia's death was finally over for both of them. A short time later Harte left his grandmother and came toward the house.

Lily ran to the top of the staircase to await him. When he came into view below and saw her on the landing, he took the steps two at a time until he had her enfolded in his arms.

"I'm going to try to come to terms with all of this," he whispered gruffly against the top of her head. "I don't know if I can forgive Grandmother or not, but I'm willing to give it a try."

"You will. I know it," she whispered.

"Let's go back to Moon Cove, Lily. I can think better there," he murmured, seeking her lips. Lily smiled as they shared a tender kiss. She knew then that everything was going to be all right. She could sense it in him, and her heart was filled with joy.

# *Epilogue*

*Bermuda*
*Late July, 1865*

Harte lay back in the hammock and laced his fingers behind his head. Early-morning mists still hung in patches over the peaceful glade, but the summer sun would soon burn them away and warm the dark-blue water. He was so glad he had brought Lily back to Moon Cove. More than anywhere else, his coral house on the sea felt like home to them. They would return here often in the future, he decided. Perhaps they could even make the island their annual refuge against the cold New England winters.

Down the bank from his comfortable retreat in the shade of the palms, Lily was strolling along the edge of the water, gathering a bouquet of Easter lilies. She wore a dress of lemon-yellow dotted swiss, and she had the tail of her skirt tucked into her waistband. She stooped and broke the stem of a particularly beautiful blossom, then held it to her nose and inhaled the fragrance.

Pleasure spread through Harte's consciousness. In the last few months Lily had begun to show her condition. Her flat belly was now mounded and firm as his son formed inside her slim body. *Oh, God,* he thought, *how lucky I am to have found Lily.* Sometimes it frightened him to think how accidental their meeting had been—completely by chance and under such dangerous circumstances. What if he hadn't happened onto Ringer in the saloon on that particular day? What if he had never experienced Lily's sweet love?

Perhaps Lily had been able to see him during her childhood dreamings and had been aware that he was waiting for her somewhere, but Harte hadn't had that assurance. If he had known early in his life the happiness and contentment she would bring to him, he would have searched the world over for her long before the day he had stepped inside Ringer's barn.

As he watched, she looked up and waved to him, then turned back, her arms full of the trumpet-shaped white flowers. Although she had said little about his grandmother's terrible deception and Camillia's unfaithfulness, she had helped him come to terms with his past. When he wanted her with him, she had been eagerly at his side, but she had allowed him to go off by himself when he needed to be alone, never imposing unwanted questions or expectations.

Her understanding of his needs had sped

the process of healing the internal pain he had endured since his grandmother's confession. In the last few weeks during his long, solitary walks on the warm coral beaches, he had made a great many decisions that would affect their lives in the years to come.

Now that the war was over and the Lincoln conspirators had been found guilty and hanged on the seventh day of July, Harte was ready to resign from the military and get on with his life. The country was still in turmoil, people on both sides were still gripped by bitterness and anger, but the United States of America would be rebuilt and Harte wanted to have a part in the reconstruction.

One night in bed, when Lily lay cuddled in his arms, he had told her as much, and she had whispered that perhaps he should reach out and try to heal the rift in his own family first. After thinking about her words, he realized that she was right.

No matter what Cassandra was up to at the moment with Derek Courtland and the *Mamu*, Harte had no doubt that she would one day want to return and claim her beloved Twin Pines. If the Federal occupational forces had confiscated his mother's plantation, Harte could make the necessary arrangements in Washington to get it back. The Virginia property had been as much a part of his ancestry as the Delaney estate at Newport. He had decided to take over the helm of the Delaney business enterprises, as Sarah had always wanted him to, and perhaps it was also time to acknowledge his mother's branch of the family.

A frown creased his forehead. But that left Stuart. His feelings for his younger brother were more complex and harder to come to terms with. It wasn't hatred that he felt. Nor was it anger. Instead, a strange sort of nostalgic sorrow had lodged itself deep within his chest—a melancholy wistfulness for the brotherhood they had lost since they had grown into men.

As boys they had been close friends, allies against their mother and grandmother, and even Cassandra. Now they didn't know each other. Harte hadn't seen Stuart in nearly fifteen years; he probably wouldn't even have recognized him. Had Stuart suffered with guilt over Camillia all these years? Was that the reason he had left Virginia so young and gone his own way?

Thoughts of his brother fled when Lily reached Harte's side and smiled down at him, a look of pure love softening her eyes. She laughed as Harte welcomed her by pulling her into the hammock with him, lilies and all.

"Close your eyes, Harte," she whispered once she was snuggled up close against him.

"Not if you're going to jump off the rocks again and scare the hell out of me," he murmured with a lazy grin.

"Oh, no. I learned my lesson the last time. This is much better. Now close them, and don't peek."

Harte did so, smiling as Lily lifted his hand, then opened his fingers. She pressed her lips against his palm; then she laid it gently on her rounded abdomen. Almost at once he felt a slight flutter, then a rather emphatic push. His eyes flew open, and Lily laughed at his startled expression.

"He moved for the first time earlier this morning while you were walking on the beach. I've been waiting for hours for him to wake up and kick me again so I could show you how strong he is."

Harte felt his throat fill with an overwhelming surge of emotion. He would soon witness the greatest of miracles. He would see his own flesh and blood reborn from the loins of the woman he loved more than life itself. He felt so blessed and happy that tears burned the back of his eyes and he fought his absurd urge to weep.

"I love you, Lily," he said hoarsely, cradling her face in his hands so he could look into her eyes. Even now, after willingly giving Lily all his love and devotion, it was hard for him to say the words aloud. But he wanted to. He no longer feared that she would hurt him or betray him as so many others had. Lily gave him nothing but joy.

"See, that wasn't so hard to admit," she murmured, closing her eyes for a kiss.

Harte was eager to oblige, and he savored her lips for several long, leisurely moments, but he kept his palm on her stomach in case his son should move again. When he felt the gentle stirrings from inside Lily's womb, he made another decision that he had been contemplating for several weeks.

"I'm going to tell Stuart that he has a daughter," he whispered against Lily's cheek. "I'd hate to think that I never knew you had borne me a child."

Lily lifted her head, surprise evident in her eyes before pleasure darkened them to molten gold. "Oh, yes, darling, I think you're right. Every man has a right to know about his children."

Harte hesitated. "Maybe we should go down to Virginia and try to find him. He might need our help now that the war's over."

Lily's smile was quick and delighted. "Oh, Harte, that's a wonderful idea."

"But I don't know. Maybe we should wait until after you've had the baby. Traveling might not be good for you."

"All right. Whatever you say is fine with me."

"You're awfully agreeable."

"As long as I'm with you," she murmured, nibbling the base of his throat where his gold medallion lay at the end of the chain, "I'll do anything you want, any time you want."

"Anything, you say?"

"Yes."

"That does sound intriguing."

Harte and Lily shared an intimate smile, then their lips met and melded together igniting a familiar, gentle passion. Even without Lily's dreamings to predict their future, Harte knew in that moment that the most wonderful life stretched out before them and their children, one full of love and tenderness and joy. He would savor each and every day, just as long as Lily was at his side.